SHELTER COVE

A Resurrection Man Novel

Colin Campbell

ISBN: 978-1-4834-8806-6 (sc)
ISBN: 978-1-4834-8805-9 (e)

Library of Congress Control Number: 2018908056

Lulu Publishing Services rev. date: 07/12/2018

Also by Colin Campbell

Resurrection Man
Beacon Hill
Snake Pass
Adobe Flats
Montecito Heights
Jamaica Plain

Vince McNulty
Northern Ex

UK Crime
Blue Knight White Cross
Ballad Of The One Legged Man
Through The Ruins Of Midnight

Children
Gargoyles – Skylights And Roofscapes

Horror
Darkwater Towers

Praise for Colin Campbell

"Very real. And Very good." - *Lee Child*

The Resurrection Man Series

"A cop with a sharp eye, keen mind, and a lion's heart." - *Reed Farrel Coleman*

"Campbell writes smart, rollercoaster tales with unstoppable forward momentum and thrilling authenticity. The Resurrection Man series is a blast." - *Nick Petrie*

"Grim and gritty and packed with action and crackling dialogue." – *Kirkus Review (Jamaica Plain)*

"Action packed. Tough-as-nails. The pages fly like the bullets, fist-fights and one-liners that make this one of my favourite books of the year. Top stuff!" – *Matt Hilton (Jamaica Plain)*

"Campbell's wry maverick Grant never fails to entertain." – *Kirkus Review (Montecito Heights)*

"Harkens back to the gritty action series of the 70s and 80s, with a stylish noir voice." – *Kirkus Reviews (Adobe Flats)*
"Crackerjack entertainment: taut, gritty and full of devilish twists." – *Kirkus Reviews (Snake Pass)*

"Campbell's BEACON HILL is a great tale of violence and intrigue, stretching across the Atlantic and back again. In it, Jim Grant proves he is the real deal." – *Reed Farrel Coleman (about Beacon Hill)*

"The Resurrection Man series is a blast, and BEACON HILL tops the list — until the next one." – *Nick Petrie (about Beacon Hill)*

UK Crime Novels

"This is police procedural close-up and personal. A strong debut with enough gritty realism to make your eyes water, and a few savage laughs along the way." - *Reginald Hill (about Through The Ruins Of Midnight)*

"An excellent story well told. A mixture of The Choirboys meets Harry Bosch." – *Michael Jecks (about Through The Ruins Of Midnight)*

"Campbell's 30 years as a Yorkshire policeman infuse this unusual procedural with grim reality and the harsh humor that helps keep the coppers sane." – *Kirkus Review (Blue Knight White Cross)*

"Every detail feels authentic, and Campbell's dark, muscular prose suggests the best pulp writers of the '50s." – *Kirkus Review (Northern Ex)*

For my daughter, Ann
Love always

PART ONE

The Man With The White Bottom

"You talk funny. I think that's why I like you."

– Holly West

ONE

*

TROUBLE COMES IN THREES. Always has and always will. If Cole Thornton had recognized that he might have avoided much of what was to come. If he'd realized that the car crash was the beginning of his personal trifecta he could have upped sticks and moved on before Shelter Cove became a killing jar instead of a safe haven. Of course hindsight is always 20/20, another undeniable truth, so Thornton didn't see the warning signs. He didn't up sticks. And the crash was just an accident. But before the crash there was the book. Hindsight would later go 20/20 that that's where it really all began.

*

"YOU GOING TO USE that to beat miscreants into submission?"

"Miscreants?"

"Thieves and vagabonds."

"You talk funny. I think that's why I like you."

Cole Thornton talked funny because he wasn't from California. He wasn't from America at all. He was just another ex-pat Brit making a living abroad, in this case running Rocky Coast Books, Shelter Cove's only bookstore, and enjoying the view across the common towards Rockaway Beach. This morning he was also enjoying the view of Holly West as she stood at the window with the sun forming a halo around her short-cropped hair. "Even so. You hit any trouble-makers with that, you won't need your Taser."

"I never need my Taser."

"I'll bet you don't."

The hint of suggestiveness brought a smile to Holly's lips. The part time deputy was in uniform even though she wasn't due on shift until noon. Discussing handcuffs and physical restraints with a man with an English accent was always the highlight of her day. Managing the Arguello Boulevard Motel wasn't exactly her life's ambition and becoming a full time police officer wasn't an option. Budget cuts and a freeze on recruiting meant that being an auxiliary was as good as it was going to get. Having the Englishman seek out books she wanted to buy gave her the excuse to stop in for a chat.

History Of The Ocean Shore Railroad

The book this time was big enough to knock sense into anybody. She hefted it in both hands then took a playful swing, two-handed like a baseball player. She smiled at Cole then put the book on the counter. "How much I owe you?"

Cole moved behind the cash register and flicked open the cover. "Wasn't that hard to track down. Picked it up from a remainder supplier."

"Not for free."

"No."

"So how much?"

Cole felt uncomfortable. He'd known Holly for almost three years, just after he moved to Pacifica then settled in the south at Shelter Cove. He'd spent his first six months at her motel before he bought the bookstore and moved into the apartment round the back. She was divorced. He was single. She loved Englishmen. He was English. They were a match made in heaven but he resisted the urge to pursue a relationship. He wasn't ready for a relationship. There was too much baggage in his closet. They were friendly but Holly wanted to be friendlier. Making her pay for the book felt like being a cheapskate.

She leaned on the counter. "You are running a business here aren't you?"

Cole stood back. "Sort of."

"Sort of yes or sort of no?"

Cole shrugged. "More like a hobby."

Holly tapped the book. "A redistribution of wealth kind of hobby?"

Cole shrugged again.

Holly gave him her best police officer stare. "Over here that'd make you a commie. You aren't a communist are you?"

Cole gave her a disarming smile. "That still a problem over here? You do know the wall came down years ago."

She braced her shoulders. "Not in California."

Cole held out his hands, wrists together. "Then you'd better arrest me."

Holly smiled. "Furry handcuffs?"

Cole waved a finger. "Naughty girl. I think I'd better charge for the book."

Holly looked disappointed. She took out her purse. "So how much I owe you?"

"Call it ten."

"That all? Maybe I should cook you dinner."

"You did cook me dinner. For six months."

"A long time ago."

Cole peeled off a sheet of wrapping paper from a dispenser and laid the book flat. The cover photo was of a sweeping railroad track coming round the headland. He'd seen similar shots of steam trains on the North Yorkshire moors back home. Always a curved track. Always the sun coming over the back. Sometimes it seemed like the further he went the closer to home he became. He supposed most ex-pats felt that way.

Holly looked out of the window while Cole wrapped. As soon as he knew she wasn't looking he slowed down. He didn't want her to leave but he wasn't ready to ask her to stay. It was more of a catch 22 situation than the one he'd left back home. Some things you tried to ignore but those things never ignored you. Hence travelling halfway around the world to get away from them. He folded the paper in nice straight lines but his eyes wandered around the shop.

Rocky Coast Books was a throwback to the backstreet bookshops he used to frequent as a boy. Stripped pine bookshelves and carved wooden picture frames. He had sandpapered the wood himself and was pleased with the carpentry smell it gave the shop. The only smell as nice as planed wood was freshly baked bread but he was no great shakes at baking. Wood he could work with. There were wooden bowls scattered around the shop with carved wooden fruit shapes dipped in scented oils. The smell complimented the wood shavings. It made the place feel like a meditation retreat. He was particularly pleased with the doublewide shop window. It was big and bright and split in two by an ornate wooden support. It made the place look even older. Gave it an air of authenticity that not many places in America had. To him everything looked like it was built yesterday. There was no history before the old west. John Wayne was as far back as most people went.

Holly turned back and Cole picked up the pace. He folded the ends into neat triangles then dabbed a strip of Sellotape to hold them down. Not too much so that opening the parcel became a recruiting test. Not so little that it looked like he was skimping. She nodded her approval. "You should run your own business."

Cole slid the book across the counter. "I do run my own business."

Holly gave him ten dollars. "No. You redistribute wealth. I don't know how you make enough to keep the place open."

Cole shrugged.

Holly left the book where it was. "He still trying to strong arm you into selling?"

"Arlo? He's still leaning some."

Holly tilted her head. "You on first name terms with Shelter Cove's biggest landowner now?"

"Not exactly. I just like the name. Reminds me of Arlo Givens in that TV show, Justified."

"The crooked father?"

"That's the one."

"You saying Arlo Rankoff's a crook?"

"Wouldn't be much of a stretch, would it?"

"Just because he's bought most of the businesses west of Cabrillo Highway?"

Cole looked out of the window. A car drove past, slow and steady. There wasn't much need for speed on San Pedro Avenue. There wasn't much traffic. The network of streets round the back of the bookstore was quiet and residential. The Fresh and Easy Neighborhood Market was the only other business still open and that was only because it was part of the Pedro Point Shopping Center just across the common. Too big for Rankoff to buy out. Not far enough west to encroach on the tract of land he now owned. Everything leading into the hills and across to the crescent of beach that gave Shelter Cove its name. Cole leaned on the cash register, a symbol of the last business standing, and turned back to Holly. "Somebody once said that business is simply theft by other means."

Holly surprised him. "Don't you mean; war is a continuation of politics by other means?"

Cole raised his eyebrows. "You heard that too?"

"Carl von Clausewitz. Yeah."

"You must have too much time on your hands."

"Time enough to cook you dinner."

Cole ignored the suggestion. "Von Clausewitz huh?"

"Business and politics. Not exactly the same thing."

"Not much of a stretch either though. And Von Rankoff's definitely playing fast and loose with the rules of engagement."

Holly folded her arms across her chest. Official stance. "So, back to my question. He still trying to strong arm you into selling?"

Cole repeated his answer. "He's still leaning some."

Holly let out a sigh. "And you still play fast and loose with your answers."

Another car drove past the window going the other way, almost identical to the previous one. There wasn't much variety beyond Shoreside Drive. Cole tracked it until it turned the corner towards the Pedro Point firehouse. The distraction gave him time to marshal his thoughts. "I've been leaned on before. It's no big deal."

That piqued Holly's interest. "Who'd have thought being a bookseller could be so dangerous?"

"I haven't always been a bookseller."

"And you haven't always answered my questions."

Cole put on a stern face. "Am I being interrogated?"

Holly responded with a stern face of her own. "Interviewed. Interrogation is electric shocks and waterboarding."

Cole's stern face set a little harder. "Well I've been interrogated before."

Holly's stern face showed a hint of concern. "Electric shocks and waterboarding?"

Cole softened his expression. "Asked questions I didn't want to answer."

Holly looked embarrassed. "Am I being nosey again?"

Cole felt bad about embarrassing her. He smiled and shook his head. "You're showing an interest. Not the same thing."

Holly held up her hands. "Invading your privacy. I do it all the time. Sorry."

Cole took one of her hands in both of his. "Maybe I'll tell you over dinner sometime."

Holly brightened up. The car came back around the corner from the Pedro Point firehouse. The same car. Cole was sure of it now. He glanced at the car then turned back to Holly. "You've got history. Divorce and stuff. Things you don't want to talk about. I've got history too. And I want to keep it in the past."

He thought about that for a moment. Catch 22. Some things you tried to ignore but those things never ignored you. The act of trying to forget inevitably meant you remembered. He tried to put a positive spin on the rebuff. "I like it here. Arlo Von Rankoff isn't going to move me on." The car was going faster than before. Cole divided his attention between it and Holly. Mainly Holly. "I like the company too." He slid the book across the counter. "You're my best customer."

She took it and smiled. "I've never been anyone's best before."

A squeal of tyres sounded outside. Cole glanced through the window. Holly followed his gaze. The car was going too fast and careered across the road as it lost control. It mounted the sidewalk at an angle, sun glinting off the windshield. Cole lunged across the cash register but Holly was out of reach. The car bounced up the curb at speed and left the ground, heading straight for the ornate wooden support of the doublewide window.

TWO

*

GLASS EXPLODED INTO BLADES of shrapnel. The carved wooden centerpiece splintered and buckled. The car tilted as it bounced off the curb, the passenger side higher than the driver's. It carved a path through the window display and the bookshelves, destroying the sales counter. The cash register was flung aside catching Cole in the chest and shoulder. He threw an arm up to protect his eyes from the glass and didn't see the impact of metal on flesh but he did hear Holly scream. The sound rang in his ears long after the collision ended. He was slammed into the wall so hard he dislodged the overhead shelf. Planed wood and a pile of books came down on top of him as he dropped to the floor. The world became dull and grey then it blinked out altogether.

The bookstore descended into silence. Complete muffled nothingness. Cole opened his eyes and for a moment thought he was still unconscious. He couldn't see anything. He blinked twice just to make sure. Yes, he was awake. No, he still couldn't see anything. Then he shoved the books that were covering him and the world became bright again. Too bright. The window display had gone. The sales counter had gone. The first two rows of bookshelves that had given the shop its intimate feel were just so much splintered wood beneath the squat ugly shape of the wrecked car. Sunlight streamed through the gaping hole of the storefront.

Sound returned. Slowly at first because Cole's ears felt numb, like when you're coming in to land and they haven't popped yet. Noises were muffled and distant. Pieces of broken glass fell out of the window frame. A bookshelf toppled over spilling books onto the floor. The engine continued to rev, the gas pedal jammed by some unseen object. Debris propped up the front of the car. The drive wheels were spinning.

Cole shook his head clear. It hurt but no more than a severe headache. His eyes searched the debris under the car. His nose quested for the smell of death. All it came up with was wood shavings and scented fruits. Then exhaust fumes invaded the pleasant aromas. And leaking gasoline.

Cole struggled to his feet. He stepped around the front of the car, careful not to step on Holly's legs or arms. He couldn't see them. He glanced around the devastation. No sign of her. That only left one place and his heart sank when he realized what the scream implied.

The windshield was cracked and splintered but the laminated glass was still in place. The side windows had been smashed into diamond cubes that carpeted the floor. Cole looked through the opening to see how badly the driver was hurt. The seat was empty. But his foot was still there, wedged between the gas pedal and the brake. Cole turned his head to avoid being sick. When his stomach settled down he opened the door and reached in. He turned off the ignition and the engine died. The wheels continued to spin but eventually slowed and stopped. The engine ticked as it cooled. The smell of gasoline was strong inside the car. The exhaust fumes drifted out through the shop window. He held his breath then reached down to release the gas pedal. His stomach did a lazy roll. Then he let out a sigh of relief and almost laughed as he dislodged the shoe that he'd mistaken for a severed foot. He stumbled back out of the car and tossed the shoe onto the backseat.

There was a cough behind him. A groan of pain. More books slid off an overturned bookcase as somebody pushed from underneath it. There was only one other somebody in the shop. Holly. Cole let out another sigh of relief then called her name. She didn't answer but the bookcase moved again. He stepped over piles of books and broken glass and yanked the bookcase free. It came up easily. Holly was curled in a fetal position amid a litter of books and spilled wooden fruit. The scented oils mingled with her perfume and this time he did laugh. "Holly."

His voice was dry and harsh but the sound of it stirred her to respond. "If this is how you treat your best customer…"

She didn't finish. A jolt of pain made her gasp and Cole leaned forward to look for blood.

"Lie still. Where does it hurt?"

She got her breath back. "Everywhere."

"That's not helpful."

He ran through his training. Something he thought he'd left behind along with the North Yorkshire railway. Visual examination. Check the extremities and the core and the head. Talk to the injured party. A screamer was better than a silent casualty because that meant they were alive. A talker was better than a screamer because they could tell you where it hurts. Most times. It didn't take long to see there were no broken bones and no major cuts. Cole helped Holly into a sitting position. He rummaged through the remains of the sales counter and found the plastic bottle of water he always kept under the cash register. Surprisingly, amid all the destruction, it was still intact. He poured some into his hand and dribbled it over Holly's mouth. Once it was clear of muck and dust he let her take a drink.

A siren sounded in the distance. Another one sounded closer by. There was a screech of tyres and a door slammed then a grey haired man wearing the same uniform as Holly clambered through the front window. The same uniform but a higher rank. Shelter Cove's chief of police.

Holly handed the bottle back. "Oh, oh. Now I'm in trouble."

*

ONE THING COLE KNEW for sure, after Ben Gardner crouched beside Holly for five minutes waiting for the ambulance to arrive, was that Gardner's part time deputy wasn't in trouble with him. Cole watched the police chief talk calmly and sternly while holding Holly's hand, letting her know that none of this was her fault. The sideways glances and whispered platitudes left Cole in no doubt who the veteran cop blamed, and it didn't seem to be the driver. Gardner instructed the paramedics as if he were their boss as well and generally behaved like a concerned father. So no, Holly wasn't in trouble with the police.

She was in trouble with the paramedics though, as she argued that her neck had been good enough when she sat up so why did she need a neck brace to ride in the ambulance? She tried to get up but they insisted that she be strapped to a backboard and carried into the rig. They settled her onto the gurney and one of them continued treatment while the other updated the dispatcher.

Gardner kicked enough debris aside to clear a path to the car without twisting his ankle and opened the driver's door. He gave the interior a cursory once over then reached inside and retrieved the shoe Cole had tossed onto the backseat. Letting it dangle from one hand he stepped back and closed the door. Cole joined him and nodded towards the ambulance. "Thanks chief. She thought she was in trouble."

Gardner turned as if noticing Cole for the first time. "I'm not the chief."

Cole gave an apologetic shrug. He didn't know what the rank structure was in Shelter Cove. He knew it was a subdivision of the Pacifica Police Department and that Gardner was the head of that subdivision. Apart from that it was either sergeants' stripes or collar insignia. Looking at the ill-fitting uniform Cole had no idea what any of the badges meant. Gardner elaborated, but not much. "I'm just the guy trying to keep Shelter Cove safe."

Cole tried flattery. "Always feels safe to me."

Gardner pointed at the car wedged in the front of the bookstore. "Not too safe today."

Cole made a squiggly motion with one hand, like a fish swimming. The fish followed an arc from the road across the sidewalk and into the shop. "Accidents happen."

Gardner jerked his chin across Shoreside Drive where the tide was coming in. "Yeah well. Surfers can't drive for shit. Surprised more of 'em don't drive into bookstore windows."

Cole raised his eyebrows. "The driver was a surfer?"

"That'd be my guess."

Cole was intrigued. "How d'you work that out?"

Gardner deadpanned his reply. "With superior intellect and the application of finely honed observation skills."

Cole played along. "Not like Johnny Utah then. The FBI lab identifying surfboard wax at the scene of the crime."

Gardner leveled his stare at Cole. "You said this was an accident."

"Okay. Scene of the accident."

Gardner shook his head. "Surfers aren't like them guys in Point Break."

Cole tilted his head in query. "So it wasn't the board wax?"

Gardner held up the Converse Classic sneaker. "It was the sand."

He turned it upside down and dried sand spilled onto the floor.

Cole was impressed. "Elementary."

Gardner ignored the Sherlock Holmes joke. "Shouldn't be too hard to find. Just match the shoe."

Cole was skeptical. "You going to call on all the fair girls of the land?"

"What?"

"To try on the glass slipper?"

Gardner glanced at the fire truck pulling up outside. From the Pedro Point Firehouse. Not as far to travel as the police and paramedics but last on the scene. The senior cop looked back at Cole. "Cinderella wasn't a surfer. They're always getting their stuff mixed up." He turned the top of the sneaker inside out. "They write their names on everything."

*

TWO FIREFIGHTERS CONNECTED a hose to the hydrant outside and began to sluice the gasoline spillage. It didn't take long. The car must have been running on empty. Adding water damage to the clean up wasn't going to take any more time than removing the debris. Firefighters had a habit of making more damage than the fires. This time they weren't that bad.

Gardner moved his patrol car and parked it further up the street. He climbed into the back of the ambulance and waited for the second paramedic to finish with Cole. That didn't take long either. Cole identified the correct number of fingers held up in front of him and only had a few scrapes and bruises. The paramedic went through his list of questions. "Did you lose consciousness at any time?"

Cole thought about the world going dark and his hearing being muffled. He knew what the next question was going to be depending on his answer. It was a choice between, "Take two aspirin and go to bed," or, "We'll take you to hospital for a complete check." Cole went for option 1. "No. Just a headache is all."

The paramedic seemed satisfied. He gave the required medical advice then joined his colleague. The ambulance pulled away just after the fire truck and the bookstore descended into silence once again. Cole stood in the middle of the carnage. Gardner had requested a local garage come out and recover the wrecked car but it was going to be half an hour before they arrived. All Cole could do until then was stand the bookcases back up and sift through the debris for undamaged books. The book he was looking for was under the overturned cash register.

History Of The Ocean Shore Railroad.

The wrapping paper was torn and the Sellotape had peeled off so he ripped the paper away and put the book in a carrier bag instead. He looked out through the front of the shop and suddenly felt alone. San Pedro Avenue was empty apart from the parked police cruiser. His gaze followed the route the ambulance had taken. There wasn't even the sound of a siren to guide him.

THREE

*

THERE WAS NO SIREN BECAUSE Holly West wasn't being rushed to hospital. She was being transported there at a safe speed with as little swerve and bump as possible. The ambulance headed along the Cabrillo Highway towards Pacifica at a stately pace that gave Ben Gardner plenty of time to express his opinions. When it came to Holly he had plenty of opinions. "I keep telling you reading is bad for your health."

Holly tried to turn her head but the neck brace wouldn't allow it so she spoke to the ceiling instead. "You don't do any reading?"

Gardner leaned forward so she could see him. "Only police reports and books with pictures."

Holly jerked a thumb back the way they had come. "The book I was buying had pictures."

"Not the kind of pictures I like looking at."

"Those would be magazines, not books."

The ambulance swayed gently as it rounded the bend at Vallemar. Gardner leaned across the gurney and planted a hand against the wall to steady himself. His eyes were directly above Holly's without her having to turn her head. Concern furrowed his brow, adding weight to his words as he got the conversation back on track. "I keep telling you not to hang around with strange men."

Holly glared defiance. "I was married to a strange man."

"Exactly."

He pushed away from the wall and rested his elbows on his knees. Just far enough away that Holly couldn't focus on him. Close enough that she could catch him out the corner of her eye. She lowered her voice. "We wear the chains we forge in life."

Gardner let out a sigh. "There you go. Reading too much again."

The ambulance picked up speed on the straight. Still smooth. No bumps. They were only a few minutes from the hospital. Holly stopped struggling against the neck brace. Gardner glanced towards the front of the ambulance, glad that both paramedics were sitting in the cab to give the cops some privacy. Holly watched his face out of the corner of her eye and tried to gauge the level of his concern. Judging by the look on his face it was somewhere between mild and a heart attack. The father and daughter dynamic let her speak her mind. "Why don't you just come out and say it?"

Gardner looked down at her. His eyes crinkled in a half smile that was more pride at her forthrightness than humor. He nodded his approval. "I'm not sure Cole Thornton is right for you."

Holly's tone hardened. "It's not for you to be sure."

Gardner wasn't intimidated. "There's something off about him."

"I'm not planning on marrying him."

"Not being married makes no difference. You know that."

Holly kept the exasperation out of her voice. "From running a motel or being a cop?"

"Both. Single men beat on women the same as husbands." As soon as he'd said it he wished he hadn't. Holly sucked in her breath. The ambulance slowed before the turn into the hospital. Gardner wrung his hands. "I'm sorry."

Holly watched the struggle on her mentor's face and softened her tone. "Don't be. Wasn't you married him. Bad choice, that's all."

"I should have done more."

She reached a hand out and stopped him wringing his. "I run a motel. I see unhappy couples all the time. One thing I know is you can't do more. You're a cop. You know that. You take one side, you get it in the neck from the other. You go against the husband and it's the wife who'll resent it. I know. I was the wife."

Gardner nodded. "I don't want it to happen again."

Holly squeezed his hands. "It won't."

Gardner fell back on his old argument. "Something's off about him."

Holly tried to lighten the mood. "He's English. They have white bottoms and drive on the wrong side of the road. Of course there's something off about him."

Gardner frowned. "You've seen his ass?"

Holly looked shocked. "No. But it rains a lot. When are they gonna get their backsides tanned?"

Gardner locked eyes with her. "I'm serious."

Holly didn't blink. "So am I. It's the right time. He's intelligent. He's handsome. And he's a gentleman. He's perfect."

Gardner shook his head. "Nobody's perfect. You read a lot. So you'll have heard this saying." Holly waited. Gardner lowered his voice. "If something's too good to be true." He leaned forward. "It isn't true."

FOUR

*

You shouldn't be doing this.

Cole told himself that, as he stood outside the hospital in the gathering gloom. The sun had set way out to sea but it left a ribbon of fire on the horizon that was fading fast. The streetlights had come on. The bright red sign above the emergency department bathed the street in blood.

You shouldn't be getting involved.

His inner voice didn't convince him. Phoning the hospital to check how Holly was doing was one thing. Coming to visit because she was being kept in overnight was a step too far. For a man looking to keep a low profile. For a man trying to avoid another catch 22 situation.

Pacifica General Hospital was a low wide building preserving the tone of the coastal strip at the northern edge of the city. The same as the schools and the office buildings and the small businesses that dotted the outskirts. Even the hotels along the shore were only three stories high. The emergency department was over to the right. The main entrance was just left of center.

This is a very bad idea.

Even as a child Cole had needed telling three times before

anything sank in. Tonight three times wasn't enough. His mind kept trying to dissuade him but his heart was in charge. He held the carrier bag in folded arms across his chest. Three ambulances were parked in the emergency bays. Pacifica's full compliment. Nobody was out on a run tonight. There were no emergencies. Cole hoped getting involved with Holly didn't provoke an emergency of his own.

You need to be light on your feet. Ready to leave at a moment's notice if the shit hits the fan. You can't afford extra baggage.

Cole felt pressure building in his forehead, like the barometer dropping before a storm. He shook his head clear then rubbed his temples. Not a storm. Just indecision. Best way to clear that was to put up or shut up. Shit or get off the pot his brother used to say. Thought of his brother brought the pressure right back. He shook his head again and this time spoke out loud. "Fuck it. Baggage is what makes life interesting."

He let the carrier bag swing from the handles and went through the main doors.

*

"YOU COME TO SEE IF I'M going to sue?"

"I wasn't the driver."

"It was your shop."

Cole pulled up a chair and sat beside Holly's bed. The private room wasn't reserved for special cases, the hospital was so small that most of the observation rooms were individual. Anybody needing a longer stay would be shipped up north to San Francisco. It reminded Cole of Wharfedale General Hospital before they discarded the pre-war buildings and put up a modern facility. Long corridors and narrow rooms. Emergency treatment for the local community with a touch of intimacy that was lost in the big cities. Everybody knew everybody. At least that's what it felt like to Cole. He smiled at Holly, who even managed to look good in a hospital gown. “Back home I remember this lad smashed his car into a tree. Swore blind the tree jumped out in front of him.”

Holly rested on one elbow so she could watch him. “You saying the shop jumped into the road?”

“I’m saying it wasn’t the tree’s fault.”

Holly smiled. “Okay. I won’t sue then.”

Cole nodded. “I keep forgetting this is a litigious society. Poodle power.”

“You mean the woman dried her dog in the microwave?”

Cole raised his eyebrows. “What was General Electric thinking? Not putting that in the instructions.”

“I think it was a Samsung.”

“Whatever.”

“And they have a warning sticker on the doors now.”

“Must have been a huge microwave. Barely fit a curry in back home.”

“I think it was a small dog.”

Cole nodded and let out a sigh. There was an awkward pause. All this small talk was just both of them avoiding the issue, the issue being how Cole felt about Holly and what Holly thought about the Englishman. Neither of them wanted to broach the subject. Cole found the easiest way into it. “How you feeling?”

“I got hit with a car. How you think I’m feeling?”

“Actually you got hit by a bookcase.”

“A bookcase that was hit by a car. Same difference.”

Cole softened his eyes. “What I’m saying is I’m worried about you. Asking how you’re feeling. Expression of my concern.”

Holly pushed the pillows up the back of the bed and sat up. Her movements were labored and she fought back the moan building in her throat. She settled against the pillows and flexed her shoulders.

Bruises stood out against her pale skin. There was a graze on her forehead that had already scabbed over. "I've felt better. Could have been worse."

Cole let out a sigh. "Yeah. I try not to think of worse."

Holly looked at the man sitting beside her bed and realized something she hadn't asked. Concern mingled with embarrassment at her oversight. "Must have come pretty close to hitting you as well."

"The bookcase or the car?"

"Both."

Cole shrugged. "Closer to you. I thought…"

He didn't say what he thought. He fell silent. Holly filled the void. "All the same. You okay?"

Cole smiled but his eyes remained sad. "Got knocked out of the way by the cash register."

He let the smile reach his eyes. "Goes to show that money helps."

Holly looked at the slight discoloration down one side of Cole's face. She stopped trying to be the street-smart cop and asked her first real question. "Has Ben found the driver yet?"

Cole raised the carrier bag so Holly could see it. "I'm a bookseller not the police. He doesn't confide in me." He put the bag on his lap and lowered his voice. "Tell you the truth. I think he blames me more than the driver." He pointed a finger at Holly then at himself. "For you being there in the first place. I don't think he approves."

Holly slumped against the pillows, keeping Ben Gardner's warning to herself. There was no point spreading the veteran cop's doubts. She toyed with the bedclothes and didn't notice Cole avert his eyes. He was struggling with his own demons. His own sense of guilt at not telling Holly the truth. The truth being that Ben Gardner was right not to trust the Englishman. He thought about the past and how much of it he was keeping from Holly. How much of it he was trying to keep from himself. Some things were best kept secret.

Some secrets were safer buried deep. *You need to be light on your feet. Ready to leave at a moment's notice if the shit hits the fan. You can't afford extra baggage.*

Cole peeled back the carrier bag just to give himself something to do.

Holly seized on the distraction. "That my book?"

Cole was happy to change the subject. "Yes. I thought flowers would send the wrong message."

She made a gimme gesture with both hands. "What message is that?"

Knowing exactly what the message was. Both of them did, but neither would speak the words they both wanted to hear. They were damned by secrets and lies. It was safer to focus on the small stuff. Cole took the book out of the bag and handed it over. Holly ran her hands over the cover. "Not a scratch."

Cole held his hands together as if in prayer. "It must be blessed. Only thing survived unscathed in the shop."

That wasn't entirely true but it sounded good. It sounded safe. Away from the dangerous ground of relationship talk and hidden pasts. Holly followed his lead and gave the book a little shake. "Thanks."

"Least I could do considering what you went through to buy it."

Holly laughed and kept on safe ground. "Shouldn't take Ben long to find Cinderella."

Cole looked at the twinkle in Holly's eye. "He told you about that, huh?"

"I don't think he was impressed with the glass slipper joke."

"I don't think he's impressed with me at all."

Which brought them right back where they didn't want to go. A siren started up outside. An emergency had finally arisen and one of the ambulances was heading off towards it. That was the thing about police, fire, and ambulances. Always rushing headlong into the next emergency. For the rest of the world it was the other way around, emergencies always hurtled towards you. Cole made one last attempt to steer the conversation. "When he finally retires you'll be a shoe in for the job." His smile looked a little strained. "I can see you as top dog at Shelter Cove."

Holly shook her head. She didn't realize what she said until after she'd said it. "Ben won't retire. He'll die first."

FIVE

*

THE SHELTER COVE POLICE office was on Linda Mar Boulevard and shared the parking lot with McDonalds next door. It was called the police office and not a police station because that's exactly what it was. An office. There was no custody area and no jail cell and no radio room. It was a single story outpost that didn't need to exist but it appeased the local community so the Pacifica Police Department paid lip service and gave Ben Gardner the job. It was almost a ceremonial position. The old cop had no staff apart from a couple of part time auxiliaries and no real power. He dealt with local issues like school crossing patrols and missing dogs. Having a car smash into the bookstore and injure his best deputy was the biggest thing to happen in the cove since Carl Anderson hit the surf shack in his pickup last year.

Gardner swung the patrol car into the parking lot and opened the office. The streetlamp outside blinked and went out again. He made a mental note to have the town council get it fixed. Light from McDonalds spilled across the parking lot so he could find his key. He flicked the fluorescents on and flopped into his chair. The leather creaked in the silence. He put his feet up on the desk and leaned back. "Well howdy doody."

His voice sounded tired in his own ears. Talking to an empty office sounded even worse. He thought about Holly convalescing up in Pacifica General and wished she were here. She was his best deputy, which wasn't saying much since young Bret Harding, the only other part timer, couldn't find his ass with both hands. The college graduate only worked three days a week and on those days Ben prayed that nothing happened to tax the football star's mind. Nothing ever happened at Shelter Cove. Until now.

Gardner let out a sigh and looked at the wall map pinned to the notice board. It showed Pacifica in all its glory, a six-mile stretch of coastal beaches nestling in several valleys between Sweeney Ridge to the east and Montara Mountain to the south. The bulk of the city was up in Fairmont and Westview, spreading down through Pacific Manor into East Sharp Park. The other residential neighborhoods were Vallemar, Rockaway Beach and Linda Mar. Tagged onto the end of that was Pedro Point and Shelter Cove but Shelter Cove had become the coverall name for the southern tip. The outpost that Ben Gardner would work until he retired.

He held his arms out wide. "One day Holly, all this will be yours."

Talking to himself was becoming a habit. He'd have to make sure he didn't do it when anyone was listening. He let out another sigh and considered what he'd just said. There were plenty of people in the cove who would agree that Holly was the perfect replacement but he knew that was never going to happen. The only reason this office was open was as a favor to the veteran cop. Somewhere for him to feel useful as he saw his time out. When he called it a day the PPD would close it and extend patrols from the city instead. Emergency cover was from there anyway.

His stomach rumbled in the quiet. "Down boy. I'll feed you."

Talking to himself again. He shook his head and considered completing the accident report but then his stomach rumbled again. He could smell the food over in McDonalds. He dropped the Converse Classic sneaker on the desk and swung his legs down. Police work could wait. It was time to eat.

*

FILLING IN THE ACCIDENT REPORT took longer than he expected. That was partly because he still wasn't proficient with all the modern technology. Back when he started, reports would be filled in by hand then typed up by the typing pool and faxed. Later he'd mastered typing up his own reports and had to fax them himself. Now it was all done online then printed for the records if needed.

The Converse Classic stood on the desk in front of him, the ankle folded down so he could read the name. Matthew King. Surf dude of the lowest order. Part of the delay was checking the vehicle details and registration, the upshot of which was that it wasn't King's car. According to DMV the surfer had a driving license but not a car. According to local knowledge that wasn't unusual because the surf community used pool cars to get around. They would share a car with anyone. If you touched their surfboard however you'd be in trouble.

Gardner checked the registration to see which surf dude owned the car. The computer blinked and came up with no name. He squinted at the screen to make sure he'd typed the number correctly. His stubby fingers were notorious for hitting two keys at a time. The number was correct. The car was not. Not according to the computer. It was shown as a scrapper that had been written off in an accident six months ago and taken to Driftwood Auto Wreckers off Crespi Drive for spare parts. It shouldn't have been in one piece never mind on the road. He marked that down as an enquiry for tomorrow then pulled up King's address and date of birth. He filled in the driver's section of the report then moved on to the witnesses.

Holly West and Cole Thornton.

He drummed his fingers on the desk. Injured party first. That would be Holly. He pushed back from the desk and went into the small kitchenette to make a fresh coffee. Working late meant keeping awake. School crossing patrols and missing dogs didn't need late night policing. Gardner rarely worked after dark. It wasn't the lateness of the hour that gave him pause though. It was the thought of Holly almost getting killed at Rocky Coast Books by a car from Driftwood Auto Wreckers. The bookstore that Arlo Rankoff was trying to buy and the wreckers yard that he already owned. That was another enquiry for tomorrow.

The kettle boiled. He brewed the coffee, strong and black with three sugars. He sat at the desk and continued. His typing got faster as he filled in Holly's details. He knew them off by heart. Arguello Boulevard Motel was just around the corner. The rest he knew from her employment records. He copied her injuries from the paramedic's report and marked that she was being treated overnight at Pacifica General.

He paused again and took a drink of coffee. He typed in the next name. Cole Thornton. That was all. He drank coffee and stared at the name. *There's something off about him.* He'd said it to Holly and he felt it now. He tried to rationalize the thought. Maybe he was doing the overprotective father thing. That was possible. He'd always felt paternal towards his young ward, feelings that were mixed with guilt at not having helped more with the abusive husband. Thornton seemed to be a quiet and respectful guy but there was something in his eyes that always set Gardner on edge. Something blank, like looking into a shark's eyes. A shield that was hiding something behind it.

He opened another screen on the computer and ran the name for criminal activity. Not for the first time. The computer was slow.

Gardner took a sip of coffee. Then the search came back negative. Not for the first time.

Gardner glanced at the wall clock. It was getting late. He finished the report with a brief summary of the accident then hit enter. The computer took a few seconds to save and send then emitted a musical ping. Job done. The file went to the PPD headquarters for attention in the morning. The first official police document to have Cole Thornton's name on it since he arrived in Shelter Cove.

SIX

*

THE NEW WINDOW DIDN'T FIT. After spending all day clearing up the carnage inside the bookstore Cole struggled to find a, *this glass is half full*, way of looking at that. He let out a sigh and put his hands on his hips. "What do you mean it doesn't fit?"

The workmen used suction cups to carry the window to one side and set it down carefully on the wooden stand. The glazier unfastened the cup with a hiss and came back to the front of the shop. "It's not the window. It's the frame."

Cole stood on the inside looking out. "The frame was here first. You cut the glass to fit."

The glazier defended his work. "The size is right. It's the shape."

"You cut the wrong shape?"

"The frame's the wrong shape."

"It's a rectangle. What's wrong with that?"

The glazier shook his head. "More of a rhomboid. Angles are a bit off."

"You saying my window's a parallelogram?"

"Not even that. Angles are uneven."

Cole wasn't getting anywhere. "You measured it."

"And it's the right size. Just not the right shape."

Stalemate. Cole climbed through the gap and stood looking at the front of his shop. All the broken glass had been cleaned out of the frame and the carved wooden center spar removed. He would miss that. The new window was one big sheet of glass, a rectangle trying to fit into a rhomboid. The frame looked rectangular to Cole. "How much out of shape?"

The glazier looked at the frame. "Not much."

"So what you gonna do about it?"

The glazier held both hands up, palms twelve inches apart, like showing the size of the fish he'd caught. The palms were both at an angle. He straightened them until they were square. "Shave a bit off the inner lip. Then it'll fit like a glove." He drew the shape of the window in the air with one finger. "Once it's sealed and beaded you'll be fine."

"Without it looking like a rhomboid?"

The glazier indicated the opening. "Does it look like a rhomboid now?"

Cole took the point. What the eye couldn't see the heart wouldn't grieve over. That sounded fine when it came to the window. He'd have a different opinion if he'd known what was coming down the line. Something his eye didn't see. He stepped back into the shop and let the workmen finish their job. By mid afternoon the window was fitted and the glazier was packing up. That's when the big guy came through the front door and turned the sign from OPEN to CLOSED.

*

"LOOKS LIKE YOU'VE BEEN having a bit of trouble."

The sign flip-flopped on its string as the door swung shut. It settled at an angle. One more misshape in a day of misshapes. Cole looked at the door and then at the man who'd just come through it. He was bigger and rougher than the ones who'd been sent before but the agenda would be the same. "No trouble. It was time I got a new window."

The man looked at the surviving bookcases lined up in one half of the shop and the piles of books neatly stacked against the back wall. All the splintered wood and broken glass had been cleared away but the shop still looked a long way from being open for business. "You call this no trouble?"

Cole picked up a heavy book and dropped it on the new sales counter. "I call it stocktaking."

The man flicked the latch on the door and took two steps into the shop. "Well it's about time you took stock of your situation."

Cole rested a hand on the book. It was bigger and heavier than the one he'd sold to Holly. More pictures. Different subject. Good for beating miscreants into submission. "A Catch 22 situation?"

"What?"

"A no win situation."

The man forced a smile. "You win if you sell the shop."

Cole kept his face blank. "But I don't want to sell the shop. So if I sell against my will that's not a win."

The smile faded. "If you keep having cars smash through your window, that's not a win either."

This time it was Cole's turn to smile. "Exactly. No win. Catch 22."

The man looked around the shop then let out a sigh. "We don't want anyone getting hurt."

Cole lowered his voice. "Somebody already got hurt."

The heavy thought about taking the bait but kept it simple. "We don't want anyone else getting hurt."

Cole picked up the book and dropped it back on the counter. A solid thud. "Is that the royal we?"

The big guy tilted his head to one side and focused on Cole. "My boss. The man offering more than this dump's worth."

Cole rested one hand on the book. "Your boss, Arlo Rankoff."

The heavy shook his head. "My boss, who wants to keep his name out of it."

Cole feigned understanding. "Ah. Yes. No names, no pack drill."

The man was starting to get angry. "Do you always talk in fuckin' riddles?"

Cole slid the book to the edge of the counter. "An English saying."

"Well I'm not fuckin' English."

"It means if Rankoff's name isn't mentioned he won't get punished."

The man looked confused and tried to overcompensate. "Mr Rankoff doesn't get punished. He does the punishing."

Cole smiled. "So, you admit it is Rankoff trying to buy me out."

The man back-peddled. "Won't be his name on the contract."

Cole braced his shoulders. "It won't be mine either. Place isn't for sale."

The man reached into his pocket and took a step towards Cole. He stopped in front of the bookseller and stuck his chin out. "You don't want any more accidents."

Cole gripped the end of the book. "They're not accidents if they're done on purpose."

The big guy ignored the interruption. "People could get hurt."

Cole slid the book closer to him and repeated the point. "People have already got hurt."

This time the man took the opening. "Your girlfriend?"

"Deputy West."

The man began to bring his hand out of his pocket. "The motel owner. Motels can have accidents too."

The hand wasn't empty. Sunlight from the new window glinted off the knife handle. One finger pressed a button and the switchblade snapped open. Cole didn't wait. He grabbed the book in two hands and swung it forward and upward, his best imitation of a baseball swing. The book was heavy. Weight and momentum took it straight through the knife hand and up into the face. One blow. A solid follow through. The knife flew across the room. The big guy's face crumpled sideways and he went down like a felled tree. Cole stood over him with the book. In case he needed a second swing. "Just like a Californian. Brings a knife to a book fight."

He didn't need a second swing. The big man was dazed and confused at how he'd been caught by surprise. Cole stepped back and put the book on the sales counter. He was going to make a comment about the book being mightier than the sword when a knock on the door broke the spell. His head snapped round just in time to see Ben Gardner kick the front door in.

*

"HE SLIPPED ON A BAR OF SOAP."

Cole indicated the man groaning on the floor. Gardner picked up the twisted door latch and closed the door. "That joke only works if you're in the shower."

Cole looked down at the man who was sitting against the counter. "Principle's the same though."

Gardner looked down at the fallen man. "Meaning he had an accident. You didn't hit him with a book when he came at you with a knife."

Cole shrugged. "What knife?" Safe in the knowledge that the knife had vanished under a bookcase. "No. He tripped just as I was showing him the book." Cole indicated the book on the counter. "I think I may have ruined the sale." He kicked the man on the floor. "That's what you said isn't it? No sale?"

Gardner helped the big man to his feet. One hand snagged a wallet out of his back pocket. He opened it and read out the name so the big guy understood that the police knew who he was in future. He handed the wallet back and sent him on his way. Once he'd left Gardner looked at Cole. "So you're not pressing charges then?"

Cole shook his head. Keeping a low profile meant keeping his name off official complaints. He didn't want his name recording anywhere. The accident was bad enough but he reckoned only being a witness might just be safe. "Accidents happen."

Gardner didn't look convinced. "Not having a good day then are you?" He dropped the damaged latch in Cole's hand. "Sorry about the door."

Cole changed the subject. "How's Holly?"

Gardner acknowledged Cole's concern without condoning it. In his view Holly wouldn't even be in hospital if she wasn't mixed up with the strange Englishman lying through his teeth. "All clear. They're letting her out this evening."

Cole deflated with a sigh. The post adrenaline dump left him feeling shaky and tired. Knowing that the crash was aimed at him made him feel even more responsible for Holly. "She need a lift?"

Gardner jerked a thumb towards the police cruiser parked outside. "She's got a lift. I think you've done enough. Don't you?"

There was no answer to that so Cole changed the subject again. "You found the driver yet?"

"I know where to find him."

"Reckon he'll tell you why he did it?"

Gardner scrutinized Cole's face. "He'll tell me he lost control driving too fast. That's what happened isn't it?"

Cole nodded. "As far as I could see. Yes."

Gardner watched for signs of a reaction. "I'll be more interested in knowing how come he was driving a scrapper from Arlo Rankoff's auto wrecker's yard that shouldn't have been on the road in the first place."

Cole felt the heat spread up his neck. He kept a straight face but wasn't sure if his face was reddening. Gardner's tone became playful. "You know, I had the chance to buy a couple of houses over towards Shelter Cove a few years ago. Could have made a killing, prices Rankoff's been paying to buy 'em all now." His face softened but his eyes were still watchful. "Who'd have thought those rundown beach homes would be worth so much he'd spend a fortune buying everything leading to them?"

Cole raised his eyebrows and shrugged. As conversations go this was a definite no win situation so he decided to let Gardner run his string. "I don't imagine Rankoff really wants to own a bookstore."

Gardner took the cruiser keys out of his pocket and headed towards the door. He stopped with the door half open and gave an exaggerated double take. "Oh, I almost forgot. Reason I came over here." Cole waited for the hammer to drop. He could feel the cop's eyes burning into him. "Somebody was asking about you up in San Francisco." Gardner paused for effect. "Another English guy. Any idea who that might be?"

The heat burst through Cole's brain. His eyes swam in and out of focus and he felt out of breath. *Time to shit or get off the pot*. His brother's favorite saying. Cole picked up the book from the counter to give him time. He rubbed the greasy smudge off the cover where it had smacked the big man in the face. Gardner watched the pantomime from the open door. Cole lowered the shield behind his eyes and shook his head. "No idea. Sorry."

SEVEN

*

IT TOOK THE REST OF THE afternoon for Cole to finish rearranging the shop. He didn't have any spare bookcases to replace the ones that were smashed so he used what he had more economically. He left the space in front of the window empty and arranged the bookcases around the edges of the shop leaving plenty of floor space in the middle. It made the room seem bigger. He had to admit it made the store look better too. Better than the outlook for Cole's immediate future. He stopped and slammed a hand against the bookcase. "Shit."

The hand stung. That was the idea. He would have slapped himself across the face to sharpen himself up but his face was still sore from the accident. Sometimes pain was your body's way of telling you something was wrong. If his brother was close to finding him then something was very wrong indeed. "Fuck."

He slammed the bookcase again. *Time to shit or get off the pot.* In this case it was time to face his brother or get out of town. He thought about that for a moment as he looked out across the field. The ocean looked calm all the way to the horizon but Cole wasn't fooled. There was a storm coming and it was coming in the shape of his younger brother. Question was should Cole ride out the storm or get out while the going was good?

Shelter Cove. The name implied a place of safety. For the past three years that's exactly what it had been. Somewhere to shelter from the slings and arrows of outrageous fortune, but now outrageous fortune was coming to get him. If there was any truth in the good brother, bad brother dynamic then Cole's brother was definitely the bad one. Violent. Angry. Short tempered. Vengeful. He ticked all those boxes and a few more besides. He wasn't the forgive and forget type. Cole doubted his brother would forgive him. Not considering why he was coming.

The money. It wouldn't matter if Cole explained. He'd want to take it back and he wouldn't take no for an answer. Vengeful. Resourceful too. If he'd tracked Cole down to San Francisco then it wouldn't be long before he rolled into Shelter Cove. Tidying the shop didn't seem important any more but Cole continued anyway, like a kind of therapy. The routine helped calm him. Replacing the bowls of scented wooden fruit brought order where chaos would soon reign. The smell was pleasant. It mingled with the wood shavings from the window frame. He could almost believe the accident had never happened.

The bookcases were in place. Cole filled them with books from the pile against the back wall. Those that wouldn't fit he stored in the back room. He didn't put the shelf above the cash register back up. Standing under something that had already crushed him made him nervous. The thought of being crushed again brought him right back to his brother.

He made his decision, stored the last of the books and closed the shop.

*

HIS APARTMENT WAS ROUND the back of the bookstore but Cole used the connecting door from the shop. He locked it and stood in the hallway for a moment. The apartment was neat and tidy, the product of a strict upbringing and a military background. His father would have approved. His mother never got the chance to see her good son grow up.

Cole walked to the storage cupboard near the back door and took out a suitcase and a battered leather holdall. He paused and looked at the scuba gear stored against the wall. He'd have to use it one more time before he left. For now it was time to pack.

He went into the bedroom and dropped the case on the bed. The wardrobes were as tidy as the rest of the house. Clothes hung from hangers in colour order. Light colours on the left ranging to the darker ones on the right. Denim jeans and tracksuit bottoms were in a separate cupboard. He took out the ones he wanted to take with him and laid them out on the bed. He removed the hangers and folded them so they'd fit in the case.

T-shirts and socks and underwear were in the chest of drawers beneath the window. He used the t-shirts to pad out the top of the case and put the rest in the holdall. He lined the top of both with towels from the bathroom then packed his toiletries in a plastic wash bag and looked in the mirror.

He stopped.

He didn't like what he saw.

Concern showed in his eyes. Not fear exactly, he was the older brother after all, but something close. He knew that if it came to a fight they would be closely matched but there would be blood and pain and neither would come out unscathed. Fighting with family was never good. Running away from family was even worse. That was the other look that Cole saw in the mirror. Guilt. Shame.

He pulled the draw cord on the wash bag and went back into

the bedroom. He was almost ready. He thought about Holly. About running out on somebody else. He felt guilty about that as well. He told himself she'd be better off without him but that lie never worked.

He fastened the suitcase and zipped the holdall. He was swinging them off the bed when a knock came at the door. Not the heavy copper's knock of Ben Gardner. A gentler knock that was almost apologetic. He went to the window and looked out. The suitcase dropped from his hand. He put the holdall down next to it.

He hadn't seen the woman outside for over three years.

His brother's ex-wife, Sarah.

EIGHT

*

BEN GARDNER COLLECTED Holly from the hospital at 5.30pm. If Pacifica had any kind of rush hour traffic that would have been a problem. It didn't so it wasn't. Cabrillo Highway was busy but nothing like the nightmare of Los Angeles and San Francisco. Surface streets from the hospital to the highway flowed easily, giving Ben plenty of opportunity to talk without compromising his driving. "I see he brought you the book."

Holly glanced over her shoulder at the carrier bag. "You'll be making detective in no time."

Ben looked across at his passenger. "And they'll be making you the town smart ass."

Holly smiled. She'd known Ben ever since he witnessed her job application. Testy banter was par for the course. As she'd settled into being a cop instead of a motel owner it became a job requirement. She understood now why cops used gallows humor to get through their daily grind. It took the edge of the dark stuff and allowed them to function. She looked at Ben. "You going to give me another lecture?"

Ben concentrated on merging onto the highway. "No lecture." He allowed himself a quick look at Holly. "I still don't like him though."

"You're not dating him."

Traffic moved over to let the patrol car in and Ben settled into the flow. "That what you call it now? Buying books and getting knocked down?"

Holly blushed. "Well, maybe not dating. Yet."

"But it's on the cards?"

Holly tried not to look too far into the future and was embarrassed that Ben was getting ahead of her. She knew what her feelings were for Cole. What she didn't know was how he felt about her. She reckoned he liked her but he'd never pushed his advantage. That worried her slightly. She sometimes wondered what he was hiding. He was hiding something, she was sure of that, and a cold dark worm of doubt was creeping into the back of her head. What if he was married?

Ben took her silence as a warning to mind his own business. The fact that Thornton was lying to him about the accident and the Rankoff intimidation didn't mean he was lying to Holly. He'd give high odds that he was though, and he didn't want to see her get hurt again. Not so much physically, because he didn't think Thornton was a violent man, but emotionally.

Holly's uniform was creased and dirty. Ben hadn't brought her fresh clothes. The uniform reminded her that she was a cop. Part time. "Have you found the driver yet?"

Ben took the exit onto Linda Mar Boulevard and slowed to a crawl. "Going to check his address after I've dropped you off." He drove past the police office and McDonalds. "You want anything to eat?"

Holly watched the fast food outlet drift by on the right. "Not a Big Mac and fries. I've got stuff at home." She watched the police office drift by too. "What's my shift tomorrow?"

Ben took a left and a right into Arguello Boulevard. The motel was just along the road on the left. He pulled into the parking lot and stopped outside the bungalow round back. "Your shift's covered."

"Bret? Don't you think we're in enough trouble as it is?"

Ben turned the engine off. "There aint no trouble apart from some surfers can't drive for shit."

Holly looked at Ben. They both knew there was more to the accident than that but neither spoke of it. Ben didn't want to concern Holly. Holly didn't want to give Cole more problems than he already had. She twisted in her seat to get the carrier bag but stopped short. Pain shot through her ribs and spine. Ben saw the look on her face and jumped out of the car. He opened the back door and brought the book round to her side. She got out gingerly. Ben started to give her the book then pulled it back out of reach. "You're taking a few days off. Don't you have sheets to iron?"

Holly straightened and flexed her back. "I've got staff for that."

Ben nodded. "And I've got staff for you."

Holly gave an unbelieving smirk. "Bret Harding?"

Ben shrugged. "He can string a sentence together and not step on his dick."

Holly smiled. "He's a muscle hound. I've heard about their dicks."

"At least he doesn't have a white bottom."

Holly feigned shock. "You've seen his ass?"

Ben gave her the book. "Two days off."

"One."

"Done." He nodded towards the caretaker's bungalow. "Now go and take it easy."

Holly took out her keys and crossed to the front door. She turned and waved her thanks as Ben got back in the car and reversed out of the parking bay. He spun the car around and raised a hand then watched her go inside. Once the door was closed he checked the map inside his head and pinpointed Matt King's address. He swung out of the lot and headed east.

*

HOLLY KEPT IT TOGETHER until she got inside then sat on the couch and burst into tears. The tension had been building for weeks, ever since she decided to move forward with Cole, but the last few days had been the worst. She liked him. She was sure he liked her but his lack of action was frustrating. She'd run out of veiled suggestions and was about to make a bolder move when the car smashed through the window.

Bad timing.

Bad omen?

After that she couldn't help falling back into cynical cop mode. It's what cops did to get through the day and sometimes it spilled over into their personal lives. That's why so many cops were divorced. Not because they were fooling around or out all hours on shift, because their nearest and dearest didn't understand the deadpan humour and abrupt responses. The stress of pretending to be calm and collected when what she really wanted was to hold him in her arms finally boiled over. The tears were hot and violent. She sobbed for three minutes. Then it was over.

She noticed the dirty uniform again and went into the bedroom. She undressed and dumped the clothes in the wash basket. The shower was hot as she soaped away the hospital smell. Her hands were gentle over the cuts and bruises, soaping her shoulders and breasts and the firm hard muscles of her stomach. She closed her eyes and thought of Cole. What she wished they could do together. One hand moved south and soaped between her legs. The moisture there wasn't all soap and water.

She stopped and opened her eyes.

Her hands were shaking.

You're a grown woman. Don't be such a wuss. And that's how the decision was made. Holly finished showering and washed her hair. She toweled down and dabbed herself with perfume. The hair drier made quick work of her short hair. Clean clothes and a milky coffee completed the transformation. From a female under stress to a woman in charge of her own destiny. It was time to find out if Cole felt the same way about her. To stop pussyfooting about and lay her cards on the table.

She washed her cup and took her car keys out of the drawer. The bookstore wasn't far but this felt more like a driving situation than a walk. She squeezed the keys in one hand, took a deep breath, then set off to visit Cole Thornton at home.

NINE

*

"YOU CAN'T HIDE FROM HIM."

"I have so far. I can disappear again."

Cole and Sarah were sitting at the kitchen table, Sarah looking as good as Cole remembered. She had a few more lines on her face but they added character to her natural beauty and her figure was as toned as ever. She didn't explain how she'd found him. He didn't ask. There was no point wondering about the how, she was here, that's all that mattered.

Sarah leaned forward, elbows on the table. "He can find you again."

Cole shook his head. "Not today."

She sat back in the chair. "What makes you think he's not here already?"

Cole pushed his chair away from the table and stood up. "Because he's in San Francisco." The kettle began to boil. Cole raised his eyebrows. "You still take it strong and black?"

She shook her head. "I've changed since the old days. Milk and three sugars."

Cole pulled a face. "Urgh. Same as he liked his coffee."

"He never liked coffee. He was always a tea drinker."

"Maybe he's changed as well."

Sarah indicated the suitcase and the holdall standing in the hallway. "That why you're heading for the hills?"

Cole shrugged. "You know why he's coming. Change don't come into it." He made two coffees, killing Sarah's with milk and sugar. Cole needed the caffeine fix to help him on his way. He slid her cup across the table and sat down with his. "Funny thing about brothers. It's always the second born goes off the rails."

Sarah took a sip of her coffee. "That's because they have a lot to live up to."

Cole thought about his childhood. He remembered his father and the trauma his brother had to live with. He considered why the brothers started life at loggerheads and the reason it got worse from there. He tried to forget his own part in that. "Sometimes older brothers have a lot to live down."

Sarah knew the history. She'd been married to the bad boy long enough to hear it many times. Not from her husband but from those around him. "It wasn't your fault."

Cole's shoulders sagged. "It wasn't his either."

Sarah pushed her coffee away. "You didn't turn him bad. The badness was there all the time."

Cole accepted the platitude. "And that's why I'm going to disappear."

Sarah looked crestfallen. She spoke slowly, fighting back the emotion. "Take me with you. Don't leave me this time."

Cole looked at the woman he'd once loved. "I didn't leave you last time. You chose him over me."

She let out a sigh. "I shouldn't have married him." Then held her hands together as if praying for forgiveness. "We all make mistakes."

Cole reached across the table and enclosed her hands in his. He gave them a gentle squeeze. "Well your mistake is on his from San

Francisco." He let go of her hands. "And mine would be hanging around to greet him."

Sarah pushed her chair back from the table. The legs screeched on the floor. "Take me with you then."

Cole looked into her eyes and tried to recall the feelings he once had. There was a time when he would have done anything for her, before she married his brother. That had changed things but it hadn't changed the way he felt about Sarah. There were some things a man just didn't do and one of them was messing around with your brother's wife. He looked deep into her eyes. She was still beautiful. She still owned a piece of his heart. And now she was his brother's ex-wife. That should carry some weight. He almost gave it serious consideration but then she spoke again and ruined everything.

"You've got the money. We could go anywhere."

*

COLE WASHED THE CUPS and prepared to leave. Even when abandoning ship he was still a tidy person. That was his father's influence. The naval commander had influenced other things too, like his other son turning out the way he did. Cole had a part to play in that too and it was another reason why he couldn't hang around to face his brother again.

Sarah recognized the pain on Cole's face. "You don't have to do this."

Cole put the dried cups on the shelf and closed the cupboard door. "And you didn't have to marry him."

Sarah sounded exasperated. "I know. That wasn't your fault either. How many times do I have to say I'm sorry?"

Cole put the teaspoons away then leaned against the washbasin. He faced the wall for a moment then turned to face Sarah. "I should have done more. I didn't like the way he treated you."

"I was his wife. It wasn't up to you."

"He was my younger brother. Of course it was up to me."

They weren't going to agree about this but Sarah tried one last time to soften the impact her husband had had on both their lives. "He didn't beat me if that's what you think."

Cole looked surprised at the suggestion. "He'd never hit a woman. Just everybody else."

"He didn't hurt me."

Cole disagreed again. "Yes he did. Every time he left."

"You know why he left."

As soon as she'd said it she wished she could take it back. They both knew why her husband, Cole's brother, and their father's second son kept finding reasons not to be at home. Because home was something that had been taken away from him at an early age. Cole could have helped with that but took his father's side against his brother. The die was cast. Conflict was inevitable. The brothers became combatants. The younger brother had been fighting ever since.

There was a thud at the back door. Cole spun to face it. There was another knock. Then three dead birds slammed into the kitchen window and cracked the glass.

TEN

*

MATT KING'S HOUSE WAS as run down and scruffy as the surfer himself. In fact it wasn't a house at all, it was the groundskeeper's cabin in the grounds of Frontier Land Park at the top of Yosemite Drive. It was a steep climb past expensive houses on the very edge of Linda Mar. The drive stopped in an abrupt turnaround next to Humboldt Court, a winding cul-de-sac of even more expensive houses.

Ben Gardner pulled up to the park entrance just beyond the turnaround and swung the patrol car round so it was facing back downhill. The forested hills that formed the outlying neighborhoods hid the coastline but the view was no less spectacular for that. Gardner knew where the police office was from here but couldn't see it. Sometimes he couldn't see the woods for the trees when it came to policing either. Maybe he'd settled into retirement mode too early, almost giving up on police work before he'd actually left. This felt like he was doing his job again. Checking the address of a dangerous driver.

The sun was low in the west and not far away from setting. It was another beautiful evening in California. Pacifica was up north beyond the trees. Linda Mar and Shelter Cove lay below towards the coast. San Andreas Lake and the San Francisco International Airport were over to the east across Sweeney Ridge, with San Francisco itself way up north along the eastern shore. Gardner took a moment to savor the peace and tranquility then got out of the car and savored it some more. Birdsong in the trees enhanced the calm. Cooked meat smells from a midweek barbecue drifted up from the houses. The smell of pine and wood bark drifted down from the park. The barbecue made his mouth water. The pine reminded him where he was going.

Gardner stepped over the padlocked chain across the entrance and followed the driveway through the trees. The park opened onto a large playing field at the middle of a bowl between rolling hills and woodland. Trees climbed the slopes on three sides, petering out to scrub and brush halfway up. A gravel footpath circled the field meeting at the children's play area, dressed up like a frontier fort, on the opposite side. The log structure and picnic tables were in keeping with the setting, the groundskeeper's cabin nestled in the left corner between a stand of trees and a supplies compound. It was as far from the surf dude image as you could imagine.

The park was empty. A gentle breeze coming in off the coast rustled the trees. Gardner stood at the mouth of the field and paused to take stock. He wasn't much of a cop but he knew enough to always check your approach before calling on a suspect. The early evening picnics were over. Any children that played in the park had gone home. A wisp of smoke hung over the barbecue pit, not completely damped down by the last user. The cabin stood dark and motionless in the lea of the fort.

Gardner took one step into the arena. The birdsong stopped. The breeze dropped and the trees fell silent. There was no movement. There was no sound. The pleasant California evening became cold and foreboding. He looked at the frontier fort. He glanced at the barbecue pit. He took a final look at the picnic tables then turned his attention back to the cabin. Nothing moved. There was no light. It was a dark corner of a summer park.

Waiting over. His feet crunched on gravel and movement and sound returned. The birds sounded louder. The trees swished harder. He turned left and followed the footpath clockwise around the park. Tree branches waved. Leaves rustled. His heart pounded a deep and rhythmic thud in his ears. His eyes flicked between the front door and the windows and the side of the cabin nearest the compound. There was no greeting. There was no warning shot.

He climbed the steps to the front porch and rested with one hand on the railing. He let out a sigh of relief and chided himself for being so melodramatic. Too many late night movies. Too many school crossings and missing dogs. He'd forgotten what knocking on a suspect's door felt like. He stepped forward and raised a fist then stopped.

The door was open.

*

SURFERS WERE NOTORIOUSLY loose with their lifestyles but this felt bad even before Gardner pushed the door open and looked into the gloom. The living room was untidy but not enough to suggest the place had been turned over. Clothes were scattered on the couch and two surfboards leaned against the wall. A TV in the corner played the weather channel to the empty room. There were half a dozen empty beer cans on the coffee table. It didn't look like Matt King drank much coffee. Gardner looked at the hallway towards the back of the cabin. "This is Ben Gardner. You in there?"

He paused for a moment and tried to figure the layout. Living room at the front. Dining kitchen to one side. That left the bedroom and bathroom along the hallway. The most likely place to find a drunken surfer.

"This is the police."

That sounded more official. He hadn't seen any movies where the cops announced themselves on first name terms. He nudged the kitchen door open with one foot. Empty. No cooking smells. Nothing recent. He walked slowly down the hallway. Bedroom on the left. Bathroom on the right. The bedroom door was open so that's where he started.

He stood in the hall and listened. The only sound was the weather reporter trying not to sound bored repeating the same forecast all day long. There was no snoring. There was no heavy breathing. There was no rustling of bedclothes as the occupant dived under the covers. Gardner put one hand on the gun in his holster. He considered drawing it but figured, how dangerous could a one-shoed surfer be?

He gave a quick nod of the head around the corner then back into the hallway. He gave a second look to be sure. Then he stepped through the door and surveyed the empty room. The bed was unmade. There were more clothes scattered on the floor.

A bang sounded behind him and he spun around.

There was nobody there. The noise came again. Across the hallway in the bathroom. Gardner unclipped the holster and gripped the butt. He couldn't remember the last time he'd drawn his weapon apart from cleaning it. This felt like a good time to start. "Is that you Matt?"

No reply.

"It's Ben Gardner."

Back on first name terms. He crossed the hallway and drew the gun, holding it down by his side in exactly the wrong way. The bathroom door was open six inches. Something was stopping it from closing. Gardner looked down at the matching Converse Classic sneaker lying on the floor. Cinderella. The bang sounded again and he jerked the gun up in front of him. "Matt. Cover your love muscle."

He nudged the door open with his foot and stepped into the bathroom. The open window swung in the breeze and banged against the frame. Gardner let out a sigh and holstered his weapon. He shook his head at the irony of finding an oceangoing surfer drowned in his own bath.

ELEVEN

*

THERE WERE FIVE DEAD birds altogether, two at the bottom of the door and three outside the window. The window had cracked but not broken. Cole wasn't having any luck with windows today. He nudged them into one pile with the side of his foot then scanned the rear garden. The garden was small but heavily wooded. Trees and bushes took up most of the space beyond a narrow lawn. He glanced up Livingston Avenue, the tree-lined street that ran up the side of the bookstore. Nice houses. More trees. Plenty of cover.

The sun was almost dipping into the Pacific. The street was draped in shadows and darker places beneath the trees. Cole had heard about freak events where flocks of birds got their navigation wrong and flew into tall buildings. He'd never heard of five birds flying round the back of a secluded house and slamming into the windows. He stepped inside to get a bin liner. "He's here."

Sarah sat heavily and leaned on the table. She looked around the kitchen as if searching for inspiration. Her eyes focused on the cracked window. "Are you sure? I had a bird smacked into my window once."

Cole looked down at her. "Did he have four friends did the same?"

Sarah was clutching at straws. "It happens. I saw it in a film."

Cole opened a cupboard under the washbasin and pealed off a black bin liner from a roll. He rubbed the plastic to open the bag. "That's why it's him. Hitchcock's The Birds. He loved that film." He closed the cupboard. "That and Saturday afternoon westerns and The Godfather. I'm surprised he didn't put a horses head in the bed."

Sarah sat back with a start. "There isn't one is there?"

He flapped the bag to fill it with air. "I think I'd have noticed when I packed."

She realized how silly she was being and tried to redeem herself. "Birds through the window. Is that why you got a new shop window today?"

Cole stopped in the doorway and looked at Sarah. He wondered how long she'd been watching before coming to see him. He thought about something else too. The threat levels had been increasing. Bullying tactics. Car crash. Knife attack. Maybe this was just another turn of the screw. "A car lost control in the street."

Sarah didn't look convinced. "And five birds lost control in the garden." She turned to face him. "You know what they say about trouble always coming in threes."

Cole nodded and glanced where the scuba gear was hidden in the hallway cupboard. At the suitcase and the holdall standing next to it. "That's why it's time to go. Before number three catches up with me."

Sarah stood up. "Catches up with us. He's not going to like me coming to see you."

"Then you shouldn't have come to see me."

That was harsh and unfeeling. He flapped the bag one last time to cover his thoughtlessness and went out to dispose of the dead birds. A car pulled up beside the house. The engine was turned off.

A door slammed. Cole looked up in time to see Holly West crossing the garden.

*

HOLLY SAW THE WOMAN in Cole's kitchen a split second too late. She was already smiling at Cole and indicating the cracked window. "You're not having much luck with windows today."

Cole flinched at the twinning of his own thoughts. Holly mistook the flinch for something else, as soon as she saw the beautiful woman sitting at the kitchen table. The woman looked up and smiled unconvincingly. Cole scuffed the last of the birds into the bin liner and tied the neck. "Not having much luck with birds either."

He doubted if Holly understood that in England birds was a euphemism for women but the laugh behind him meant that Sarah got the joke. There was a strained silence. Nobody moved. Nobody spoke. Holly looked at Sarah. Sarah looked at Holly and then at Cole. It was the very epitome of an awkward situation. If this were a romantic comedy there'd be a hasty exchange of lies that would only make the situation worse. This wasn't a comedy, this was deadly serious. The only thing to do was come clean. More or less. Cole put the bag down and indicated Sarah. "Holly. This is my brother's wife. Sarah."

Holly looked confused. "You've got a brother?"

*

IT WAS COFFEES ALL ROUND again, milky for Sarah and black for Holly and Cole. Making a quick exit wasn't on the cards any more so Cole resigned himself to the delay. He put the bag in the trashcan and gave one last look around the garden then locked the door and put the kettle on.

He was glad that Holly had come to see him. Her presence made the threat seem less real. He felt guilty at running out on her. At least this gave him the opportunity to explain. Leaving certain things out. Sarah went to the bathroom to freshen up and give Cole some privacy. Cole sat opposite Holly at the table. "We don't get on."

Holly sipped her coffee. "You and your brother?"

Cole nodded. "He's a rough diamond. A nasty piece of work. And he holds it against me."

"Holds what against you?"

"His life."

"What's that got to do with you?"

"A lot."

Cole drummed his fingers on the table while he considered how much to tell her. She was a cop so there were some obvious omissions. There were some things he was too embarrassed to admit so he left them out too. That left the husband and wife situation. He felt on safe ground with that. "He wasn't the greatest husband."

Holly put her cup down and listened.

"He had a lot of anger in him." Now Cole had her complete attention. He looked down at his hands as if he didn't know what to do with them. He stopped the drumming and jerked his head towards the bathroom. "I should have done more to help her."

Holly let out a sigh. Deja vu settled over her. She wanted to tell him that she'd been in that situation but wanted to keep that part of her life private. She opted for police experience instead. "That's a no win situation. If you go against the husband the wife ends up resenting you. If you don't..."

She shrugged, implying violence that could only be solved from within. She hoped that got the message across. Cole shook his head. "It was more delicate than that." He paused to gather his thoughts. "Before she was with my brother." He didn't need to say anything else.

Realization dawned on Holly's face. "Whoah. That *is* a Catch 22 situation."

Cole was struck again by the twinning of his thoughts. Holly was more in tune with him than anybody he'd ever met. It made it even more difficult to leave, but leave he must. He dropped both hands on the table. "He's not a forgive and forget kind of fella."

Holly looked towards the bathroom. "And she came here to you."

Cole focused on Holly's eyes. "Not my choice."

"But she's here."

Cole nodded. "And he's coming to get me."

Holly nodded at the suitcase she'd seen on the way in. "So you're leaving."

Cole let out a sigh. "For now. I don't want to bring trouble. You've had enough." Holly opened her mouth but didn't speak. Cole gave her a sympathetic smile. "Shelter Cove is a small place. In three years, people talk. It's none of my business. We've all got a past. I don't want to bring mine into yours."

"You are in mine. The past is history."

Cole kept his eyes on hers. "I don't want history to repeat itself."

Holly stared back. "It won't."

Cole nodded and smiled. It wasn't a happy smile. "I need to sort this out first. Away from here. I need to keep you out of it."

Holly sat in silence for a moment. They had reached an understanding. She'd got her answer. Cole Thornton did like her as much as she liked him. The question was, would he come back? That was a question she couldn't bring herself to ask. She nodded her understanding and stood up. "Okay. Sort it out."

Cole accompanied her to the door. They didn't hug. They didn't kiss. It was a muted farewell. He watched her get in the car and drive off. When she was out of sight he went inside and closed the door.

TWELVE

*

"SHE FANCIES YOU, YOU KNOW."

"You fancied me. Look how that turned out."

Cole leaned with his back against the door as if keeping anyone from coming in. Sarah was standing in the hallway from the bathroom. She'd heard the door close and knew it was safe to come out. Cole stood with his head lowered. Sarah pointed out the obvious. "You fancy her."

Cole avoided the obvious answer. They both knew that Cole had fancied Sarah but Sarah had chosen his brother. Who you fancied didn't always lead to the person you ended up with. Happy ever afters almost never happened. Even if you ended up with the right person it hardly ever lasted forever. Things changed. Life got in the way. Sad but true, in Cole's experience. "Holly's a good woman. She doesn't need our shit messing her up."

Sarah came into the kitchen but didn't sit down. "Maybe you should let her decide."

Cole pushed off from the door and went to the window. "She doesn't know all the facts."

Sarah folded her arms across her chest. "And you're not going to tell her."

Cole looked at Sarah. "Would you?"

Sarah shrugged. "She might understand."

Cole snorted a laugh. "She's a cop. She might arrest me."

Sarah shook her head. "That's not the reason."

Cole looked out of the window but it was getting dark outside. With the lights on in the kitchen all he could see was a reflection of the interior. He drew the curtains so nobody could see inside then turned back to Sarah. "No it isn't. You know what he's like. When he gets going people get hurt. Not always the one's he's aiming at. I don't want Holly getting caught in the blast."

Sarah dropped her hands to her sides. "Then you're right to go."

She looked at the dirty cups on the table. Cole had washed them up earlier, when he'd been preparing to leave. Now he made no attempt to clear the table. The cups stood there like signs of his defiance. She nodded at the cups. "But you're not going are you?"

Cole linked his fingers together and flexed them outwards. Bones cracked in his knuckles. His hands formed into fists. "It's too late if he's already here. No point trying to outrun him." He put the kettle on for fresh coffee. "Better to face him on home ground. Easier to defend."

Sarah looked doubtful. "Have you got a gun?"

Cole let out a sigh. "He won't use a gun."

Sarah tilted her head to one side. "This isn't Home Alone you know. You're not going to beat him with booby-traps and marbles."

Cole held up a finger. "Back home. If you smacked a burglar with a baseball bat. You'd have to explain why you had a baseball bat." He went to the utility cupboard next to the back door. "But this is America. Everyone's got a baseball bat."

THIRTEEN

*

BEN GARDNER ENTERED the police office and turned the lights on. It was almost full dark outside now. He put the Big Mac and fries on the desk and sat down. Whenever he had something on his mind he ate. Having McDonalds next door was convenient because he had a lot on his mind right now. He unwrapped the burger and took a bite. Chewing helped him think.

He couldn't get the pain on Holly's face out of his mind. He considered warning her to be careful of Thornton but reckoned he'd already overstepped the mark in that regard. He needed to pull back from thinking of her as the daughter he never had. It wasn't the best working relationship but he wasn't a very strict boss. He wasn't a very strict cop either. At this stage of his career all he wanted was a quiet life. The past two days had been anything but quiet.

He took a mouthful of fries and went into the kitchenette to put the kettle on. He never got a drink with his burger, preferring coffee at the station. He stopped himself in mid thought. It was the first time he'd thought of the office as a Police Station in a long time. Doing police work today must have rekindled his enthusiasm. Writing a report for the coroner reminded him of the parts he didn't like.

He finished the Big Mac and fries then reviewed his notes over coffee. The ambulance had taken Matt King away after Gardner had taken half a dozen Polaroids and checked for signs of foul play. He didn't check very hard. Drowning in the bath was as open and shut as it was ever going to get. There was no sign of a struggle. There were no injuries apart from some scrapes to his knees and elbows, no doubt when he dived from the car before the crash. He'd contacted the dispatcher on the radio but headquarters told him to fill in an accidental death report and inform the relatives.

There weren't any relatives.

Matt King was as loose as the driftwood that washed up on shore, a lone surfer who followed the waves but kept to himself. How he managed to be driving a car that had already been written off would never be known. That troubled Gardner but he did as he was told and wrote the report. It was the second time that King's name had been sent to headquarters.

Gardner leaned back in his chair and put his feet up on the desk. The chair creaked. He put his hands behind his head and stretched his neck, first to the left and then to the right. He could feel the bones grate. He looked at the map on the wall. Pacifica, California. Not the biggest police force in the world. The southern tip was even smaller. Linda Mar and Shelter Cove, the quiet backwater where he was destined to end his career. A concession to his service over the years. As he brought his hands forward and folded them across his chest he wondered if that was a good thing or just the final nail in his coffin.

He wasn't a cop anymore.

That grated more than the bones in his neck.

He swung his feet off the desk and stood up. The desktop was awash with food wrappers and empty cups. In his early days a senior detective had told him that a tidy workstation was the sign of a bad cop. The only person who kept his desk tidy was somebody who wasn't out there doing the job. Gardner had a different view now. Being untidy was the sign of a cop who didn't do any work at all. He swept the food wrappers into the bin and took the cups into the kitchenette. The water was cold. It took a few minutes to warm up. It felt like another indication of where he was in his career. Cold and in need of warming up before he'd be of any use.

He washed the cups and stacked them on the drainer. His hands warmed up as he toweled them dry. Making the enquiries today made him feel useful again. It felt like he was warming his police skills at the end of his career. The enquiries had drawn a blank but there was somewhere else he could visit tomorrow. The car had been scrapped at Driftwood Auto Wreckers. The scrapyard was only half a mile away between the Pacifica Skatepark and the Crespi Shopping Center.

A musical ping came from the computer. Gardner folded the towel and went back into the office. It was half an hour since he'd filed the coroner's report. He hoped he hadn't made a mistake. A car with a throaty exhaust rumbled past McDonalds. The tailpipe popped twice and the explosions made Gardner jump. The exhaust faded in the distance. Gardner's hands were shaking. He'd not felt this jumpy since his army days. The nerves needed help so he made another coffee and ignored the computer.

Traffic noise dwindled to nothing. The lights went off at McDonalds. Doors rattled and a car set off. The world descended into quiet and darkness. Gardner glanced at the wall clock. He hadn't realized how late it was.

The musical ping sounded again. Reminding him that he hadn't acknowledged the first message. He sat down and checked the screen, expecting to find some minor discrepancy in the coroner's report. He frowned when he saw the notification. It wasn't about the drowning. It was about yesterday's accident.

He opened the folder to see what they wanted. The accident report was all in order apart from one field that hadn't been filled in correctly. Gardner scrolled down to the offending section. Witnesses. Holly West had been accepted but the other witness was the problem. Headquarters had searched all systems to verify the identity and drawn a blank. The message field asked Gardner to check that the details had been input correctly. He checked the name and date of birth against his notebook. They were accurate. Pacifica Police Headquarters disagreed.

According to government records Cole Thornton didn't exist.

FOURTEEN

*

THE MAN WHO DIDN'T exist went around the house drawing the curtains. The baseball bat hung loose in Cole's hand, ready to bring it up into a two handed swing if needed. It would be needed soon. The sky had gone from dark blue to black in fifteen minutes. The streetlamps had come on but they were few and far between on Livingston Avenue. They weren't much better on San Pedro Avenue out front of the bookstore. The apartment round the back was in the shadows between lights.

"You going to stalk around with the bat all night?"

Sarah craned her neck from the kitchen table to look down the hallway, dividing her attention between watching Cole and drinking her third cup of coffee. If she had any more she'd be spending all night in the bathroom. If her ex-husband came to visit she reckoned that might be the best place to be.

Cole came back into the kitchen. "It won't take all night. Now it's dark outside he'll be coming."

Sarah let out a sigh. "Don't you think you're being a bit melodramatic?"

Cole turned the hall light off, leaving the kitchen as an oasis of light in the darkened apartment. He left all the internal doors open so he could hear any approach from the other side. The utility room was unlocked, as was the kitchen door, giving his brother an easy way in. Cole wasn't trying to keep him out and there was no point having him kick the doors open. He raised his eyebrows at Sarah. "You've just spent half an hour telling me how dangerous he is."

Sarah nodded. "So do you really think closing the curtains will make any difference?"

Cole rested the baseball bat on one shoulder. "There's no point letting him see where I am."

Sarah held both hands up as if testing for rain. "It's the only room with the lights on."

Cole looked down at her and smiled. "Who said I'll be waiting in here?"

*

HOODED EYES WATCHED from the safety of the trees across the street. In deep shadow now that day had turned into night. He glanced up and down Livingston Avenue. There was no traffic. There were no pedestrians. The nearest streetlamp was fifty yards up the slope. The nearest one the other way was on San Pedro Avenue round the corner from the storefront. There was no light on this part of the street apart from the glow through the curtains of the kitchen window.

A dog barked in the distance and the eyes darted in that direction. The trees rustled in a gentle breeze coming off the coast. The movement enhanced the smell of pine and night flowers, everything overlaid by sea air and salt. There were no cooking smells, it was too late for that. Canned laughter from a TV comedy drifted from one of the houses over his shoulder. He ignored the laughter and shifted his weight, getting ready to stand up.

The dog barked again. A cat hissed and a dustbin was knocked over. The dog gave chase until a rough voice shouted for it to come inside. The street fell silent again. Almost silent. The trees still rustled. Some kind of bird cooed or hooted, he couldn't tell which. The TV went quiet.

He stood up and waited a moment. He gave one last look around to make sure he was alone then crossed the road walking upright. There was no need to crouch and there was no need to tiptoe. He walked briskly to the edge of the lawn then stopped beside the flower border. He could see movement through the curtains. A changing of the kitchen light as somebody moved from left to right. He nodded to himself and fingered the haft of the knife in his belt.

The lawn was small and square and bordered by trees and bushes. It was completely dark, barely touched by the glow through the curtains. He took one step then paused. There was no sudden activity in the kitchen. Confident that nobody was watching he crossed the lawn and almost made it all the way before the twig snapped loud in the cold night air.

The kitchen light went out.

*

COLE DIDN'T HAVE to tell Sarah to turn the lights out. Having her move around the kitchen had been the plan. She was to turn out the lights at the first sign of activity or on Cole's signal. He was glad it was the snapped twig because calling out would have given his position away. He was no master tactician but there was no need to give his brother the advantage.

Time to shit or get off the pot. His brother had been full of useful sayings. He had also been full of youthful confidence even as a kid. Despite being five years older Cole had never beaten him in a fight. He'd never bested him at sport or games or TV quiz shows. There was a competitive streak in his younger brother that came from the school of hard knocks he'd been brought up in.

The snapped twig sounded like a gunshot in the quiet.

It came from the back lawn over towards Livingston Avenue.

The direction Cole was supposed go.

Time to shit or get off the pot. Maybe. But, *distraction* was the saying that sprang to mind. In all the games and sports they'd played it was his brother's favorite technique. Send you going one way then he came at you from the other. Cole wasn't falling for the broken twig this time. The noise had come from the lawn approaching the kitchen door. Cole went the other way, towards the utility room door on the opposite side.

Sarah watched his shadowy figure go down the hallway. She moved away from the door and stood against the washbasin, holding her breath and folding her arms tight around her waist.

Cole didn't have to open any doors. He'd left them all open. He made no noise as he moved through the apartment to the far side. His eyes had already adjusted to the dark because he hadn't been in the kitchen.

He went into the utility room. The washing machine was a dull shape in one corner. A separate tumble dryer stood next to it. Stray light from a neighboring house played across the window. Tree shapes and branches were silhouetted against the glass. They danced in the breeze, too faint to light the room but bright enough to highlight the more solid shadow approaching the outside door.

Cole raised the baseball bat in two hands, just like he'd seen on TV. This was one sport he was determined to beat his brother at, with a home run across the side of the head.

The shadow reached the door.

The handle began to turn.

Cole took a deep breath and tightened his grip. The shadow merged with the door as it began to open. A couple of inches at first to make sure it didn't creak. Just like his brother to be cautious even at the point of attack. The door opened six inches. Cole flexed his arms. Twelve inches. He tightened his grip. The door opened all the way and the shadow came into the room.

Cole swung the bat as hard as he could. A roundhouse swing aimed at the head. He wasn't thinking about how much damage the blow would cause, he was just thinking about getting the first strike in. The bat went through the air fast. The head ducked even faster. A strong hand caught Cole's wrist on the follow through and twisted the bat out of his hand. It bounced twice as it fell to the floor.

Then Jim Grant stepped into the room and kicked the bat away.

FIFTEEN

*

GRANT DODGED TO HIS right, the opposite direction to where he'd kicked the baseball bat, and flexed his knees ready for the counter attack. The fugitive had the advantage of knowing the layout of the utility room. Grant had the advantage of speed and strength. Thornton ignored the bat and spun round with a low punch to Grant's stomach. Grant blocked downwards with his forearm then slapped Thornton across the face.

The slap was loud in the silence. The sting and the shock stunned Thornton's eyes wide open without risking the bones in Grant's hand. He'd been taught to never punch if you could avoid it. There are too many small bones in the hand to come up against the more solid bone of the skull. Use the elbows for attack or a slap if you don't want to cause too much damage. Grant wanted Thornton distracted not disabled.

Thornton swayed back from the slap. Grant knew what he was going to do even before Thornton started to move. The baseball bat. It was the only chance the bookseller had of shifting the balance of power. He ducked and turned and followed the roll of the bat. In the dark it was hard to track. In the confined space it was impossible to miss. The trouble was that the slap had disorientated him. Grant let Thornton take two steps then followed. The bookseller missed his footing, stepped on the bat, and the foot shot up like he'd stood on a banana skin. Grant caught him under the arms and twisted him face down. Thornton hit the floor. Grant knee-dropped onto his back and grabbed his hair. He pushed Thornton's face against the floor and leaned forward.

The lights came on. Grant jerked his head towards the corridor. Sarah stood with a hand to her mouth, eyes wide with shock. Grant didn't have time for niceties. "Turn 'em off."

His voice was so commanding that she did what he said. The lights went out but Grant's night vision was ruined. He muttered under his breath but they all heard the movement outside the kitchen door. Thornton's voice was a distorted whisper from the corner of his mouth. "The broken twig wasn't a distraction?"

Grant took his knee out of Thornton's back. "The twig was a twig."

He dragged Thornton to his feet and both dashed past Sarah into the kitchen. The door was kicked inwards despite being unlocked, splintering the frame and breaking the windowpanes. A hulking shape lurched into the room, ungainly and off balance from the kick. Grant yelled at Sarah again. "Lights, now."

The lights came on again and the big guy from the shop was surprised to see two men before him. He pulled the hunting knife out of his belt. "Who the fuck are you?"

*

THERE ARE TIMES FOR engaging in conversation and there are times when actions speak louder than words. Grant always liked to talk people down if he could but when a man waves a knife at you it's time to keep talking to a minimum. "I'm the police. And you're breaking and entering." He glanced at Thornton. "Twig."

The heavy looked at Grant. “What?”

Thornton nodded his understanding. “Distraction.” And kicked a chair away from the table. It fell sideways and bounced at an awkward angle. The legs stuck up like an impromptu obstacle course. The man couldn’t help but look at it. He stood in the doorway with the knife in one hand and his legs settling from kicking the door open and glanced from Grant to Thornton to the fallen chair. A split second cycle that gave Grant just enough time. While the big guy’s eyes cycled through the threats to his right Grant went the other way. He grabbed the door and slammed it shut. Right into the knifeman’s face.

The rest of the panes in the door shattered. The knife hand was caught in the window frames. The face was cut and grazed, adding to the bruises he’d sustained in the bookstore that afternoon. Grant stepped forward, grabbed his head, and dragged it through the top half of the door. He brought his knee up in a crushing blow and the man dropped like his legs had been broken.

Grant picked up the knife and tossed it into the washbasin. Thornton stood the chair back up and sat heavily. His hands were shaking. The man groaned. Sarah came in from the corridor and sat next to Thornton. Grant looked at the two of them then indicated the man wedged in the doorway. “What you want to do about him?”

Thornton calmed his hands. “You speaking as a policeman?”

Grant shrugged. “It’s not my house.”

“Meaning do I want to press charges?”

It was the second time today he’d been asked that question. Against the same man under the same circumstances. He gave the same answer with a shake of the head. “It’s a misunderstanding.”

Grant picked the knife out of the washing up bowl. “You think he was here to sharpen your pencils?”

Thornton looked at Grant. “I think you’re here for more than breaking and entering.”

Grant nudged the big guy with his foot. “It’s still police work.”

“But it’s not why you’re here.”

Grant nodded. “The bigger picture.”

Thornton let out a sigh. “They still want me for that?”

Grant began to fill the kettle. “The Force was embarrassed. They’ll hunt you to the end of time.”

Thornton jerked a thumb at the intruder. “Then you’d better let this fella go.”

Grant opened the door and emptied the kettle over the big guy’s head. He spluttered and got to his knees. Grant stepped back out of his fighting arc. Waking an injured man was a dangerous time. His first instinct is often to lash out. Grant was ready in case he did. He kept his voice low but forceful. “It’s your lucky day. On your bike.”

The man looked confused again. “D’you two ever speak English?”

Grant twirled a finger then pointed out the door. “We are English. Go. Or I’ll call the local police.”

The man looked at the knife on the drainer and held out a hand. Grant raised his eyebrows and snorted a laugh. “Really?” He jerked a thumb towards the street.

The man looked crestfallen and wet and more than a little shaky. He glanced at the Englishmen as if formulating a parting shot but couldn’t come up with anything so he turned and walked into the dark. Grant closed what remained of the door and turned to Thornton. “Cole Thornton?”

“I always liked that film.”

“I know. Sunday afternoon westerns.”

Sarah shifted in her seat with a bemused expression on her face. Cole explained. “The Sons Of Katie Elder. John Wayne. Four brothers seek revenge after their mother’s death.”

Grant pulled out a chair and sat down. “Except you’ve got it wrong. He was John Elder in that one. He was Cole Thornton in Eldorado."

Thornton rubbed his chin. "Damn. I've been living a lie."

Grant leaned back in his chair. "Story of your life."

Thornton wasn't fazed. "Same difference. It's still John Wayne."

The kitchen went quiet. Sarah looked at the two men in her life and felt like crying. Thornton blew out his cheeks as he emptied his lungs. Grant focused on the man he'd come all this way to arrest. "Okay. So, if you're thinking The Sons Of Katie Elder. You're John Wayne. Which one does that make me?"

Thornton leveled his gaze at Grant. "Take your pick. You're my younger brother."

PART TWO

BROKEN SHELTER

"Hundred and fifty thousand reasons, I'd say."
– Jim Grant

SIXTEEN

*

GRANT LOOKED AT HIS brother but didn't speak. Hearing himself referred to as the younger brother brought back a flood of memories that he struggled to suppress. On his way down from San Francisco he'd tried to imagine how he was going to feel when he finally caught up with the man he shared a family name with but not a family. The man who Grant had buried so deep that he never mentioned him or thought about him or gave him any consideration at all. Sitting here in the battered kitchen he didn't know how he felt so he reverted to type. "Whose pot you pissing in now?"

"Why? You worried about me? Left it a bit late haven't you?"

"Look who's talking." Grant kept his hands under the table in case they began to shake. "Should I call you Cole Thornton or Andrew Grant?"

"Should I call you Jim or James?" Cole leaned forward. "Or The Resurrection Man?"

Grant flexed his neck. A bone cracked, loud in the silence. "You heard about that, huh?"

"I get American news. Shelter Cove is in America."

"It was the press came up with that. Not me."

"They didn't come up with Jim Grant. Why's that? James?"

"Why do you think? Andrew?"

Sarah banged the table. "Stop it."

She didn't say anything else. She didn't need to. Both brothers knew they sounded like squabbling children. Grant nodded and gritted his teeth but it was hard to contain the years of resentment. His brother reined it in. "Call me Cole. It's been three years. You'll only confuse me."

Grant didn't. "Call me Grant. I don't want you getting too familiar."

Sarah looked exasperated but had no strength to argue. She was contending with her own flood of memories, none of them good. The man responsible for most of them was sitting across the table from her. She didn't trust him. The powder keg could explode at any time. It often had. Never at her but when he went off somebody always got hurt.

Grant glanced at the broken door. "Thugs always kicking your door in?"

Cole looked at the door then back to Grant. "They're like buses." Grant tilted his head. Cole's smile was cold and humorless. "You wait for ages then two come along at once."

Grant frowned. "You think I'm a thug? Haven't been keeping up have you?"

Cole watched his brother. "I've been keeping away. Safer option."

Grant lowered his voice. "You're not here to keep away from me, and you know it."

Sarah couldn't stand the tension any longer. She stood up and went to the washbasin. Cold water hissed into the kettle and the noise broke the spell. She got three cups out of the cupboard and waved them in the air. "I'm going for a caffeine overdose. Anyone else?"

Cole nodded but didn't trust himself to speak. Grant looked at his ex-wife then scanned the open cupboard. "You got any tea?"

*

TEA AND BISCUITS ALMOST civilized the gathering. If they'd thrown in scones with jam and cream the kitchen could have been a café in the Yorkshire Dales. They didn't, and only one of them was drinking tea anyway. Grant marveled at the drink the Americans never seemed to master. Sarah had always made a good pot of tea. Thinking back to married life Grant decided it was time to open up a little. He dunked a custard cream in his tea and ate the soggy biscuit. "I'm not the man I used to be."

Cole accepted the olive branch. "How so?"

Grant backpedalled slightly. "I never thought of myself as an angry man."

Sarah put her coffee down. She sounded almost wistful. "James. You were angry at everything."

Grant looked at her. "The army changed me."

Cole's mouth was dry. He took a drink so his voice wouldn't sound harsh. "You joined so you could get into more fights."

Grant shook his head. "I joined to be part of a family." He realized he was back on the old subject so he tempered it. "They taught me that the best fight is the one you don't get into." He looked at Cole. "That the best family is the one that's got your back."

The old subject again. He couldn't seem to keep away from it. Maybe he hadn't changed as much as he thought. He dunked another biscuit. Cole fought back the urge to join the argument and took a sip of coffee. Sarah did the same. The group sat in silence for a moment, each locked into their own memories of a past that was fraught with danger. Practically any subject could lead to an argument. Almost everything they touched had the potential for conflict. Cole was the first to come out of the reverie. "Let's cut the crap shall we?" He pushed his cup away. "You didn't come here to reminisce." He sat back in his chair. "And you're not in the army any more."

Grant put his cup down. "No. I'm in the police."

"Up in Boston. Yes, I know. But it's Yorkshire you're here about."

Grant kept his face calm. "Back when you were in the police as well."

Sarah prepared for the explosion. Grant rested his hands on the table. The kettle ticked as it cooled and the breeze through the broken door wafted coffee smells around the kitchen. Cole folded his arms across his chest. "You come for the money?"

Grant shook his head. "I've come for you. The West Yorkshire Police want the money." He couldn't keep the disappointment out of his voice. "The money you stole before you left the Underwater Search Team."

SEVENTEEN

*

THE HOMELY KITCHEN round the back of the Rocky Coast Bookstore felt like a powder keg waiting to explode. The tension was palpable, so thick you could almost taste it. Cole swallowed to cover his discomfort. He hadn't thought about his police service for years. No, that wasn't true. Only yesterday he'd recalled his police training when triaging Holly. Casualty management had been a big part of a beat copper's duties. He wondered how many casualties there would be tonight. He looked at his brother. "Is that what you think? That I stole the money?"

Grant kept his eyes flat and level. He held his emotions in check. "It's what the police think."

Cole felt sadness crawl up his throat like a whimper trying to get out. "That's not the question."

Grant scrutinized Cole, his eyes taking in every detail. "You left pretty damn quick."

"You left first. We were still kids."

Grant's eyes hardened. The emotions bubbled to the surface but he still held them back. This was the first time he'd talked about the deep past since, well, since the deep past. "When I joined the army? Or when I was sent to boarding school?"

Cole ignored the accusation. “Do you think I stole the money?”

Grant gave up. “How the fuck should I know? Since when did I know a single damn thing about how you grew up?”

Cole looked disappointed. The fight drained out of him. “Yeah. Not exactly a close family are we?”

Grant leaned forward. “You should have tried growing up at Moor Grange School For Boys.” He lowered his voice to a whisper. “I was eight years old.”

Cole rallied his defence. “You think I had it any better? A navy dad and an empty house?”

Grant clenched his teeth. “I’m getting all weepy.”

What Grant was really getting was all angry. He’d bottled up his frustrations for thirty-odd years. He’d buried his emotions deep beneath military service and police work. Weepy was the last thing he was feeling. Cole however was trying hard to match his younger brother’s composure. “All I’ve got is a box of photos and five years with a mother before she died.”

Grant saw his chance to turn the screw. “At least you had five years. I never met her.” But all that did was give Cole the perfect weapon. “And whose fault is that?”

*

COLE’S ACCUSATION EVEN shocked himself. Sarah began to cry. Grant was stung as if he’d been slapped. As soon as he’d said it Cole wished he could take it back but like so many things from his childhood up until now there was no taking back what he had done. The most shocking thing of all was that he sounded just like his father. The strict disciplinarian had taken a stance and Cole had gone along with it. If he couldn’t forgive himself for that how could he expect his brother to forgive him? “I’m sorry. I shouldn’t have said that.”

Grant was staring so hard that his eyes were beginning to water.

He refused to wipe his eyes. He refused to blink. He relaxed his eyes instead and that stopped the tears from spilling over. They were there though, and both brothers knew it. Grant spoke slowly and quietly. "That's where it all started though isn't it?" He breathed in deep and let it out slow. "Before I came along everything was okay. When I turned up, she's dead and I'm cast out."

Cole tried to redeem himself. "It was childbirth. You can't blame yourself."

Grant didn't look convinced. "You've changed your tune haven't you?"

"It's been a long time."

Grant blew out his cheeks. "My whole life. Dad didn't see it that way back then. And neither did you."

Cole still tried to pour oil on troubled waters. "I was too young to understand."

"He wasn't."

"He was hurting. He blamed you. That was wrong."

Grant rubbed his eyes and blinked them wide open. A long day's travelling would be his excuse. A hard night of revelations was the truth. "He had eight years to get over it. But the first chance he got he farmed me off to Moor Grange. And you went along with it."

Cole fell silent. There was no answer to that. He'd abandoned his brother in his time of need and he was about to hurt him again if Grant insisted on pursuing the stolen money. The way this was going there'd be no avoiding it. He kept quiet. Grant brought things up to date. "Now it's your turn to get farmed off. To prison instead of boarding school." He pulled a grim face. "You'll find there's not much difference." Then leaned his elbows on the table. "I'm investigating the seized cash taken from the evidence locker." He interlaced his fingers. "And the West Yorkshire Police have you down as prime suspect."

Cole shook his head. "I didn't take it."

Grant leaned forward. "Bit of a coincidence then. You dashing off just after it happened."

"I had my reasons."

"Hundred and fifty thousand reasons, I'd say."

"No."

Grant nodded towards the bookstore out front. "Where'd you get the money to start your own business then?"

Cole felt the room growing smaller. He'd known this moment was coming ever since he learned his brother was looking for him. Hard truths and bad lies. Not the best foundations to build a new life. Holly was better off without him. He agreed with Ben Gardner about that. Tearing his brother's heart out again was a high price to pay but he would do it anyway, to make a clean break. "It's my inheritance."

The answer caught Grant by surprise. "Mum didn't have that kind of money."

"I haven't got that kind of money. It's a lot less."

"She didn't have that either."

Cole looked at his brother and prepared to put the boot in. The kitchen felt cold despite the hot cups of coffee. The breeze through the broken windows flapped the curtains. Sarah couldn't stop looking at the train wreck that was happening right in front of her. This was news to her as well. Cole's eyes held a world of sadness. "It's from dad."

He let the words sink in and watched his brother's reaction. At first there was none as Grant collated the information but then his eyes opened as understanding dawned on his face. There was only one way to get an inheritance. "Bullshit."

Cole shook his head. "Kind of a legacy. He left it all to me." Grant's shoulders sagged but Cole hadn't finished. If he was getting this out he needed to tell it all. "He said he was disowning you. That he didn't want you to know. That's why I had to leave. I couldn't hang around after that."

Cole watched his brother's world come crashing down. He didn't know how much Grant believed but judging by the look on his face enough of it hit home to stop him in his tracks. The two men looked down at the table. Neither spoke for several seconds. Distant sirens were a welcome distraction. Grant tried to decipher if they were police or fire. Then the air horn sounded and other sirens joined in. Fire *and* police. Probably ambulance too. The noise grew louder. Blips of light started small then blue lights flashed as the convoy past the front of the bookstore. A helicopter thudded overhead.

Grant got up and went to the window. Cole stood next to him. A coastguard horn joined the cacophony of sound. Whatever had happened it had happened in the west. Beyond the rocky outcrop that protected Shelter Cove.

EIGHTEEN

*

"YOU GOT A FLASHLIGHT?"

Grant was back in his own headspace. Emergency situations always did that to him, focused his mind and highlighted what was important. People were in trouble. He was a cop. Maybe he could help. Cole hadn't become as American as Grant. "What?"

Grant translated. "A torch. Have you got a torch?"

Cole snapped his fingers, nodded his understanding and went to the hallway cupboard. He rooted around for a moment then came out with a long black flashlight and a battery powered storm lantern. He glanced at the scuba gear in the corner and considered bringing that but grabbed his coat instead. He was sticking one arm in the sleeve when he returned to the kitchen. Grant looked at his brother. "Where d'you think you're going?"

Cole put the lantern and the flashlight on the table then shrugged into his coat. "To help."

Grant shook his head. "Forget it. I'm a cop. You're a bookseller. Stay here."

Cole fastened his coat and picked up the flashlight. "You're a cop, but I'm a diver. If there's people in the water I can help."

Grant couldn't argue with the logic of that. His brother had always been the stronger swimmer but he didn't want Cole with him. Right now he didn't want Cole at all. Grant prepared to back his brother down but Cole strengthened his argument. "This is a quiet place. The police here? It's one cop and two part-timers." He nodded through the window. "All the rest have come from somewhere else. Ben'll need all the local help he can get."

Local knowledge. In situations like this it went a long way towards making sense of the chaos that a major incident could descend into. Grant had come from Boston. Local knowledge rested with Cole. Grant breathed out slowly and drummed his fingers on the window. He began to compartmentalize and put his family revelations in a lockbox deep inside. This needed affirmative action. Cole was the best man for the job. Grant stopped drumming and nodded to his brother. "Okay." He opened the door and waved Cole forward. "Lead on."

The sirens had stopped but the helicopter was still thudding in the distance. Red and blue lights flashed against the low clouds of an overcast sky. Cole went through the door first and Grant followed. After three steps across the lawn they disappeared into the night together.

*

THE SIRENS MIGHT HAVE stopped but the engine noises were loud enough to guide them towards the rendezvous point. In an emergency there was always a rendezvous point. In this case it was along the coast road where Shoreside Drive became Shelter Cove, the road not the row of beachfront houses across the ridge. Cole followed the sound of the fire trucks. Even though they weren't using their pumps the engines were still loud and throaty. He turned right off San Pedro Avenue and followed Danmann Avenue to the coast road. Grant kept pace with him, one step to the side and half a step behind. This was no time to worry about who was in charge.

They came out opposite the boathouse diner and turned left. The coast road was narrow. Fire trucks were lined up at the head of the column. Three ambulances were parked behind them with two police cars bringing up the rear. Roadside flares had been deployed just in case any stray motorists didn't realize the road was closed. You'd have to be blind or stupid not to realize that. The road was completely blocked with emergency vehicles flashing red and blue lights. Red sulphur burned bright, sending clouds of luminous smoke into the air. There was a boat in the water to the right but most of the activity was beyond the headland.

A gust of wind cleared the smoke for a second and a police uniform stood out, painted red by the flares. A broad shouldered college football type glanced nervously around. Bret Harding looked like he'd be out of his depth in a puddle, standing guard at the biggest incident to hit Shelter Cove this century was more than he could cope with. Cole stepped between the flares and Bret jumped as if he'd seen the devil himself. The way the flares lit Cole's face it was an easy mistake to make.

"Halt. Who goes…" He didn't finish the challenge. Embarrassment flushed his cheeks as he recognized Cole. "Mr Thornton, sir. Sorry. But you can't come past."

Grant stepped forward and flashed his badge. "Police. We've come to help. Where's forward command?"

Harding couldn't read the ID in the dark; Grant could have shown him his library card and still got through. Harding blustered indecision, looking more at sea than the boat coming ashore along the road. Cole put a reassuring hand on the part-time cop's arm. "Where's Holly?"

Hearing a familiar name bolstered Harding's confidence. He

waved a hand in the general direction of the fire trucks. "She's co-ordinating." He raised his hand and waved some more. Beyond the ridge. "Ben's at the forward command post."

Grant was about to ask what had happened but Cole was already striding past the police cars toward the fire trucks. Grant broke into a trot to catch up with him. The patrol cars were empty but the ambulances were open and active. Paramedics were preparing for casualties. The back doors were open and the footplates lowered. The gurneys were unstrapped and ready.

Cole ignored the ambulances. He focused on the solitary figure standing at the end of the road where the tarmac stopped in a tangle of bushes and trees. Grant was more interested in the rescue boat coming ashore on the shingle beach. The helicopter was thudding away somewhere beyond the headland. Cole shouted above the noise of the fire trucks. "Holly."

Holly didn't hear him. She'd been deployed at the head of the column to guide any rescuers to the forward command post, her days off cut short. She was an auxiliary. Full time professionals would shoulder the brunt of the work. That annoyed Cole. As far as he was concerned she was worth a dozen Ben Gardners. He shouted again, closer this time. "Holly. You okay?"

Holly was watching the boat being dragged up the shingle beach. Her face betrayed sadness and strain that was framed by square jawed stoicism. She caught movement out of the corner of her eye and turned to see Cole. The sadness was dialed back a bit but she didn't smile. "Cole. You can't be here." She saw a guy in a bright yellow windcheater with Old Town Trolley Tours on the breast come up behind Cole but didn't ask who he was. "Either of you."

She looked back towards the beach. Grant followed her gaze. Two men in life preservers jumped out of the boat and dragged it further up the shingle. One climbed back in and began to manhandle something towards the bow. Grant didn't need telling what it was. He turned back to the woman in uniform and flashed his badge again. "I'm a cop. We thought we could help."

Holly glanced at the ID then looked Grant in the eye. "Boston PD? A long way from home aren't you?"

Grant nodded. "More than you know. What's going on?"

Holly looked at Grant then Cole then back to Grant. "Mexican washed ashore. Probably illegal."

They all looked at the body being dragged over the bow. It was limp and heavy and difficult to carry. Dead people always were. Two paramedics from the first ambulance wheeled a gurney across the road. One began to unfold a black zippered body bag. This casualty was beyond medical attention; it was a coroner's transport job now. Cole felt the sober reality of life beside the sea settle over him. Grant waved at the column of emergency vehicles. "Seems a bit excessive for one illegal."

That sounded harsh but it was true. Holly wasn't shocked. She shook her head and waved a hand towards the ridge of trees behind the road. "Not one. Seventeen. Bodies have been coming ashore all along the cove."

NINETEEN

*

HOLLY POINTED THEM IN the general direction but had to maintain her position at the end of the road. This time Grant took the lead but only because he was first out of the blocks. Landslips and foliage made the path treacherous but not impossible. It had once been the main access road to houses in the cove but years of neglect and a costly lawsuit meant that Arlo Rankoff hadn't got permission to rebuild it. In places there was only enough room to walk single file. Grant's eyes focused on his footing, ignoring a drop on the right that ended where the shingle beach surrendered to jagged rocks. His night vision strengthened the further they got from the flashing lights and the flares. He was saving the torch for later.

Cole followed his brother, watching Grant's feet to avoid any nasty surprises. It didn't help. Halfway along he stood on a section of loose scree and one foot slid over the edge. Grant turned and grabbed Cole's arm. Gravel and rocks bounced down the cliff. Cole nodded that he was okay and they continued, keeping as far to the left as the hillside allowed where trees and bushes rose to the houses up on Kent Road. The path curved left and climbed towards the ridge.

When they fought through the bushes and crested the ridge the cove opened out below them. Shelter Cove proper was a seventeen-acre beachfront neighborhood along the crescent beach between San Pedro Point and San Pedro Rock. Thirteen dilapidated rental cottages hugged the shoreline with a hardscrabble path along the hillside above them. The cottages were on stilts. The stretch of beach in front of them was mainly sand petering out to shingle and rock beyond.

The bodies were lined up on the sand.

Grant paused on the edge of the ridge. Cole stood beside him gasping for breath. He didn't need to ask what the row of zippered bags was. He'd been a policeman too. He knew all about body recovery. He couldn't count them from here but it looked like they'd surpassed Holly's original seventeen. "Jesus."

Grant let out a sigh. "Them being Mexicans, that'd be Hay-soose."

Cole didn't argue pronunciation. Anything to make the tragedy feel less human. They both scanned the scene with professional eyes. A coastguard cutter stood off beyond the surf. Smaller boats had been launched and were darting about in the shallows. Torches and searchlights combed the area. Reflective jackets stood out in the gloom, especially around the body bags where somebody was collating information on a clipboard and fastening toe tags to the zippers. A rescue helicopter hovered over the beach but didn't land. Landing on damp sand was a recipe for disaster. Two smaller helicopters were vying for position out across the bay. News choppers doing what they always did, getting in the way of the rescue effort while broadcasting it live to the world. There was nothing like a good tragedy to make your viewers feel more alive.

Grant saw what he was looking for. "Over there."

A circular block of concrete stood on a small hilltop over to the right, the base of a long abandoned gazebo or bandstand or something. At the beginning of a rocky outcrop that stretched become San Pedro Point. It was the perfect vantage point and therefore the best place for a forward command post. A handful of uniformed men stood in a huddle, directing operations and sending rescuers where they were most needed. Most were firefighters and paramedics. One wore the same uniform as Holly West. Cole saw what Grant was looking at. “Ben Gardner. He’s the local man.”

Grant nodded. “A small police section. He won’t be in charge for long.”

Cole bridled at the suggestion that Ben wasn’t capable, even though he’d had similar thoughts himself. He felt protective of the place he called home. That included the people who served there. “He’s got plenty of service.”

Grant looked at Cole. “Operation like this. Until it’s declared a crime scene. It’s search and rescue. That puts the fire chief and the coastguard in charge.”

There was a rustle from the bushes behind them and Holly pushed her way into the open. Cole was surprised to see her. Grant was not. He’d sensed that she was a capable officer when she’d read his ID in the dark. She wouldn’t want to be sidelined for too long. Cole threw her a look and raised his eyebrows. Holly jerked a thumb back the way she’d come. “I got Bret to relieve me. They don’t need him at the flares.”

Cole pointed to the concrete circle. “Ben’s over there.”

Holly nodded but looked at Grant. She still didn’t ask what he was doing in Pacifica but her eyes kept jumping from Grant to Cole and back again. She settled on Cole. “Thanks for coming out.”

Cole jerked his chin towards the coastguard boats. “Looks like they’ve got the water covered.”

Holly scanned the shoreline then focused on the forward command. “I’d better go see what Ben wants me to do.”

Grant was listening but his eyes were searching the track behind the cottages. Something caught his eye but it was too far away to see. He tapped Cole on the arm and spoke to Holly. "We'll leave you to it. We're going over there."

Holly looked at them both again, her face betraying her uncertainty. She didn't speak. Cole looked sheepish. Grant led him away from the auxiliary cop and along the footpath. Towards the beach cottages that hadn't been lived in for years.

*

THE FOOTPATH BECAME A dirt track by the time it ran along the back of the beach shacks. Once it reached the last three cottages it was hardly a track at all. It overlooked the back of the houses and the steep slope down to the beach. Rough grass and scrub bushes dotted the slope. The hillside above it was more densely covered and it was the edge of that where Grant concentrated his search.

The torn white shirt was snagged on a thorny bush beside the track. The shirt had blood on it. "Andrew." Grant stood over the shirt but Cole didn't respond. "Cole." Now he turned towards his brother. He'd been right. Three years of using one name had softened the recognition of his given name. Grant indicated the shirt then fanned his hands out on either side of the track. "Somebody crawled up here. You check that side."

They split up without further discussion. Training kicked in. The urgency of the situation calmed any dissension. Cole used the flashlight to scour the track going back towards the command post, focusing on the side of the hill dropping down to the beach. Grant went the other way, doing the same with the lantern. He wasn't a hotshot tracker but any casualty dragging himself up the hill would leave a trail like a slug. He didn't find it.

Grant stopped when he reached a narrow dirt path leading down to the beach. There was no sign of blood or disturbance but he hadn't expected to. It was too far from the shirt. If the casualty had crawled up here he would have gone straight across the track not further along before cutting up the hill. He turned back and retraced his steps, this time concentrating on the other side of the path. When he reached the shirt again he still hadn't found a trail.

Cole joined him and shook his head.

Grant picked up the shirt. It was plain heavy cotton. Rough material, not some designer shirt. A poor man's garment. The kind of man who would risk being smuggled into America from Mexico. He checked inside the collar. Unlike school kids and surfers the owner's name wasn't printed on the label.

He took a deep breath then turned to view the rescue operation. The boats had moved across the bay and were concentrating on a small area near San Pedro Point. The final leg of the search. The helicopter kept the spotlight over the boats. There didn't seem to be any more bodies added to the row of zippered bags. Maybe the owner of the shirt was already there.

A groan sounded behind Grant and he spun towards the bushes. Leaves rustled six feet up the hill. A hand slapped the foliage trying to get a grip. The fingers were too weak. Grant waded into the bushes and shouted over his shoulder. "Cole."

Cole dashed after him. When Grant reached the naked torso the man tried one last time to pull himself up. The hand failed again and the man slumped onto his side. He adopted a fetal position and prepared to die. Grant could see the hope drain out of him. He knelt beside him and cradled his head. "It's okay. We've got you." The man didn't respond. His chest and arms looked as if they'd been flayed. Scratches from the thorn bushes were deep and bloody. Cole looked down at his brother. Grant jerked his head towards the command post. "Go for help."

Cole nodded and was moving before Grant turned back to the injured man. His trousers were as rough as the shirt and he was barefoot. Grant slipped out of his windcheater and wrapped it around the man's shoulders. There was a shiver of acknowledgement but the eyes didn't open. His breathing was so shallow it was hardly there at all. Grant leaned forward. "No. Hang on." The shiver trembled again. "Stay with me."

The man was giving up. Grant sensed it even before the final death throes. At the last moment the eyes blinked open and the lips began to move. Grant leaned closer but even then could barely here the whispered farewell. "The train did not come." A final trembling shiver. "It was late." Then the Mexican died in Grant's arms as voices shouted in the distance.

TWENTY

*

"WE DON'T HAVE ENOUGH personnel to search the entire cove."

Ben Gardner answered Grant's question and the fire chief nodded his agreement. Search and rescue were winding down their sweep of the bay but even if they were redeployed on a hill search it would be needle in a haystack time. Grant stood on the edge of the concrete circle. He was back wearing his yellow windcheater despite the bloodstains. He shook his head. "Just the lower slopes behind the beach huts?"

Gardner bridled at the downsizing. "They're three-bedroom beach cottages."

Grant shrugged. "So they're supersized beach huts. Shower and change after a dip in the sea."

Gardner thought about Matt King and got protective again. "This is surf country. They don't take a dip in the sea."

Further along the path the paramedics were zipping the Mexican into a body bag. Holly and Cole stepped aside while the body was taken down to the beach and lined up with the others. Twenty two corpses in a neat row on the sand, plus the one that had been fished out of the water around the headland near the coast road. All but one of them had been found in the ocean. The Mexican had dragged himself up across the path. If they'd found him earlier he might have survived. Searching for any others who had clambered ashore was the priority now. Not arguing over the size of a beach hut. Grant focused on the positives. "If we leave it 'til daylight we're looking for bodies. We do it now we might find more survivors."

Gardner let out a sigh. He was close to retirement but he'd been a cop long enough to know that Grant was right. He looked towards the hillside above the cottages, a few trees and bushes on the slope down to the beach, dense foliage on the hillside above the path. It made sense to check the crescent immediately behind the houses. That didn't change the fact that he didn't have enough manpower. He rubbed his chin in frustration. "We're gonna need more help."

Holly came along the path and joined her boss. She kept her voice down so only Ben could hear. "I've still got the numbers for the volunteer group. You know? Helped search for that missing girl last summer? And Cole knows a few people."

Gardner looked up at the mention of Cole's name. He glanced at the bookseller standing away from the group but this wasn't the time to voice his doubts. Holly was a good cop. She was right. He nodded. "Get as many as you can. Flashlights and lanterns. Keep it tight. We'll search as much as we can before dawn." He patted Holly on the back then looked over to Grant. "You got it." He nodded again. "Thanks for your help." Then glanced towards Cole. "We'll talk later."

*

IT TOOK LESS THAN AN hour to get the search party together. That was pretty quick considering the time of night. By one-thirty in the morning there were thirty-two volunteers lined up along the hardscrabble path together with the search and rescue crews not engaged in body removal and securing the area. Grant pointed out where the Mexican had been found. Holly coordinated the search. They started twenty yards south, beyond the furthest house, working in predetermined grids, from the path down to the beach first then from the path up the hill. Everyone an arm's width apart. Flashlights scouring the ground for any survivors.

The helicopter thudded overhead, concentrating its searchlight beam on the beach where paramedics were engaged in body removal. They'd discussed using it on the search but decided that while it would provide light in one area it would throw everything else into darkness and make it harder to see. Each person having their own flashlight gave them more control over what they were looking at.

The first grid was empty. Between the path and the beach beyond the houses. The hillside above it was empty too. After the third and fourth grids Holly was beginning to think this was a wild goose chase. It had to be done though. Calling off the search and then finding a body in the morning would throw up the worst kind of shit storm. The line was spread thin. Cole was down the far end. The search and rescue crews were in the middle. Holly was on the left next to Grant. As they moved from grid four to grid five she spoke to him. "What was it he said again?"

Grant crossed the path in line with the others. "Hay-soose?"

"Yes. At the end. What did he say?"

Grant thought for a second, getting the words right. "The train didn't come. It was late. Something like that."

Holly raised her voice to shout along the line. "Okay. Last two sections. Stay focused." The line of flashlights began to flick side-to-side going down to the beach. Holly kept here eyes peeled but returned to the conversation with Grant. "You sure?"

Grant held the lantern out in front of him. "Close enough."

Holly shook her head. "Ocean Shore Railroad shut down in

the twenties. Parts of it were still used near San Francisco until the mid-eighties." She focused on the narrow patch of ground directly in front of her. "Hasn't been a train along here in fifty years."

The line reached the bottom of the slope then climbed back up for the final leg, the thorn bushes above the track. Grant gave Holly his hand and pulled her up the last six feet to the path. Once the line had reformed the search continued. Grant spoke in measured tones to cover being out of breath. "He was pretty far gone. Maybe he was doing a Michael Caine."

Holly stopped and looked at him. "Michael Caine?"

Grant kept swinging the lantern to see ahead. "In Zulu. He said the marching sounded like a train in the distance."

Holly glanced over her shoulder towards the beach. The helicopter was drowning out any sounds of the ocean but she played the sound in her head. "Could be the surf breaking I guess. Comes in regular. Like a train."

Grant frowned. "Who knows? He wasn't making much sense."

The searchers reached the designated point and stopped. Pockets of conversation broke out and one or two even lit cigarettes. Grant turned towards the top of the hill. The sky had been lightening for the last half an hour and now it was pre-dawn grey. The clouds were beginning to thin in preparation for another sunny day in Pacifica. Down on the beach the bodies had been removed and the coastguard dinghies winched aboard the cutter. The helicopter finally drifted north then swung away. The news helicopters had gone long ago. There was nothing else to see until daylight.

There were no survivors.

There were no fresh corpses.

The final tally was twenty-three.

Holly gathered the volunteers back on the footpath and pointed them in the direction of the coast road where a mobile canteen had been set up. It was cold and grey and everyone had been scouring the hillside for hours. Cole came over to join Holly and Grant. "It was worth a try."

Grant reckoned that was more to appease Holly than him. They all knew the search had been necessary. The Mexican might not have been the only one to crawl ashore. Cole looked as if he had something to say but there were too many people around. Holly definitely had questions for the bookseller but again, this wasn't the time. The command team began to drift apart, each faction gravitating towards its own personnel. The fire chief led his men back to the rendezvous point where the fire trucks were parked. The paramedics did the same. Ben Gardner stood alone on the plinth. His only members of staff were Bret Harding and Holly West. Grant broke off from the volunteers to join him. "Tough night. You okay?"

Gardner looked exhausted. Everyone did. After an incident like this there was always a let down, an empty feeling when the adrenaline dump wore off and the body hit bottom. Gardner had hit bottom and was still going down. He glanced at Grant and then saw Cole talking with Holly. It reminded him of something else he'd have to look into when he got time. "Are you the guy been looking for Thornton in San Francisco?"

Grant tensed. He hadn't decided what to do about his brother yet. "That's me. Yes."

Gardner let him off the hook for now. "Come see me at the office later. We need to talk."

Grant nodded and followed the crowd heading along the coastal path. He watched Cole chatting with Holly then glanced up the hill at the expensive houses overlooking the bay. The lights were out but the sky was bright enough to pick out the windows and patios with an ocean view that must have been a huge selling point when the houses came to market.

Seagulls screamed overhead. Surf broke on the shingle beach below, sounding nothing like a train in the distance. He considered what he might say to the local cop when he saw him later but there was something else on his mind. He put a spurt on to catch up with Cole, the person he really needed to talk to.

TWENTY-ONE

*

THE FIRE DEPARTMENT WAS packing its equipment into the trucks and preparing to leave. They wouldn't be leaving any time soon because the narrow road was blocked with a convoy of ambulances that had arrived to transport the bodies. Three hearses were parked in support of the ambulances. This was bigger than Pacifica's normal body run for the coroner. The police cars were still parked at the entrance but the flares had burned out.

Half the volunteers had gone home but quite a few were gathered around the mobile canteen. Grant caught up with Cole just after Holly went to help Bret Harding control the traffic. "A bit dangerous isn't it? Cozying up to the police in your situation?"

Cole moved away from the canteen queue. "I didn't have a situation until you arrived."

Grant went with him. "You're being naïve if you think that's true."

They were standing on the edge of the road overlooking the beach.

"It wasn't on a cliff edge anyway."

Grant looked over the cliff. "You mean do you stay or do you jump?"

Cole looked at Grant. "I mean do I jump or do I push you?"

The cliff was high and steep but even with a solid push it was only a leg breaker not a life ender. It was symbolic anyway. Both men knew that Cole wouldn't hurt his brother and that Grant wouldn't hurt Cole either. Not physically. Grant closed his eyes as the night's revelations flooded back. He'd understood from an early age that his father blamed him for the death of his mother. In a practical sense he was right, death by childbirth wouldn't be death without a child to birth. That child had been James Grant. How could he expect his father to forgive him if he hadn't forgiven himself? But shutting his son out even at the end of his own life? That hurt. If Grant had still been the angry young man of the past he'd be busting heads right now. The new, calmer, Jim Grant took a deep breath and opened his eyes.

There was chaos all around him. Volunteers mingled over coffee in Styrofoam cups. Paramedics transferred body bags from stretchers to their rigs. Firefighters loaded emergency gear that hadn't been needed since there'd been nobody to rescue. Noise and movement and chaos, conditions in which Grant worked best. He breathed in through his mouth and out through his nose and set the ghosts aside. "She seems like a good cop."

Cole glanced over his shoulder where Holly was creating order out of chaos. "She's good all round."

Grant zoned out the activity around him and concentrated on his brother. "Are you good enough for her?"

Cole snapped his eyes back to Grant. "Were you good enough for Sarah?"

Grant turned his back to the cliff but didn't move away from the edge. "Not when I should have been. I'm a better man now."

Cole looked at his brother then down at the rocks below. "Now that you're an American?"

Grant huffed a laugh. "I'll always be a Yorkshireman. Just wasn't always a good man."

"And you're good now? What? You don't hit everyone that crosses you?"

"I try not to hit anyone at all."

Cole tilted his head in disbelief. "That's not the way it looks on the news."

Grant shrugged. "You can't believe everything you see on TV."

A van skidded to a halt at the police barricade and a helicopter began to thud its way along the coast. Grant spun towards the noise, thc van not the helicopter. Another news van pulled up behind the first. The media circus was gathering for the emotional aftermath shots. The vans had camera platforms on their roofs but the cameras hadn't been mounted yet. It wouldn't be long though. A female news reporter climbed out of the first van. She fluffed her hair and picked the microphone off the seat. Her eyes scanned the crowd for newsworthy interviews.

Grant knew from experience that the situation was about to degenerate into a media free for all. He watched the news crew fight its way into the volunteers then turned to Cole. "And right now being on TV is the last thing you need."

Cole turned his back to the camera crews setting up beside the vans. "I'm with you there."

Grant took three steps away from the mobile canteen and two from the edge of the cliff. The volunteers were thinning out but the ones remaining split into two factions, those who wanted to get away from the cameras and those who began straightening their hair. Grant and Cole kept their heads down and walked towards the patrol cars. The flares had gone out and Bret Harding was having even more trouble controlling the scene. Grant didn't have time to help. He was looking at the building further down the road towards

Linda Mar. "Let's grab some breakfast." Grant didn't wait for Cole's answer, striding to the Boathouse Diner instead.

*

THE DINER WAS FAR ENOUGH away that the media didn't come anywhere near it and close enough that Grant could watch the recovery effort winding down. He found a booth along the back wall and sat facing the full-length windows. Two more news helicopters came thudding along the coast. Dawn pictures of an aftermath always made good TV. The networks could edit in some moody effects and a bit of music and they'd have their very own disaster movie. Cole followed Grant's gaze. "They love this shit don't they?"

Grant watched the activity further along the shore. "It makes the world go round. They hate nothing more than a slow news day."

Cole looked at Grant. "Didn't do you any harm."

Grant turned steady eyes on his brother. "You think? I can't go anywhere without people asking where's the orange windcheater?"

Cole looked at the yellow Old Town Trolley Tours windcheater. "And where is it?"

"In Texas."

Cole raised his eyebrows.

Grant waved a hand. "Don't ask."

The waitress brought their order over. Scrambled eggs on toast and a pot of English breakfast tea. Grant had learned not to risk what Americans called bacon, the rashers of blackened meat that was so crispy it was inedible. He seasoned his eggs with salt and pepper and poured two cups of tea. Englishmen abroad. Some habits died hard.

They ate in silence. It had been a long night and the hot food was good. Grant ordered more toast and some of those little plastic portions of orange marmalade. He had to explain what he meant. The waitress wanted to sell him pancakes and syrup. When they were both full Grant ordered a refill for the tea so they had an excuse for sitting there and waited for the waitress to leave. "Did you hear anything on the news about this last night?"

Cole stirred sugar into his cup. "I was out with you. Remember?"

"Before that. Shipwreck or anything like that?"

Cole put his spoon down. "Before that I was packing. I knew you were coming."

Grant took a drink of hot tea. "Yeah, well. I'm here now. And last night we were both out there on the peninsula. Did you see any shipwreck?"

Cole knew where his brother was going with this. "No."

Grant held his hands out to indicate the air around him. "Calm night. No storm. Just twenty-three bodies washed ashore." Cole waited while his brother got to the point. Grant pushed his cup away. "I checked before we left. Twenty-three people. Not one had any ID." He tapped the table with one finger. "No wallets. No money. No phones. Out of twenty-three."

The door opened and three volunteers came in. Coffee at the mobile canteen wasn't enough. They wanted breakfast as well. One of them recognized Cole and threw up a lazy wave. Cole nodded but turned back to Grant. "Some were kids. They wouldn't have any."

The volunteers sat in a window booth to give Cole some privacy. The waitress got busy taking their orders. The smell bacon and coffee soon filled the diner. Grant leaned forward. "Three kids. Seven women. And thirteen adult males." He lowered his voice. "And not a thing on any of them."

Cole tried to rationalize it. "Illegals. They travel light."

Grant shook his head. "They didn't swim from Mexico."

Cole let out a sigh. "No they didn't."

Grant waved at the view beyond the windows. "And they weren't in any shipwreck."

Cole ran out of counter arguments. He leaned back in his seat. Grant leaned further forward, maintaining the distance between them. "I don't believe in coincidences."

Cole wasn't following. "Twenty-three bodies on the night you turned up, you mean?"

Grant shook his head. "Twenty-three bodies on the night some guy comes in your house with a knife. Half a mile from where the bodies washed ashore." Now Cole was shaking his head. He didn't reply so Grant pushed on. "Why was he at your house last night?"

TWENTY-TWO

*

THE STORY TOOK LONGER than one cup of tea. The rest of the breakfasting volunteers finished and left. Grant ordered a fresh pot and the waitress talked him into trying pancakes and syrup. Even then they'd only eaten half of what a traditional American breakfast covered. The syrup was sickly sweet. The story was harder to swallow.

*

"SO THIS RANKOFF. He likes bookshops?"

Grant had listened to the early approaches and tempting offers. At first Cole had been flattered that someone as influential as Arlo Rankoff was interested in buying his shop. Cole had bought the business when it was a rundown hairdressing salon and transformed it into Shelter Cove's only independent bookstore. He'd done most of the work himself. The stripped wood and potpourri theme gave it a calm and welcoming vibe. The plain and uncluttered layout meant that shoppers could browse in a natural environment and a friendly atmosphere.

Grant didn't ask about Cole's stake money and Cole didn't mention it. It wasn't relevant to the tale of a man who was used to getting what he wanted being told he couldn't have the latest thing he wanted. Rocky Coast Books. The offers grew. They outweighed the value of the bookstore. Cole still turned them down. Then the negotiations took a turn for the worse.

The businesses on either side of the bookstore sold out. Doggie Daycare closed down and nothing opened to take its place. The Curio Shop on the other side did the same. Cole learned that several homes along San Pedro Avenue had been sold but nobody moved in. Arlo Rankoff was buying everything in his path and that path was leading to the peninsula at San Pedro Point and the crescent of beach that gave Shelter Cove its name. Rocky Coast Books was the only business left, and the veiled threats became a car through the window and the man threatening him at the shop.

Grant pushed his pancakes away. He'd only managed half of them and the sweetness was making him feel queasy. He took a drink of tea to rinse his mouth and resisted the urge to gargle. "You sure the car wasn't an accident?"

Cole gave Grant a curious look. "You're the one doesn't believe in coincidences."

Grant shrugged. "I believe in evidence though."

Cole frowned. "What evidence you got connects the bodies with the man at my house?"

Grant put his cup down. "That's what I'm trying to find out. But what connects the car to Rankoff?"

Cole was going to say the timeline was what connected the car to the threats but then he remembered something that Ben Gardner had said. *"I'm more interested in how come he was driving a scrapper from Arlo Rankoff's auto wrecker's yard."* The surf dude who'd driven through the window. "The car was a scrapper from Rankoff's yard."

"Rankoff's got a scrapyard?"

"Rankoff's got everything."

Grant considered that. He always thought of powerful men

living in New York or Boston or somewhere big on the west coast. San Francisco or Los Angeles. He wouldn't have put Shelter Cove, Pacifica, at the top of that list. Cole brought Grant up to date. "Then the same man from the shop came to the house."

"The same guy?"

Cole nodded. "Different knife."

"Rankoff's got the hots for your bookshop."

Cole echoed Gardner's supposition. "I don't think Rankoff really wants to own a bookstore."

Grant didn't think so either but he wanted to hear Cole say it. "What's he after then?"

Cole took the salt pot and sprinkled white stuff on the table. He drew the shape of the peninsula and the cove and the coast running past the diner. He stabbed little dots along the crescent bay. "Shelter Cove. You saw the beach cottages." Grant nodded but didn't speak. Cole highlighted the access road that had mostly slipped into the sea. "Big story around here is Rankoff suing the council for permission to rebuild the access road. Planning was refused last year. He's resubmitted." Cole dragged his finger along a stretch to the left of the access road. "He's bought everything blocking his way." Then stuck his finger where the bookstore would be. "Except a bookstore run by a visiting Englishman."

Grant looked at the makeshift map and nodded. He took a pinch of salt and threw it over his left shoulder. "Is it left or right? I can never remember." To be on the safe side he threw a pinch of salt over his right shoulder too. "So if he gets permission, those properties are gonna be worth a fortune."

Cole swept the salt off the table. "He's already worth a fortune. What's the point?"

Grant let out a sigh. "Point is. The rich get richer and the poor get poorer. Fact of life."

Cole shook his head. "And he's done so much to clean up the neighborhood."

Grant looked at him. "Drugs clean? Or litter?"

Cole took a drink of tea because talking had made his mouth dry. "Napoleon complex. Thinks he's going to clean up America, one stop at a time. Starting with Linda Mar and Shelter Cove."

Grant leaned back in the booth. "You'll have to explain."

Cole waved a hand to include everything around him. "Jobs in America for Americans. Some kind of white supremacy bullshit."

Grant tilted his head. "He doesn't like blacks?"

Cole looked at his brother. "He's not that keen on them. Or Englishmen." He put his cup down and brushed the salt from his hands. "But he hates Mexicans."

TWENTY-THREE

*

BY THE TIME THEY LEFT the diner most of the volunteers had drifted away but the emergency services were going to be there a whole lot longer. The end of the road had become a parking lot of oversized fire trucks and overloaded ambulances. Helicopters filled the sky over the sea and reporters swarmed across the peninsula like it was D-Day. Cole was shocked at the activity. "Christ almighty. It's a feeding frenzy."

Grant looked at the media scrum then cut through the field behind Danmann Avenue to avoid the cameras. "Pack mentality sets in. They go loco for a disaster."

Cole vaulted the fence and went down the embankment to follow his brother. "Blood in the water."

Away from the trucks and reporters the field was peaceful. Grant slowed his pace along a well-worn track across the field. "Media sharks. Strip you to the bone if you let 'em."

Cole caught up and fell in step beside him. "Is that what it was like in Boston?"

Grant watched the uneven ground as he walked. "And L.A. Not

so much after that." He threw Cole a sideways glance. "You had the best idea. Take the money and live a quiet life."

Cole avoided Grant's eyes. He concentrated on not tripping. There were things he wasn't proud of in his life. His brother took the brunt of most of them, even now. He tried not to think about the lies he'd told but as always, the more you tried to forget the more you remembered. Like a boomerang, that shit kept coming back. They continued in silence, the morning sun warming their backs. Twenty minutes later they were back at the apartment. Sarah looked at the two men as they crossed the lawn. "You boys done catching up?"

Grant shut the kitchen door behind him, the broken windows patched up with bin liners and Sellotape. He looked at his ex-wife and then his brother. "I haven't even started yet."

*

DESPITE HAVING JUST had breakfast the first thing Cole did was put the kettle on. It had practically been a ritual when they were kids. Whenever the family had been out, when they got back home it was on with the kettle. It must have been something to do with the English weather. Fruit and a cold drink didn't cut it in the British summer. Grant hung his windcheater up. He didn't explain the bloodstains. Sally stood with her arms folded across her chest. "You gonna set in on him now?"

Cole waved a calming hand and shook his head. Grant let out a sigh. He could feel the after effects of emergency action settling over him like a cloud. Not the post adrenaline shakes because he never got so hyped up that there was a comedown. It was just the focus and concentration you needed when dealing with death that took its toll when you finished holding it in. Cole knew the feeling. He'd been a cop too. Sally realized this wasn't the time for bitching. "Sorry. You okay?"

Cole nodded. Grant looked at the tablecloth. Since arriving yesterday it had been a long day merging into night. He hadn't slept since the night before. Fatigue was creeping up on him but his mind was wrestling with something else. He didn't have all the pieces yet but this Arlo Rankoff situation was shaping into a real mystery. There were questions to be answered and places to go. That was always the case with police work. Until enquiries were complete there was always somebody else to see. Add to that, the death of twenty-three Mexicans needed examining. There was also a box of childhood photos he wouldn't mind taking a look at. And the unresolved issue of the family inheritance. "Where's the rest of the money?"

Cole spilled hot water on his hand as he poured. He forced himself not to glance at the hallway cupboard where the scuba gear waited to be used. "Safe."

Grant rubbed his eyes to stay awake. "Which safe?"

Cole pulled himself together and looked at his brother. "Not a safe. Just safe."

Sally joined them at the table. Cole brewed two coffees and a cup of tea. His mind played around with the facts that he'd given and the lies that he'd told. Sorting one from the other was what usually caught liars out. Keeping it straight in his head was what would keep Grant at bay. He breathed in the coffee aroma. Not from the cups but the smell of the packet. It helped calm him, like the smell of carved wood or freshly baked bread. He put the cups on the table and pulled out a chair. "You still think I stole that evidence money?"

Grant frowned. "The police still think you did."

Cole sat down. "And the police are never wrong. Right?"

Grant took a sip of tea. "If they are we need to prove it. Otherwise they'll keep coming after you. I'm gonna have to take you back. Sort it out one way or the other."

"What if I don't want to go back?"

Grant looked at his brother. "You kidding me? You know how this works." He leaned forward. "This isn't just me. It's the entire police force. I'm just the point man."

Cole warmed his hands around his cup. "You filed a report already?"

Grant shook his head. "What? Since last night? Between your intruder and twenty-three Mexicans, I haven't had time yet. But I will." Mention of the report dragged up another thought. "The car through the window. Police handling that?"

Cole took a drink and put his cup down. "Ben Gardner. Yes."

"He took a report?"

Cole nodded. "Accident report."

Grant looked Cole in the eye. "Involving John Wayne as Cole Thornton."

Cole let out a sigh but didn't reply. Grant felt his head begin to sway. He wasn't just tired any more, he was exhausted. Before he did anything else he was going to need some sleep. He focused on Cole but his eyes felt heavy. "With all this money you've got. Did you buy any false IDs?"

Cole shook his head. Grant nodded. So that's what Gardner wanted to talk to him about. Cole saw the look on his brother's face. "Did Gardner talk to you?"

Grant rubbed his face but it wasn't working. "Wants to see me later."

Cole's shoulders sagged. Grant waved a hand. "He's got his hands full right now. I'll sort it."

Bloodshot eyes stared out of Grant's face. He wasn't going to sort anything out unless he got some sleep. He glanced along the hallway, trying to figure out how many bedrooms Cole had. "You got a bed I can borrow? I'm bushed."

Cole looked at his brother with a degree of sympathy. Grant looked pale and drawn and absolutely knackered. Cole didn't feel much better himself. The ravages of the last two days had taken their toll. A car crash and being threatened by a knifeman were bad enough but add an all night search for survivors and you had a recipe for exhaustion, mental as well as physical. Sarah was the freshest one there but even she looked tired. That threw up a problem. This was a one-bedroom apartment. There was a couch in the lounge, and that was it. Sarah saw Cole doing the math. "You boys get some sleep. I'll be fine."

Cole let out a sigh of relief. He nodded at the woman who had chosen his brother over him and went in search of bedding for the couch. Grant should have been thinking of how he was going to deal with Gardner but his mind kept wandering back to a box of photos and a childhood he never had.

*

SLEEP CAME FAST AND HARD. Grant fell into a black hole and the lid slammed shut. In keeping with everything American the couch was big and wide and soft enough to suck him down like a drowning man who'd given up the struggle. Like twenty-three Mexicans in the bay off Shelter Cove. Or going further back, like a boy building sandcastles in the North Bay of Scarborough. A boy who didn't like the water but whose brother was a much stronger swimmer.

*

JAMES GRANT PACKED THE wet sand into his bucket then upended it, slamming it onto the beach then tapping the bottom with his spade. He lifted the bucket slowly. The northern rampart of his castle had another perfect turret. James scooped more sand into the bucket and looked around for his brother. Andrew was down at the water's edge, splashing and jumping then charging into the Yorkshire surf.

The five-year-old continued to make his sandcastle while his ten-year-old brother practiced diving into the shallow waters. Five and ten. It amazed James that his brother was exactly twice as old as him. With a youthful ignorance of maths he imagined his brother would always be twice his age, even when they were grown ups, but being an adult was a long way off. For now they were a pair of carefree boys on holiday at the seaside with their father.

James looked around. Thoughts of his father made him nervous. He knew his dad didn't like him as much as Andrew but was too young to understand why. He scanned the beach but Commander Grant RN was nowhere to be seen. The pristine sands of Scarborough's north bay stretched for a mile and a half around the crescent bay, from the cliffs of Scarborough Castle to the Sealife Centre peninsula. The seawall was big and strong and protected Royal Albert Drive for half its length but it was the northern stretch that serviced the public beach. Above the promenade two rows of brightly painted beach huts overlooked the sands. The wooden huts were no bigger than garden sheds, providing washing and cooking facilities for anyone needing a shower after a dip in the sea. Building his sandcastle under the gaze of the beach huts made James nervous too. Under the gaze of his father. He turned towards the sea and watched his brother flopping about in the waves. At least James had his brother. It was good to know somebody had his back.

James made another turret, then another. The castle was taking shape. It wasn't as impressive as the ruin that overlooked Scarborough but it was big enough to draw admiring glances from the others kids. That was when the problems started.

"Hey dumbbell. Whatcha think ya doin'?"

There were four of them. Maybe eight years old. All of them bigger than the skinny kid making the sandcastle. As with all gangs, one of them was the leader and the others did as they were told. What they were doing now was watching the big fat bully pick on the skinny kid.

"Dontcha know it's babies make sandcastles?"

To prove his point the bully kicked a chunk out of the northern rampart. Sand tumbled out of the breach and one of the turrets collapsed. The other three laughed so the bully kicked again. Another section of the castle wall turned into a pile of sand.

"Are you a baby?"

James sat back on the edge of the hole he'd dug for water. He felt tears prickle the back of his eyes. He daren't look up to see if his father was watching. He'd get no help there. Instead he turned towards the sea and looked for his brother. Andrew had disappeared, probably diving underwater and pretending he was James Bond.

The bully took another kick and this time the others joined in. Their laughter was harsh and cruel. The castle walls tumbled into the moat. The carefully crafted turrets fell into the courtyard. Grant was struck dumb. He couldn't speak. The tears that had threatened now spilled down his cheeks but the anger building inside was tempered by fear. He was scared of fighting back but he couldn't stand by and watch his handy work being destroyed.

"Stop it." The sharpness of his voice surprised him. The bully stopped kicking. The other three turned to see what he was going to do. They'd seen this scenario before. They knew what came next.

"You talkin' to me? Dumbbell." The bully drew himself up to his full height. It was like a grizzly bear rearing up to attack. James shrank in the face of the overwhelming firepower. He gripped one of the paper flags that would have adorned the turrets. The wooden stake was pointed at one end. He held it like a knife, ready to plunge it into soft flesh. That was as far as he got because the bully slapped him across the face and he fell into the puddled hole. The slap stung. The shame hurt worse. He curled up in a ball and waited for the inevitable kicking. The next blow sounded louder than the slap and James prepared for the pain but it didn't come. He looked up in time to see Andrew slap the bully three times then knee him in the stomach. "Why don't you pick on somebody your own size?"

The bully doubled over and fell to his knees. Andrew stood over him. "Oh hang on. There isn't anybody your size is there?" He slapped the bully again. "Fatso."

The other three stepped back in amazement. The bully cowered down. James felt tears of joy well up but then a familiar voice shouted down from the promenade.

"Andrew. Stop that." Their father looked over the seawall and shook his head. "He's got to stand up for himself sometime." Andrew looked up at his father and then back down at James. His brother was a muddy heap in the bottom of the moat. The pleading look broke Andrew's heart but his father had spoken. James watched in disbelief as his brother stepped away from the castle and lowered his fists. Seagulls screamed overhead. Children laughed and played along the beach. The world went on around him as if nothing was happening. Along with the sandcastle, James Grant's world came crashing down.

Andrew turned and walked away. The bully got to his feet. The other three stood beside him and all four dropped into the hole where James lay on his back. He tried to stand up but he didn't have the energy. He couldn't fight back because he couldn't fight. Bullying was something his brother always took care of.

He was five years old. The beating was brief. The castle was destroyed. And the brothers were never the same again. It was the last time that James didn't fight back. Three years later he was packed off to Moor Grange School For Boys and the rift was complete.

*

IT WASN'T THE BULLYING that woke Grant up it was a warm feeling that had nothing to do with the childhood dream. The sensation was familiar and he wondered briefly if he'd segued into another, nicer dream. He kept his eyes closed in case that was the case. His dreams usually revolved around one of two things. Sometimes he'd be spending time with stars from his favorite movies, and sometimes he'd be having sex. This felt like a sex dream. He relaxed and let it happen.

A warm hand slid down his stomach and soft naked flesh brushed against him. The sandcastle was forgotten. The beating was a thing of the past. This dream was much better. He identified the soft flesh as the gentle curves of female breasts. He could feel the nipples grow hard as they brushed his chest. The hand was attached to a long naked arm. It snaked downwards until it encircled what it had been looking for. The thing it had been looking for stiffened and woke up and so did Grant. He didn't open his eyes. "Do you really think you should be doing that?"

Sarah's reply was close to his ear. "You never complained before."

Grant kept his voice low, not wanting Cole to hear. "No man ever complained about a woman stroking his cock."

"You want me to stop?"

Grant blinked his eyes open but didn't move. The curtains were drawn. The lounge was in shadow but sunlight meant it wasn't dark. The top of Sarah's head showed above the quilt but it slowly disappeared as her head followed the path of her hand. Wet lips and an adventurous tongue warmed his chest and stomach. Soon her mouth explored what she had in her hand. Then she stopped talking.

Grant looked towards the bedroom door. It was closed. It was at the far end of the hallway. It was… The warmth of Sarah's mouth enveloped him and pushed all thoughts from his head. He couldn't help but thrust slightly with his hips. Then he did something he thought he'd never do. With an effort of will he gently pushed Sarah's head away and she resurfaced on the pillow. "Something wrong?"

Grant had to get his breath back. "I'm pretty sure it said something about this in the divorce papers."

"That was when we were getting divorced. Now we're single."

Grant turned on his side to face her. "You're single and you came to see Andrew."

Sarah let out a sigh. "I fucked up didn't I?"

"Just now? Or before?"

"Marrying you."

Grant tried to ignore the fact that his ex-wife was naked beside him. "We both fucked up. Mostly me."

Sarah looked in Grant's eyes. "You had anger management issues."

"Not against you."

"No. But they were hard to ignore."

"I know. I'm different now."

"I noticed. You never stopped me before." Grant shrugged. There was no answer to that. Sarah stared at the ceiling. "But I fucked up coming here." She let out another sigh. "All this way and he's in love with somebody else."

Grant looked at her. "The policewoman?"

"Holly. Yes."

"I'm guessing she doesn't know what's going on."

"But he wants to tell her. I can see it in his eyes."

Grant shrugged again. "That's up to him."

Sarah raised a hand and stroked Grant's cheek. "Actually it's not. Not if you're going to tell the local police."

"Ben Gardner?"

Sarah nodded. "He wants to see you later?"

"He does."

"What are you going to tell him?"

Grant shifted up onto one elbow and looked down at Sarah. "I haven't decided yet."

Her hand snaked south again. "Can I help make up your mind?"

Grant stopped her hand and looked into her eyes. He shook his head. Sarah gave him a sad little smile. "You have changed. You're a lot nicer now. Maybe I should have given you a second chance."

"I wasn't ready for a second chance back then."

She lowered her voice. "Are you now?"

Grant felt a wave of affection wash over him. The divorce hadn't been Sarah's fault and he did still have feelings for her but that time had passed. He wished he could say something different but he couldn't. Sarah shifted up onto the pillow and understood his decision. She nodded. "I fucked it up with both of you didn't I?"

Grant didn't sugar the pill. "You'll get over it."

"What about Gardner?"

Grant wasn't ready to answer that one yet. "You'll get over him as well."

TWENTY-FOUR

*

IT WAS ALL OVER THE NEWS by lunchtime. The panoramic vistas of Linda Mar and Shelter Cove were plastered across network TV with helicopter tracking shots and artful close-ups of police activity on the beach. The sun was out. It was another beautiful day in Pacifica. The blue sky was bright and cloudless and a perfect backdrop for the uniforms on the sand and the green of the hillside. Hollywood couldn't have made it any better. Holly West would have preferred it if the news reporters found something else to tell their viewers about. "Hey you. Keep back there. This is a crime scene."

The cameraman lowered his shoulder rig and tried to clamber back up the slope from the beach. He lost his footing on the loose surface and went over backwards. The camera hit him in the face and blood trickled from the bridge of his nose. Maybe the news could cover that and leave Holly alone. "All the way back. Up the hill."

Holly turned back to the beach. She was overstating the facts. This wasn't a crime scene because the powers that be, Coastguard, Border Agency and Pacifica PD were playing this as a tragic accident. Twenty-three Mexicans washed overboard off the California coast. Illegal Mexicans probably but that only made it more newsworthy, not more criminal. It wasn't a murder investigation. There was no crime scene tape cordoning off the beach, that's why reporters kept getting under Holly's feet while she tried to keep order among the competing factions. The Coastguard wanted to find out which ship they'd come from. The Border Agency wanted to know who brought them into the country. Pacifica PD wanted the whole mess cleared up so they could get back to protecting its citizens and ensuring their support in the next elections. Police chiefs were more political than practical.

Two powerboats hired by competing news networks jockeyed for position for the best shots from the victim's point of view. Half a dozen local boatmen from the Rockaway Marina zipped in and out between the news crews and the coastguard. It was only a matter of time before there was another maritime incident.

Holly looked along the beach to where Bret Harding was waving his arms ineffectually at an anchorwoman trying to film an introduction from the rocky peninsula of San Pedro Point. This was more action than Bret had seen in his entire career. He looked as if he'd prefer flipping burgers at McDonalds. Holly could have managed a Big Mac right about now. Her mouth watered at the thought of the McDs restaurant opposite the police office.

*

BEN GARDNER COULD SMELL the burgers across the parking lot from his office. He'd already eaten but the smell made him hungry all over again. Not for the first time he wondered how something so devoid of meat could taste so good. It must be all that artificial color and flavoring. He left the door open to let some air in and went into the kitchenette. Coffee was the only antidote to a cheeseburger and fries. It was also the only answer to all the papers on his desk. Push them aside and have a coffee. "Goddamn paper trails."

He was talking to the empty office again. He'd have to get a handle on that. Somebody once told him that the first sign of madness was hairs on the palms of your hands and the second sign was looking for them. He reckoned number three was where he was at right now. If anybody caught him he'd be off the job in double quick time. Looking at all the reports he was going to have to write that didn't seem like such a bad thing.

He stirred his coffee and let out a sigh. That wasn't true. He couldn't imagine life without the uniform. Lot's of cops felt that way. A lifetime of service would leave a big hole to fill upon retirement. No wonder so many ex-cops ate their guns. Gardner had never fired his. He'd probably miss.

He took the coffee and sat at his desk. The Pacifica map looked down from the wall. Gardner stared back at it, ignoring the coastal strip and focusing on the crescent beach of Shelter Cove. Looking at it from above it was easier to see the full picture. He picked out where most of the bodies had washed ashore, the sweeping bay between the peninsula and the rocks. The entire beach and headland jutted into the Pacific while Linda Mar's beach cut inland more than any other stretch of the coast.

The bodies had been caught in the riptide that swirled beneath the waters of the cove. One had drifted around San Pedro Point and been picked up near the coast road. None of them had been carried further up or down the coast. That suggested they'd gone in the water closer to shore rather out to sea. Not likely to be a passing ship running up the coast. More likely to be something smaller and more personal. Something more targeted towards the inlets of Pacifica. Or Linda Mar itself. There weren't many Mexicans working in the neighborhood. Twenty-three new faces would have stood out. Shelter Cove wasn't the place to smuggle illegals.

Gardner took a drink of coffee then shuffled the papers into priority order. The maritime disaster was his first priority. Local matters were downgraded to pile number two. As he shifted that pile to one side he noticed the accident report. The car through the bookstore window. That was something he really wanted to look into but he didn't have time. "Goddamn Mexicans."

Talking to the office again. He didn't want to be writing coroner's reports on illegal aliens, he wanted to be checking who the unknown alien was that was courting his protégé. He put the accident report at the top of the secondary pile. The voice from the door made him jump.

"You talk to yourself a lot?" Jim Grant stood in the doorway. Gardner pushed back from his desk but didn't answer. Grant noticed all the paperwork and came to a decision. "About your mystery man."

TWENTY-FIVE

*

GARDNER LEANED BACK IN his chair and looked at the man in the bright yellow windcheater he'd last seen at San Pedro Point. "He's not Cole Thornton, I know that much."

"No, he's not." Just that. Grant stepped inside and closed the door. This required some privacy. He didn't want half the customers of McDonalds hearing what he had to say. He hadn't fully decided what he was going to say himself yet. Gardner looked at the dried bloodstains on the windcheater, the dark red standing out against the bright yellow. He didn't think the man was from Old Town Trolley Tours. "And that would make you?"

Grant showed his badge. "Jim Grant. Boston PD."

Gardner looked at the ID then at Grant. "This isn't Boston."

Grant stood in front of the desk. "This isn't a Boston matter."

"Then why are you here?"

That was the big question wasn't it? The next answer Grant gave would lock him into a line of action that he'd have to stick with. He needed a moment to make his mind up. He smelled the coffee and glanced towards the kitchenette as he put the badge wallet away. "You mind?"

Gardner waved a hand. "Knock yourself out."

"Thanks." Grant took a cup from the shelf and boiled the kettle. It was still warm from the last brew. There were no teabags so he made a weak coffee with lots of milk, not exactly a latte but with enough sugar he'd get by. Gardner waited patiently. He indicated the chair opposite the desk when Grant came out with the coffee. "So? What can I do for you?"

Grant sat down. He decided to be vague. "You can let me use your facilities if I need them."

"For this thing that isn't a Boston matter."

"Yes."

Gardner took a drink of coffee. "They employ a lot of Brits in Boston now do they?"

Grant raised his eyebrows. "When the job requires it."

"Like this job that's to do with Pacifica, not Boston."

Grant shrugged. "It's international."

"You saying Thornton's a spy?"

"I'm saying Thornton isn't Thornton."

Gardner put his cup down. "Who is he then?"

Grant's decision solidified. "I can't say."

Gardner looked at the second Englishman he didn't believe. "What's he here for?"

"I can't say that either."

Gardner tried a different angle. "Is he in WITSEC?"

The question threw Grant for a second. Saying that Cole had been relocated for the Federal Witness Protection Program could explain why he was living under a false name. Witness security was an important arm in the prosecution of criminals but it was run by the US Marshalls service not an English cop working for Boston PD. "No." That wasn't going to be enough so he threw Gardner a branch. "He's working undercover."

The office went quiet while both men tested the validity of that statement. Grant tested the story for holes and decided it was watertight. If he'd said it was WITSEC there'd be a paper trail that Gardner could follow to confirm the story even if he wouldn't be able to find out Thornton's name. An undercover cop would be buried deeper, especially for some international investigation. Gardner was thinking exactly the same thing but for different reasons. "Undercover? In Shelter Cove?"

Grant took a drink of milky coffee to cover his answer. "Yes."

Gardner indicated the map on the wall. "Nothing ever happens in Shelter Cover."

Grant put his cup on the desk and jerked a thumb over his shoulder. "Really? You just had twenty-three Mexicans wash up on shore."

TWENTY-SIX

*

DRIFTWOOD AUTO WRECKERS WAS in the angle at the bottom of Roberts Road just off Crespi Drive. It was hidden behind the US Post Office sorting depot and nestled in the mouth of a dry canyon that cut into the foothills above Cabrillo School. Grant didn't get the address from Ben Gardner. Conversation had kind of gone downhill after throwing in the twenty-three dead Mexicans. It wasn't hard to find though. Everybody knew where Arlo Rankoff wrecked his cars.

The afternoon sun had moved inland and was now blazing down the canyon like a blowtorch. The heat brought beads of sweat to Grant's forehead and prickled his scalp. He unzipped the windcheater but didn't take it off. He liked to be highly visible when approaching potential trouble. It made him appear less threatening. If the heavy from last night was anything to go by, Rankoff's employees might need lulling into a false sense of security before Grant turned up the heat.

He followed the dirt road round the back of the sorting depot until he came to the wire fenced compound. Dead cars were stacked four high and six deep around the perimeter, leaving a central clearing for customers to park and enough room for the ramshackle office that was a prerequisite for all scrapyards. The main gate was open so Grant didn't think he'd have to worry about a guard dog. His take on Arlo Rankoff was that nobody would be foolish enough to steal from him anyway so there was no need to feed a dog.

Grant walked through the gate and stopped in the middle of the compound. The hard packed earth was dry and dusty. It puffed little clouds with every footstep. The dust settled over his shoes when he stood still. There was no movement in the yard. The stacked cars creaked as they settled. A radio played in the office but there was no sign of who was listening. The office was the obvious place to start.

The dust cloud followed Grant as he crossed the compound, eyes checking the stacks in case anyone was clambering over them collecting spare parts. Not likely. He reckoned any usable parts would have been stripped before the carcasses were piled in the vehicle graveyard. A chunky square car with front end damage and flat tyres stood in a clearing at the base of the right hand stack. Nobody was working on it. All the relevant parts were still intact. Wheels, windshield wipers, light fittings and mirrors. It was a work in progress waiting to feed the resale market.

The music was coming through an open window along the side of the shack. Grant knocked on the faded wooden door and went in. Somebody turned the radio off. The office was empty.

"Hello. Anybody home?"

The bare wooden floorboards were as dusty as the compound. The paintwork was faded and pealing. The only furniture was a desk and a filing cabinet. There was an unplugged desk lamp on top of the filing cabinet. The leather swivel chair behind the desk was old and worn into the shape of a fat man's backside.

The fat man wasn't sitting in it.

A floorboard creaked in the next room and Grant turned towards the door. "Hello. You got a customer here."

The door opened and the man whose backside fit the chair waddled through. "What can I getcha fella?"

The man was fat but big with it. Tall, big. He was one of the few people who could look down on Grant. High wide and handsome was how they could have described him. Minus the handsome. The floor creaked again as he came into the office. "Folks normally call ahead for spares."

Grant scanned the office. There was no phone. "By bush telegraph?"

The man pulled a cell phone out of his pocket. "Business line."

Grant nodded. "Good to know. But I was just passing and thought I'd drop in."

The man put the phone back in his pocket and walked to the front window. "Whatcha lookin' for?"

Grant saw the man's eyes glance outside then back to the customer. Sun blazed in through the open door. Grant stepped away so he was facing the entrance. "I'm looking for a car that has a predilection for bookstore windows."

The man's eyes flickered. It was the only signal he gave. "Predi-what?"

Grant looked out the door. "Predilection. A preference or special liking for something."

The fat man glowered. "Do I look like I swallowed a dictionary?"

Grant didn't mention what it looked like the fat man had swallowed. "They've got one in the bookstore. The car probably understands what I mean. I'm guessing it's the one dumped round the side there."

The fat man stepped away from the window. The signal was sent. Echoing bangs and creaks broke the quiet of the compound as two hired hands climbed down from the stacked cars. They were nearly as tall as the big man but nowhere near as fat. Working in the scrap trade made them strong and hard and weathered to stone. They blocked the doorway but didn't come in.

Grant spoke to the room. "Anyone got a screwdriver?"

*

THE AIR IN THE OFFICE was stifling. It was hotter than outside and even with the door open there was no breeze to move the air around. Sweat rolled down Grant's forehead. He wiped it clear with the back of his hand and flicked it across the floor, half expecting it to sizzle on the dusty floorboards. The hired hands waited in the doorway blocking what little fresh air there was. Grant looked at the pair in the door then at the fat man behind the desk. "This your idea of customer relations?"

The fat man sat in the chair. It groaned under his weight. "It's my idea of dealing with folk sticking their noses where it don't belong."

Grant went to the filing cabinet and leaned one arm across the top. "What if I said my nose belongs exactly where I'm sticking it?"

The fat man rested his hands on the desk. "It aint your car."

"No it isn't."

"Then it aint none of your business."

Grant had his badge wallet in the hand resting across the filing cabinet. He let the wallet fall open to show his ID. "That statement suggests you know who the owner is." He wiggled the wallet. "And this makes it my business." He nodded towards the car outside. "And since the car that drove through the bookstore window was scrapped a year ago I'm interested in who put it back on the road."

Nobody moved. Nobody spoke. Silence hung in the air like fog. The fat man proved he had excellent eyesight when he broke the silence. "That badge don't give you no authority outside of Boston." He waved a hand to indicate the compound. "And in case you haven't noticed this aint Boston."

The two heavies took their lead from the man in the chair. They pushed through the door, nudging each other out of the way in their eagerness to get to the stranger leaning on the filing cabinet. Grant flicked the wallet shut and stood up. "A crime's a crime no matter where it's committed. And a cop's a cop no matter where he is. You boys come any closer and you're gonna see the inside of a jail cell."

The pair stopped in the middle of the office. They weren't used to somebody backing them down with a few choice words and a confident manner. It was the confident manner that gave them pause. They were confused and looked to their boss for a decision. The fat man nodded.

Grant stepped around the side of the filing cabinet. The fastest heavy got a head start on his partner and rushed forward. Grant waited until the last second then yanked the top drawer open. The metal was sharp and angled and heavy with papers in file hammocks. The hired hand caught it in the chest and Grant stamped hard on his shin. Boot scraped bone and the heavy reflexed forward, his chin disappearing into the drawer. Grant slammed it shut against the side of his head. The floor bounced when he hit it.

The second heavy came around his fallen partner but Grant sidestepped left, grabbing the desk lamp from the top of the filing cabinet. The cable was loose and dangling. Grant swung the plug by the cord and it wrapped around the big fella's legs below the knee. With his legs tied together he had no base for balance. Grant shoulder charged him and he went over sideways towards the cabinet. He smacked his head against the dull grey metal and looked even more confused than when he'd come in.

Grant didn't wait for them to recover. He darted around the desk just as the fat man opened the drawer. Stubby fingers reached for the gun but Grant raised a leg and stamped the drawer shut. The fingers mashed. The fat man tried to get up but being tall and overweight meant getting up from a low position was a struggle. The wheels of the chair slid across the floor and Grant leaned on the big man's shoulders. The chair overbalanced. The fat man went over backwards and the office floor shook again.

Grant took the semi-automatic out of the drawer and leaned against the wall. "You want taking in? Or answer a couple of questions?"

The fat man groaned. His two workers struggled to sit up. The tangled one was clearing his head and the first thought to go through it was attack. Being slammed into a filing cabinet wasn't going to knock either of them out. They started to get up with vengeance in their eyes.

Grant worked the slide on the gun. "Ah, ah. I know what you're thinking." He pointed it loosely between the two of them. "My advice is, don't."

The duo stopped halfway up. Grant kept his feet shoulder width apart for a solid base but didn't think any more action would be needed. The fat man sat on the floor with his back against the wall. "You just shit in your own pocket."

Grant kept the gun vague. "But not on my own doorstep. Like you said. This isn't Boston." Then he pointed it at the fat man. "Obstructing a police officer in the lawful execution of his duty. Assault with a deadly weapon. You're the one who's in deep shit." He lowered the gun. "Or we could just have a friendly chat and you tell me whose car it is."

The fat man let out a sigh. His two workers sat against the filing cabinet but didn't try to get up. Nobody spoke. Grant raised his eyebrows. "Name?"

The fat man looked up. "Matt King. Surfer dude from up the way."

Grant pushed off from the wall. "I'll be needing a chat with him as well."

The fat man chuckled. It made his entire body rumble. "Good luck with that."

Grant could feel bad news coming. "How come?"

The fat man smiled. "Drowned in his bath yesterday."

"Can't surfers swim?"

"There aint no swimming in the bath."

Grant shook his head. "Should have been careful whose car he borrowed then shouldn't he?"

The fat man pulled the chair towards him to help get up. Grant kicked the chair away. It rolled across the floor towards the door. Grant looked around the office. There was a map of Linda Mar on the wall and an address book on the desk. Grant lowered the gun. "Somebody's cleaning house."

The fat man grunted but didn't speak. Grant smiled. "I'd stick to showers if I were you." Still no reaction. "Once Arlo Rankoff finds out I got his address from you."

This time the big man spluttered and answer. "I aint given you nobody's address."

Grant held the gun out in front of him and pressed the magazine release. A few swift moves later and the gun was in pieces on the floor. He stepped over the debris and flicked open the address book. He checked the entry then glanced at the map. He wasn't surprised to see where the boss man lived.

TWENTY-SEVEN

*

"NICE VIEW. COULD ALMOST TELL if they were doing breast stroke from here."

"Only if they were swimming with flashlights. It was dark, I understand."

Grant was standing with Arlo Rankoff on the balcony of his luxury home on Kent Road, a winding cul-de-sac overlooking San Pedro Point and Shelter Cove. The three men standing behind Rankoff looked like they wanted to throw Grant over the railing. Seeing the look in their eyes made him wonder if it was a good idea coming up here alone.

*

THE SUN WAS LOW IN the west by the time Grant followed Essex Way up the hill to Kent Road. He'd just turned off Sussex Way, all the streets named after English counties. It would have made him feel at home if it weren't for the big wooden houses and the American cars in the driveways. That and the palm trees and yucca plants in some of the gardens. Plants that were more at home in California than England.

Kent Road took one final twist then came to a stop at the end of the promontory. Trees shrouded the horizon. If he went any further he'd drop off the edge onto the landslip road where he'd walked with Cole last night. Around the bottom of the hill where the rescue operation was winding down.

Grant stopped on the final bend and leaned against a lamppost. A long steep footpath between the houses ran all the way down to the beach cottages. Hundreds of steps cut into the hillside. With the access road wiped out by avalanche damage this was the only way down to Shelter Cove. Steep and narrow and treacherous. The next house along was Rankoff's. The last house on Kent Road. It was big and modern and had outbuildings that disappeared into the trees. There were a couple of smaller houses on the inland side and one on the corner behind Grant. House to house enquiries would be an easy choice. Looking for witnesses to last night's tragedy. Grant's excuse for being here. Except police work was never that easy.

Grant pushed off from the lamppost and crossed the road.

Five minutes later he knocked on Arlo Rankoff's door.

*

A SMALL TOUGH LOOKING man led Grant into the living room to meet Rankoff. He wasn't what Grant had expected. Rankoff was as short as the man who'd answered the door but nowhere near as tough looking. He was round-shouldered and balding with a Viva Zapata moustache and a dark complexion. Grant's first thought was that for a man who hated Mexicans he looked a lot like a Mexican. Standing in front of a large stone fireplace he looked like a land baron lording it over his domain. His domain at the moment was all the land leading to Shelter Cove.

"Welcome officer. How can I help you?"

Grant put his badge wallet away and surveyed the room. It was the centerpiece of the ground floor, taking up all the space along the back of the house. Any kitchens or dining rooms must have been off the corridor he'd walked along from the front door. The high ceiling went up to the second floor and a staircase and balcony curled along two sides of the room looking down into the lounge. Bedrooms were off the landing and another corridor towards the front of the house. Comfortable chairs and settees were arranged around a heavy throw rug in front of the hearth. The third wall, overlooking the ocean, was floor to ceiling glass. Two floors worth of patio window that made the room look like it was open to the elements. The windows were triple glazed. The elements were kept outside.

"Nice paintings."

Grant ignored the view for now, concentrating on the wall above the fireplace. There was a lot of wall, like a hunting lodge without the mounted heads. Authentic looking oil paintings hung at irregular intervals. The American west. Cattle drives. A craggy faced cowboy. The iconic image of The Alamo after the battle, more dead Mexicans than had drowned outside the windows. A few dead Texans too. Grant smiled. "Must make you feel proud to be American."

Rankoff spread his arms to encompass everything around him. "I am proud to be American."

Grant nodded then jerked a thumb back the way he'd come. "All the streets are named after somewhere in England."

Rankoff shrugged. "I am sure there are American street names in England."

Grant shook his head. "No. They're pretty much English. Maybe not in the same cities. Manchester Road isn't in Manchester but it goes to Manchester. Otley Road goes to Otley. Like that."

Rankoff waved for Grant to sit down then sat on the settee opposite. "Well, Kent Road leads to my house. How can I help you?"

Back to his original question. His expression was calm and

friendly but his eyes were hard and watchful. Looking for any sign of the lies he knew Grant would tell while trying to divine what the visiting cop actually knew. He waited patiently. Grant got the ball rolling. "A few people drowned in the bay last night."

Rankoff put on his sad face. "Tragic. I saw it on the news."

Grant nodded. "Hard to miss. All those helicopters. Must have got every angle covered."

"Seemed like it to me. They do love their disasters on TV."

Grant flicked his eyes towards the patio windows. "Only angle they missed was from up here."

"Not easy for them to get that unless they lived here."

"That's where I come in."

Rankoff draped one leg over his knee. "How so?"

Grant put his official voice on. "I'm doing house to house enquiries. See if there were any witnesses."

Rankoff leveled a searching look at Grant. "You didn't do the houses across the street."

"They don't overlook the bay."

"Or the one on the corner."

Grant smiled. "I always start at the top and work down. You are at the top aren't you?"

Rankoff's smile didn't touch his eyes. "Oh yes. I am at the top."

Two more men came into the lounge, as tough as the doorman but taller. They weren't smiling. They kept their distance but their presence changed the dynamic in the room. Hard eyes and stony silence gave off the unspoken threat. Arlo Rankoff was the top dog and his pack was here to back him up if necessary. Grant stood up and flexed his shoulders. "So? Can I take a look?"

Rankoff stood up too. The three hard men moved a step closer. "Be my guest." He snapped his fingers and the doorman pushed a button. The triple glazed patio door hissed as the seal was broken then it slid back on silent wheels. He held out a hand for Grant to go first then followed him out onto the balcony.

*

GRANT TURNED HIS ATTENTION away from the cove, where you could have seen if they were doing breast stroke, and faced the three men glaring at him from the patio doors. The doorman looked tough enough but the other two were the real threat. The knifeman from Cole's house wasn't among them. He was lower down the food chain. These guys were the real deal. "You could have heard them. People drowning tend to cry out."

Rankoff tapped the window. "These are triple-glazed against the coastal winds."

Grant took one last look at the spectacular view. Shelter Cove curved like a scimitar, slicing into the ocean at San Pedro Point and arcing towards the rocky outcrop to the west. Surf broke on the jagged teeth of San Pedro Rocks, standing out to sea like a volcanic island. He could see the concrete circle that had become the impromptu forward command post and the track that ran behind the beach huts. Beach cottages, he corrected himself, since this wasn't Scarborough. There were still a few rescue workers clearing the beach but most of the activity had died away. "You weren't out here last night then?"

Rankoff waved his attack dogs inside then stepped aside to let Grant go next. "I was watching a John Wayne movie."

Grant went inside and Rankoff followed. The door slid shut with a faint sucking noise as the seal took hold. Grant looked at the wall of paintings. It was time to probe. "Not The Alamo?" He paused and turned to Rankoff. "I heard you don't like Mexicans."

The living room was quiet. The surf breaking over San Pedro Rocks was silenced by three layers of glass and the rubber seal.

There was no clock to tick quietly in the corner. The open fire wasn't burning so there were no crackling flames or exploding knots of wood. Just five men breathing evenly. Nobody getting excited or ready for action.

The painting of the mission that became a fortress looked down from the wall. Rankoff turned his back to it. "No. I don't think this movie had any Mexicans in it." He let the silence stretch for a long moment, never taking his eyes off Grant. "Eldorado. Robert Mitchum as a drunken sheriff." This time the smile did twinkle his eyes. "And John Wayne playing Cole Thornton." Until he switched the twinkle off. "I wonder who's playing Cole Thornton now?"

TWENTY-EIGHT

*

THE FIRST THOUGHT TO GO through Grant's head was, that was quick. He'd only told Ben Gardner about Cole this afternoon. The second thought was, Ben Gardner was the *only* person he'd told this afternoon. The only person he'd told, period. It seemed that property and scrapped cars weren't the only things that Arlo Rankoff owned. He hoped none of that showed on his face. "I always thought he played Cole Thornton in The Sons Of Katie Elder."

Rankoff shook his head. "He'd have to be a stepson then. Since the sons were called Elder."

Grant shrugged. "About the same time though. John Wayne in his later years but before he was too old to play gunslingers."

Rankoff kept his face impassive. "Maybe our Cole Thornton is really John Elder."

Grant matched Rankoff's poker face. "I once arrested a kid. Back home in Yorkshire. Gave his name as Spartacus Adams. Only a teenager. Custody sergeant beat him black and blue for lying to the police. Turned out his mother was a huge Kirk Douglas fan. She wanted her son to be able to stand up when he was called and say, 'I'm Spartacus.'"

Rankoff didn't look like he believed him. Grant continued. "And then there's that war movie. Where Eagles Dare. Richard Burton played a triple agent called John Smith. You know how many people in England are called John Smith?"

This time Rankoff did respond. "Your point being?"

Grant stood near the windows and glanced along the coastline. Apart from the beach cottages there were no other buildings as far as the eye could see, just trees and shrubs and rugged hillside. The only thing of value was the row of cottages along Shelter Cove. The rest of the land was undeveloped. He turned back to look at Rankoff. "My point is there's more people named Cole Thornton than the one played by John Wayne." He lowered his voice as if imparting a secret. "And even John Wayne wasn't John Wayne."

Rankoff joined the conspiracy by lowering his own voice. "And Cole Thornton isn't Cole Thornton. Is he?"

Grant scrutinized Rankoff's face. "Is that why you want to buy him out? Keep California pure?"

Rankoff shrugged. "It pays to know who you're doing business with."

Grant kept his peripheral vision on the three tough guys. "And it pays to know whose window you're driving cars through."

Rankoff held up his hands in surrender. "An over zealous employee. I had to let him go."

Grant tilted his head in query. "Was that before or after he drowned in the bath?"

Rankoff let out a sigh. "I heard about that too. But it didn't make the news."

"A bit of a coincidence though, isn't it?"

Rankoff turned level eyes on Grant. "Life is full of coincidences. How else do you explain two Englishmen turning up in Linda Mar with an interest in John Wayne?" Back to Rankoff's original accusation, only this time including Grant in the implied conspiracy. It was time to change the subject. Grant waved a hand at the view out the window and prepared to go deeper.

*

RANKOFF ANSWERED GRANT'S questions in a dull monotone. Business answers that were as dry and boring as a science lecture. He admitted buying most of the properties leading to Shelter Cove and conceded that he owned the rundown beach cottages at the bottom of the hill. What he didn't do was accept that the holiday homes were a bad investment. "Do you know the value of beachfront property in California?"

Grant shook his head.

Rankoff rubbed the fingers of one hand together. "A lot of money." He moved to the window and looked out. "But not with an access road that's slipped into the ocean."

Grant gave an understanding, ah hah. "So you got them on the cheap." Rankoff raised his eyebrows but didn't speak. Grant spoke for him. "Then, when the new road's built." He jerked a thumb skywards. "Whoosh."

Rankoff turned away from the window. "I'm having a little trouble with the planning permission. Not everyone wants a new road built on their doorstep."

Now Grant really understood. "So you bought everything in your path."

Rankoff shrugged. "Not always on the cheap."

Grant looked Rankoff in the eye. "And not always a bookstore."

"No. And in the interests of full disclosure, not just for a row of beach cottages. The potential for redevelopment along this stretch of the coast is endless."

Grant looked up at the western paintings. “Pioneering spirit. Worth smoothing a few bumps in the road.”

Rankoff gave an almost imperceptible nod. The three hard men came out of sleep mode and moved closer to Grant. “I think I have been more than helpful. Since none of this has anything to do with a bunch of Mexicans drowning in the cove.”

Grant relaxed his shoulders and kept his hands loose. “Could put a crimp in your planning application though.”

Rankoff ignored the implication and continued. “And since house to house enquiries don’t include a scrapyard across the valley.”

The men spread out to form a perimeter. Grant focused on Rankoff but kept them in his peripheral vision. “He called you about that, huh?”

Rankoff held a hand to the side of his face with a finger and thumb sticking out in the universal telephone mime. “You should have taken his phone.”

“Self defence I can justify. Taking his phone would be theft.”

“Do you always uphold the letter of the law?”

Grant’s stare turned hard. “I always uphold what’s right.”

The men tightened the circle. Rankoff made a twirling motion with one hand above his head. “You going to lasso my men with a desk lamp?”

“Only if your men obstruct a police office in the lawful execution of his duty.”

Rankoff lowered his voice. “It’s the lawful bit I might take exception to.”

The two big men moved either side of Grant to widen his arc. The doorman stayed in the middle. Rankoff took a step back out of the way. The room fell silent. The build-up of testosterone sparked like static electricity before a storm. The tension was thick enough to cut with a knife. Grant’s yellow windcheater stood out like a ray of light. His tone lightened as well. “Just so you know. I can swim in the bath.” He reached into his pocket. “And I don’t need a lasso.”

He took his cell phone out and raised it before anyone knew what he was doing. The flash was bright in the living room as he took the photo, all three men and Arlo Rankoff in the background. “My phone’s backed up to the cloud. So unless you want my last photo and location to come bite you in the ass.”

He put his hands together then opened his arms as if parting the Red Sea. Rankoff smiled. He clicked his fingers and the three men stepped aside. The threat level dropped but the tension didn’t. Rankoff held out a hand towards the front door. “Don’t forget to complete your enquiries. The house on the corner might have seen something.”

Grant put his phone away and headed down the hallway. “Oh I think I’ve learned all I need to know.”

*

THE WALK BACK DOWN the hill was less taxing than the walk up Kent Road. Grant took the long route to let the tension ease out of his muscles. The sun had dipped into the ocean but the sky was still blue. There were no evening clouds to be painted with the dying embers of the day. Birds sang in the trees and the smell of cooked meat drifted over from after work barbecues. The hiss of a pressure washer came from a hidden driveway as somebody washed his car, no doubt one of those big American ones.

He ignored Essex and Sussex and stayed with Kent all the way down. It snaked between yucca plants and palm trees and doubled back on itself. His mind replayed the scene with Rankoff but what he was really wondering was how much does it cost to buy the local police? And how much danger did that put his brother in?

He turned right onto San Pedro Avenue and didn’t hear the car pull in behind him. The engine purred but it was the quick burst of the siren that caught his attention. The patrol car stopped beside a vacant lot loaded with builders' equipment and once again Grant thought, that was quick. He'd only just left Arlo Rankoff's house and already he'd set his pet cop on him. The car door opened but it wasn't the pet cop. Holly West got out and rested her arms across the top of the door.

TWENTY-NINE

*

HOLLY WASN'T SURE WHY she'd pulled up behind the cop from Boston. Jim Grant. The one the press had dubbed The Resurrection Man. She didn't know enough about him to ask the questions she wanted to ask but when she'd seen him coming down from the overlook, instinct took over. She followed him round the corner into San Pedro Drive and watched his easy gait as he walked towards town. He was tall and broad and English but apart from that he was nothing like Cole Thornton.

That thought right there was why she wanted to talk to him. He'd been with Cole during the rescue operation so he would hopefully know some of the answers she was after. Whereas Cole was quiet and bookish Grant was solid and confident. It came off him in waves, but what was the cop from Boston doing in Shelter Cove? That was one of the questions she wanted to ask but mainly she wanted to know about Cole Thornton.

She tapped the siren then pulled over. By the time Grant came towards her she was resting her arms across the top of the open door and trying to look casual.

*

GRANT NOTICED THE DARK rings under Holly's eyes as he drew level. During the last 24 hours she'd been on duty a long time with little sleep. Maybe none at all. He stopped in front of her and smiled. "You finished beach duty?"

Holly turned the question back on him. "You finished sightseeing?"

Grant nodded towards the top of Kent Road. "Nice view of the cove from up there."

Holly scrutinized his face. "Some nice houses too."

Not mentioning anyone's in particular. Letting the implication hang in the air. Grant ignored it and stuck with police work. "I see the beach is mostly cleared now. What was the final body count?"

That brought Holly back down to earth. "Still only twenty-three. But the riptides are treacherous around here. We could be picking floaters for a couple of days."

Grant let out a sigh. "Twenty-three's enough."

Holly's head felt heavy. Her shoulders sagged. "It is."

The radio crackled and a scratchy dispatcher's voice broke the silence. Nothing Grant could interpret. Translating radio messages was something you had to do all the time or you lost the knack. It had been a long time since Grant patrolled a beat, he'd lost the rhythm. Holly listened with half an ear. Her call sign wasn't mentioned and there was no urgency in the voice. There was nothing to concern her. She could concentrate on the visiting cop from Boston and beyond. "Did you bump into Arlo Rankoff while you were up there?"

Grant watched Holly's eyes to see her reaction. "We had a chat. He's a busy man."

Holly's gaze remained steady. "Busy trying to buy the Rocky Coast bookstore."

Grant nodded. "And employing careless surfers."

Holly played along. "Surfers?"

Grant reckoned she already knew. “Surfers that drive into bookstore windows and drown in the bath.”

The shock on Holly’s face said she didn’t know it all. “He’s dead?”

Grant watched her eyes even more closely. “Day after the crash. Didn’t Ben Gardner tell you?”

Holly got defensive. “We’ve been kind of busy. King isn’t the only person that drowned.”

“Except the others didn’t work for Rankoff.”

Holly took a deep breath and let it out slowly. She was trying to steer the conversation towards Cole Thornton. She knew Grant had been with him last night and took a gamble that he knew a little of what was going on. “And they weren’t trying to pressure Cole into selling.”

The way she’d said Cole’s name told Grant more about her feelings than anything she might say. It tied in with what he knew about Cole’s affections towards the part time policewoman. He looked at Holly with fresh eyes. She was attractive and friendly with an open face. He reckoned that whatever she felt would show in her eyes. What he saw in her eyes now was concern for Grant’s brother. What he also saw was that she was suspicious of the connection between the two Englishmen. “Yeah. He told me about that.”

Holly weighed her words carefully and watched for Grant’s reaction. “But what did you tell Ben Gardner?”

“About Rankoff?”

“About Cole.”

“What makes you think I’ve told him anything?”

Holly stood up straight but kept her hands on top of the car door. “Because he’s been acting strange.”

Grant shrugged. “Twenty-three dead Mexicans can do that.”

Holly shook her head. “No. Strange when Cole is mentioned.”

Grant thought, yes I bet he does. Especially when he’s passing info to Arlo Rankoff while investigating Rankoff's involvement in the car crash. The crash that was designed to force Cole to sell the bookstore to Rankoff. I'll just bet he's acting strange. What he said was, "You'd have to ask him. Doesn't look like he shares everything with you."

She got defensive again. "He shares enough." She thought about Cole and the brother he was trying to avoid. A bad man coming to do bad things. The sort of man the police might be in hot pursuit of. She looked at Grant. "You're a cop aren't you?"

Grant nodded. "You know I am."

She stepped around the door and closed it behind her. "In Boston. So what you doing all the way over here?"

*

THE PRESSURE WASHER STOPPED. The absence of noise made the birds sound louder. The birdsong gave the street a calm and pleasant feel that was completely at odds with the tension that filled the air. Holly's question told Grant one thing for certain. Ben Gardner hadn't told her about Grant's visit to the police office. It also suggested she wasn't part of the Gardner/Rankoff axis. That gave him confidence that he could trust her but he wasn't ready to come clean about the family connection yet. "Cold case."

Holly raised an eyebrow. "Cold case or Cole case?"

Grant kept his guard up. "What's it to do with you?"

Holly leaned against the car. "I'm a cop too. And more local than you."

Grant put his hands in his pockets to keep things casual. "So is Ben Gardner. And what I told him is confidential."

Holly ignored the evasion. She was thinking about the bad brother again. The one who Cole reckoned was on his way from San Francisco. The reason Cole was packing up and running from Shelter Cove. "This isn't to do with Boston is it? English cop comes to see an English, what? Suspect? Witness? Complainant?" She hardened her eyes. "This comes all the way from England doesn't it? What's Cole been up to?"

Grant looked into the sleep deprived eyes and saw the concern again. He held her stare for a few moments then let out a sigh. "You don't give up do you?"

Holly shook her head. Grant kept any confrontation out of his voice. "I can't tell you what this is about. It's confidential." He weighed up the gravity of the situation against Cole's affection for the part time cop. The open face and the easy manner. He wasn't surprised that his brother had fallen for her. The look on her face told him she was falling for Cole as well. Grant made a decision, tilted his head, and smiled. "What I can say is, think with your head. Go with your heart."

Her expression softened. "He's said something hasn't he?"

Grant shook his head. "He didn't have to. Don't let this get in the way."

Again she thought about Cole's brother and wondered if Grant knew how bad the brother was. Would that be too big to get in the way of a relationship with Cole? Grant seemed to be implying not. The birdsong gave that thought some credence, painting the evening in non-threatening colours. The main thing she was getting from Grant was a sense that Cole had feelings that the visiting cop had picked up on. That made her feel good while at the same time embarrassing her. She pushed off from the car and opened the door. "Tell him I said hello."

Grant nodded and took his hands out of his pockets. "I will."

Then he set off along San Pedro Avenue as he heard the car door shut and the cruiser do a U-turn back towards the coast road.

*

SARAH WAS IN THE KITCHEN when Grant came through the door. She didn't offer to make him a drink. She touched her face as if brushing away a stray hair. Her hand was shaking. Grant closed the door and looked into her eyes. "What?"

She looked down at the table and clasped both hands together to stop them shaking. When she looked up again there were tears in her eyes. "He's gone."

THIRTY

*

COLE WAS OUT OF BREATH long before he reached the spine of the ridge that ran along the western arm of Shelter Cove. San Pedro Point was the eastern arm but that wasn't Cole's destination. His usual route would have been the Kent Road stairs down to the cove then along the beach past the cottages until the rocky outcrop. Today that wasn't an option. Too many people could see him from Kent Road, one person in particular. Today he didn't want to be seen at all.

The detour took him the long way round, along the canyon road of Grand Avenue until the houses petered out and the woods took over. Then it was cut right and climb the hill until he came out of the trees onto the park trails that laced the plateau. Park benches dotted the trails but nobody came up here this late in the evening. The pathways didn't extend beyond the top of the hill. There were no lights and it was dangerous trying to find your way back after dark.

Cole put the backpack down on a bench and took a moment to catch his breath. The view was magnificent. To his left he could see all the way south along the sheer cliffs and rocky beaches to where the Old Pacific Coast Highway Trail swept around the bend. Cabrillo Highway took most of the traffic these days, cutting a direct line through the hills with the Tom Lantos Tunnels but if you wanted the scenic route it was the Highway Trail. Cole looked to his right, north along the wooded hillside towards Shelter Cove. The crescent beach stood out in the evening light but it was fading fast. Twilight was coming but there were still a few hours of daylight before getting back became a problem. Cole wasn't planning on getting back.

The beach cottages looked even more rundown from up here, probably because there were no lights on in the empty homes while the rest of Linda Mar was bejeweled with streetlamps and house lights. Scrub and brush clung to the hillside, only receding where brooding shoulders of rock jutted like broken bones through skin. Short stretches of overgrown pathway, long abandoned, disappeared into the cliffs. Surf rolled up the beach with a barely audible swish.

The sound of the water brought Cole back to reality. He hefted the pack onto his back and felt the weight of the scuba gear bite into his shoulders. With a last look at Shelter Cove and his house beyond he set off along the trail. Soon the pathways disappeared and he was clambering along the narrow spine of the headland. With sheer cliffs on one side and the rough hillside on the other it was the gentlest slope down to the ocean and the jagged teeth of San Pedro Rock. He watched his footing on the loose scree, focusing on one step at a time, and tried to forget what he was leaving behind.

*

"ARE YOU SURE?"

Grant leaned against the kitchen door and knew the question was redundant.

Sarah shifted in her seat and waved a hand towards the hallway. "Take a look. He's not here."

The kitchen fell quiet. Sarah rested her hands on the table and felt a shiver run down her spine. Her fingers trembled. She interlaced them for stability. It didn't make any difference, her entire body was trembling. A gentle breeze signaled the end of the day. It rustled the plastic bin liner taped to the broken door. The evening was closing down towards dusk. Grant flicked the light switch and the kitchen immediately felt more welcoming. "Well, let's figure it out over a drink." He betrayed his Yorkshire roots. "Put the kettle on love. I'll have a look around."

Sarah raised her chin. Her hands stopped shaking. Having something to do was the best medicine at a time like this. Grant knew that. She could either make a cup of tea or do the looking around. He remembered that she made the better tea. Sarah got up and filled the kettle. Grant went down the hall to Cole's bedroom.

The suitcase was on the bed. The holdall was on the floor. Both were open and spilling untidy clothing, an odd sock on the bedside cabinet, a couple of T-shirts on the floor, a thick webbing strap in the doorway. Grant looked at the strap for a moment. It didn't look like the kind of travelling strap for securing your suitcase, it was harder wearing than that. He looked through the door. Either Cole had dropped it going out or it had fallen on his way in. From the hallway.

Grant picked it up and stood in the opening. Opposite the door was a storage cupboard. There was a space in the corner where something heavy had been stored. A depression in the carpet gave a rough estimate of the size but not the height. He went back into the bedroom and looked at the suitcase.

There was one thing he didn't think Cole would leave behind. Grant stood for a moment, not sure whether he wanted to look for it or not. He rubbed his hands together then stopped. He took a deep breath and let it out slowly. The suitcase was open. The disarray spoke of a hasty retreat and a quick search.

Grant nodded to himself and stepped into the room. He flung the lid open and rummaged through the contents. The cardboard box was in the bottom, partly covered by the remaining T-shirts. The top was off. Grant shifted the T-shirts and picked up the box of photos. Memories of a childhood that had been too short and was too long ago. Cole had searched the box but left it behind. The top photo was of two brothers on the beach in Scarborough.

*

COLE SET THE BACKPACK down on the beach. Not the gentle sand of Scarborough's North Bay but the rock and shingle of California's Pacific coast. The light was fading but that was a good thing. It meant he'd be just about invisible to the residents of Kent Road and Olympian Way, the only houses with a view along the shoreline. He glanced over his shoulder at the steep descent he'd just completed. His legs ached from keeping his footing. His back and elbows were sore where he'd fallen on the way down.

This wasn't the time to feel sorry for himself. He sat with his back to the cliff and unpacked the bag. There were procedures to be followed, safety checks that every diver made before taking to the water. Like a parachutist checking his chute, if Cole didn't check his equipment it would be too late when he was underwater. If your chute doesn't open all you can say is splat.

Twenty minutes later everything was laid out on the empty backpack. Everything had been checked. Everything was working and the pressure gauge showed the tank was three quarters full. More than enough for one final dive. He ticked off all the pieces of equipment in his head then geared up in reverse order. The last thing was the mouthpiece. He waded into the surf and let the shock of the cold water spark his senses. It was always the same, that initial numbing cold.

He gritted his teeth and looked across the short stretch of open water to the jagged peaks of San Pedro Rock. They stood out against the darkening sky like a dinosaur waiting to strike. He spat into the facemask and swilled water over the glass then pulled it over his head. With one last look to get his bearings he clamped down on the mouthpiece and sank under the water.

THIRTY-ONE

*

GRANT FELT LIKE HE WAS SINKING. He closed the bedroom door so Sarah couldn't see then sat on the edge of the bed. His weight tipped the box over and dog-eared photos spilled across the bedspread. Pictures from a life he'd left behind. From a childhood that he'd barely lived. Some were black and white. Most were in colour but even the colour photos were faded and washed out. Pretty much how Grant remembered the years before his father packed him off to boarding school.

Two brothers on a beach in Scarborough. That was the first one. Grant was standing in a hole beside a sandcastle under construction. The ramparts were in place but the turrets hadn't been added yet. Cole, Andrew as he was then, was kneeling beside him with one arm draped casually across Grant's shoulders. They were both grinning like fools at the camera. Grant's smile looked strained, a testament to the glowering presence behind the camera. The promenade in the background was busy. Families strolled along the seafront in soft focus and joyous release. Everyone looked happy, even the two brothers on the beach.

Two hours after the picture had been taken the sandcastle was in ruins and the brotherly bond destroyed. It was the last smiling photo of James and Andrew Grant together. The rest of the photographs took Grant further back, when there'd still been something resembling a family unit. He sifted through them with his fingertips and swam towards the light.

*

COLE FOUND THE CAVE after two attempts. He'd poked his head above water twice to get his bearings during the swim along the northern edge of San Pedro Rock. He was aiming for a narrow inlet between towering cliffs halfway to the tip. Waves broke on the rocks. Strong currents and eddies tried to pull him off course. Three times he struck out for the inlet only to feel the riptides pull him back out to sea. At a different time of day those same riptides would batter him against the rocky coast. Today they tried to keep him away. Until he forged his way between twin sentinels that guarded the entrance and the pull was reversed.

That was how he'd first discovered the hidden cave. It happened again now. He felt himself being pulled beneath an overhanging shelf of rock and sucked in like water down the plughole. The plughole spat him out and he came up into a cavern of prehistoric beauty. The walls were lined with lichen and shell life. A sloping beach crawled up out of the water. Purple stripes lined the rock strata, picked out by light coming down a funnel from above. A chimney to the outside world. Down here the world was dark and private and the safest place to hide stolen money.

Cole pulled the mask onto the top of his head and took the mouthpiece out. He took a deep breath of salt smeared fresh air.

Stolen money.

Once again he felt guilty about the lie he'd told. He felt guilty about a lot of things, not least about running out on Sarah and lying to Holly. His brother was the biggest burden though. He wondered if he would ever tell Grant the truth? Some day perhaps. In the next life.

Cole waded through the water until it was only knee deep then sat facing the entrance and took his flippers off. He tossed them behind him onto the secret beach and shrugged out of the tank harness. He closed the valve and stood up. It was easier to walk now. He felt warm after the initial dive, body heat coming off him in thin tendrils of steam. The warmth of the day never touched the cave. It was better than a refrigerator. He could have stored milk and butter instead of sealed plastic bags of money, converted from English banknotes into US currency long ago.

Water dripped from the cave roof. The crustaceans on the walls showed the waterline at high tide, halfway up but not reaching the back of the cave. The beach stopped at a scattering of rocks that formed a ledge across the width of the cavern. Dry and sharp and clear of sea life. There were smaller caves back there but none of them led anywhere. The only way in was through the submerged passage, unless you could climb down the chimney with no handholds and an awkward bend in the funnel. Nobody could see in here from above. Very few could get in here from the sea and anybody who did wouldn't go into the narrowest of the chambers along the back wall.

Cole pulled his gear up the beach and stowed them on the rock shelf. It was time to take the money and run. Or swim.

*

GRANT LOOKED AT A PHOTO of the man he hadn't seen for thirty-five years and felt nothing. Knowing he'd never see him again didn't do much for him either. What stuck in his throat was the way Commander Grant RN was holding young Andrew Grant in a bear hug, both sporting grins as big as the ocean. His father had never held him like that. He couldn't remember him smiling in his presence either. It was as if Grant put a damper on the father son dynamic whenever he was in the room.

The next photograph showed why.

Grant clenched his jaw and fought back a wave of emotion he never thought he'd experience over a picture of his father. The proud naval commander was standing in dress uniform with an arm around the waist of a beautiful woman. The photo was black and white. It was creased and dog-eared and fading to grey but the woman glowed on her wedding day. The mother Grant had never met. A photo he had never seen. His father in love with the woman Grant had killed when she gave birth to him. The joy in both their faces broke Grant's heart. He sniffed and wiped his eyes.

The next photograph shook his core beliefs. He dropped it as if it had given him an electric shock. His throat constricted. No amount of jaw clenching would help this time. All his life he'd been under the illusion that he'd never met his mother. That she died in childbirth and didn't have the chance to hold her newborn son. He'd seen the death certificate. Cause of death, complications following childbirth. The 4x3 colour print told a different story.

The hospital bed was neat and tidy. The maternity ward in the background looked like something out of a Carry On film, NHS clean with flowers on every bedside cabinet. The woman sitting up in bed was as beautiful as she'd been on her wedding day. She was smiling at the camera. The boy standing in close beside the bed, five-year-old Andrew Grant, was smiling too. The baby they were holding between them looked bemused, wrapped in a white cloth that made his pale blue eyes shine out from the picture. The complications must have set in later. Whatever had gone wrong at least his mother had time to express her love for her son. To pass it on through warm affection and a loving embrace.

Grant reached out and touched the photo of the mother with her two sons. He let out a sigh that trembled in his throat and even as he tried to stop them tears began to spill down his cheek.

*

COLE WAS DOUBLED OVER on his knees as he dragged the sack out of the narrow chamber. He banged his head on the low ceiling again but didn't complain. For a few awkward moments he'd thought the money had gone. That it had been found by some adventurous surfer exploring San Pedro Rock and carried away. He backed out of the cave and sat with his back to the wall, took a deep breath and nodded his satisfaction. It was done. Now he could leave.

Dripping water echoed in the main cavern. Breaking surf sounded hushed and distant beyond the entrance. Gentle waves lapped against the sloping beach. Cole unfastened the rope on the sack and took a quick look inside. The plastic bin liners were neatly squared and packed tight. Gaffer tape sealed the gaps and protected the bundles of banknotes. The money was safe. There was a lot of it. More than he'd admitted to Grant. He closed the sack and retied the neck. He tugged the rope to make sure it was still strong. The last thing he needed was for the riptides to snap the cord and carry his future out to sea.

The cough came from behind him. At first Cole thought it was a combination of water echoes and crashing waves. It sounded again, definitely a cough followed by two or three smaller ones. He spun to his left and stared into the gloom. He wasn't armed but he did have a small knife strapped to one leg, a diver's lifeline in case he got snagged in netting or fishing line. He didn't unsheathe the knife but his hand rested on the handle.

The next cough almost choked the woman who made it. Cole saw her collapse sideways at the far end of the rocky ledge. She struggled upright and wrapped her arms around two smaller figures on either side of her. Even in the gloom Cole could see she had similar features to the other Mexicans who had drowned in the bay. She was shivering but still protecting the children in her arms. A mother with her two sons. Cole's hand dropped away from the knife and he went over to help.

THIRTY-TWO

*

GRANT SAT AMID THE RUINS of his childhood with a sheaf of photographs on his knee and a cup of tea that Sarah had brought in before tactfully retreating. He was back in control of himself. The photographs were just photographs. The past was just the past. It had no bearing on today. That's what he told himself.

He took a final swig of lukewarm tea then put the cup on the bedside cabinet. He skimmed through the last of the photos then shuffled them into one big stack and put them in the box. All but one. That one he slipped into his back pocket. He put the lid on then slid the box under the T-shirts in the suitcase. He picked up the discarded clothing and repacked the case. Once the bedroom was tidy again he stood up and smoothed the bedspread.

The photos were safely out of sight, like Kryptonite in a lead box. Pictures of the family before it broke up, before Grant was banished and Cole joined the Underwater Search Team. Before Cole became a thief. Grant picked up the cup. Did he really believe that? Did the family inheritance negate the suspicion that Cole had stolen from the evidence locker?

The outside door opened and Grant heard voices through the

bedroom wall. He drummed the cup with his fingernails then stepped into the hallway. Cole Thornton stood beside the kitchen table carrying the scuba gear and an empty sack. Water dripped on the floor. Grant looked at the sack and then at his brother. Cole returned the gaze. "There's something we need to do."

*

MORE TEA. MORE COFFEE. Split three ways. Cole had toweled dry and was wearing warm clothes. Sarah played mother, putting biscuits on the table then filling the kettle again. Grant dunked a custard cream but held it while he looked at Cole. "What she mean? The train was late?" The soggy biscuit broke and dropped in his tea. "Shit." He scooped the broken piece out with two fingers and slurped it down.

Cole smiled. His brother had always dropped broken biscuits in his tea, even as a kid. The smile covered his fears for the woman and her children. "She's close to shock. It could mean anything."

Grant swallowed the biscuit. "Except it's the same as the fella said, we found in the bushes." He swilled it down with a drink of tea. "Holly thought it might be the surf."

Cole shook his head. "I was in the cave. Surf's nothing like a train."

Sarah finished making a flask of coffee and screwed the lid down. She put it in Cole's backpack together with energy bars and cheese then slammed it on the table to get their attention. "I don't understand why we don't just call the police?"

Grant didn't want to explain why he didn't trust the local police. He glanced at Cole so he'd know to go along with him then pushed back from the table. "Coastguard have gone and the local police are down to two men. We'll be quicker getting them ourselves, then let them know."

Cole looked Grant in the eye but didn't contradict him. "We'll need some rope."

Grant nodded his thanks. "Vacant lot up the street. The builders have got a block and tackle."

Cole stood up. "That'll do it."

Grant pulled the curtain back with one hand and looked out the window. The sky had gone from dark blue to night. The streetlamps were on. The cover of darkness was one thing but the quickest way to the beach was past Arlo Rankoff's house. He had a feeling Rankoff would be interested in what three surviving Mexicans might have to say about the drownings in the bay. "Dark-light protocol."

Cole nodded. "No torches."

Grant let the curtain fall shut. He shrugged off the yellow windcheater and borrowed one of Cole's anoraks from the cupboard. A dark one. The kitchen was warm. The swim was going to be cold. He looked at the pile of blankets on the table then at Cole. "We could do with another way out there."

Cole checked that the backpack was secure then took out his cell phone. "You go fetch the rope. I know somebody owes me a favor."

THIRTY-THREE

*

THE FAVOR WAS A CAR, a small Japanese thing with barely enough legroom for a pair of six foot Yorkshiremen. The trunk was too small so they loaded the equipment on the back seat. Grant leaned on the roof and looked over the top. "What you gonna do? Drive down to the beach?"

Cole put the last of the blankets in and shut the back door. He looked over the roof at his brother, two giants leaning on a pebble. "I'm going to drive to the nearest road on the other side of the headland."

Grant tried to picture it on the map he'd seen at the scrapyard. Cole didn't need to picture it. He'd seen it from the ridge on his climb down to the beach. The Old Pacific Coast Highway Trail. The scenic route that bypassed the Tom Lantos Tunnels had an unobstructed view along the coast to San Pedro Rock and a clear run along the beach out of sight of Arlo Rankoff's house.

*

"MAKE SURE YOU TIE IT TIGHT."

Grant glanced up from securing the rope and gave Cole a withering look. "Do you know how stupid that sounds?"

Cole ignored the rebuke. Some things you couldn't help saying, like, "Be careful," when you're climbing a ladder, or, "Are you alright?" when you've just been knocked down by a truck. What he was really doing was calming his nerves by talking to his brother. Brotherly chitchat had been in short supply for the last thirty-odd years. It was reassuring to have Grant with him now.

Grant found a protruding rock and looped the rope around it. The knot was solid. He gave the rope a tug – secure – and looked back the way they had come. The coast was rocky and uneven south of the point. It hadn't taken long for their eyes to adjust to the dark, helped by a clear sky. Full night, a myriad stars and a shining moon. The ocean had calmed to a whisper during the long walk over loose shingle. They hadn't talked since parking the car in a dusty layby up on the highway shoulder. Now that the moment of truth had arrived both felt the need to talk. Cole spoke while checking the scuba gear. "Did you always want to be a policeman?"

Grant finished the knot and began stacking the blankets behind the rock. "Did you always want to be a diver?"

Cole shrugged into the harness. "Ever since the beach at Scarborough."

He paused for a moment. Not the right thing to mention. Grant looked up from stacking the blankets. "That's when I knew I wanted to stand up for what's right."

Cole tried to sound conciliatory. "A moment of madness."

Grant wasn't consoled. "I just remember him being mad. At me. All the time."

The brothers fell silent, each thinking about the man who had influenced both their lives. Both from a different perspective. Cole thought about the decisions that had been made that day. "Not a complete waste then."

Grant wasn't sure if Cole was referring to the man who'd deserted him or the character building beating he'd taken as the bullies destroyed the sandcastle. Either way the end result was the same. Two men joining forces on the California coast. "Not if we save the woman and her kids."

Cole snapped the buckle shut and spat into the facemask. "Let's do it then."

Grant brought the coil of rope to the edge of the water. Cole braced himself for the cold. With a nod to his brother he walked into the waves as Grant fed the rope out through his hands.

*

THE PLAN WAS SIMPLE. It was the execution that was going to be hard. Cole was to swim the rope across to the cave and tie it off. A tug on the line signaled Grant to pull himself along the rope and then both men were to help the children back to shore with the woman doing the same between them. A simple plan. By the time Grant finally reached the cave he realized it was going to be much harder than they'd thought.

The water was numbingly cold. The undercurrents were vicious. There was a reason they were called riptides, because they tried to tear Grant from the rope and drag him under. If they were going to bring the kids along the rope it was going to take a monumental effort.

Grant coughed water from his lungs as he clambered up the shallow beach into the cave. Cole helped him out of the water and they both sat on the rocky ledge to get their strength back. Moonlight shone down the chimney like a spotlight, painting the cavern in ghostly light. Three pairs of eyes watched them. Two of them looked sad and weary. The youngest looked bright and eager.

Cole opened the waterproof knapsack he'd brought with him and warmed the family with coffee and biscuits. They ate fast. The coffee warmed their bodies. They even ate the cheese, which in hindsight wasn't the best choice of emergency food. After they'd finished the children warmed their hands around the cup of the flask. The mother warmed herself hugging her sons. "Gracias. Gracias."

Cole nodded then mimed swimming back out of the cave. It was hard to tell in the gloom but the boys looked to be about two or three years old. They could have been older but hard life and hunger had thwarted their development, no doubt why their mother had risked everything bringing them to America. The land of plenty. Grant let Cole do his thing. He was the diver of the family. Cole pointed to the children then took a deep breath and pinched his nose. He indicated that the older boy would go with him first. Then the mother. Then the youngest would go with Grant. They all nodded their understanding but fear shrank them back against the rocks. Cole made soothing noises and told them it would be okay. The only word they appeared to understand was, okay. That would have to do.

The first part of the evacuation went smoothly. Getting the family out of the cave and into the sheltered inlet on the north side of San Pedro Rock. They rested on a table of rock that shelved into the calm waters. Calm on the surface but hiding treacherous currents beneath, nothing like the riptides that would batter them during the short journey to the main coastline.

Grant clambered onto the rocky shelf and looked across the bay. Shelter Cove was still and quiet. Surf broke on the beach in a calm unhurried line, the white tops of the waves showing in the moonlight. There were no lights on the beach. The row of abandoned cottages beneath the hillside was blind and empty, the first port of call once they got the family ashore. Hide them beneath Arlo Rankoff's nose but only because the climb up to the highway would be too strenuous. Dry blankets and more food. Then it would be time to send for the cavalry. The coastguard not the police. From Pacifica not local.

Cole put a hand on Grant's shoulder. "You ready?"

Grant nodded. Cole mimed the change of order. The youngest boy with Grant. The woman next on the rope. Cole bringing up the rear with the second boy. The mother nodded but the fear in her eyes told the truth. She tried to hide it from her sons but Grant and Cole knew how frightened she was. The last time she'd been in this bay twenty-three of her friends had drowned. Cole made encouraging noises but they fell on deaf ears. All they could do now was get on with it. Cole brought the mouthpiece to his lips and nodded at Grant. "Twenty minutes and this is over."

*

GRANT SLIPPED INTO THE water and took the youngest boy under one arm. The boy clung onto him like a limpet as Grant edged along the rope. Cole helped the woman get a solid grip on the line and didn't let go until she felt secure. She nodded her thanks and held on tight. Encouraged that two of his family were already in the water the second boy came easily. He smiled at Cole and gave him a timid thumbs-up. Then the ragged group set off from the inlet.

The first thing Grant noticed when he cleared the rocks was how heavy the surf was. The waves looked gentle and calm from the safety of the inlet but even calm waves had the power of an ocean behind them. The swell lifted him three feet then dropped him into a trough. The cycle was unrelenting. Rise and fall. Rise and fall. He reaffirmed his grip on the boy and hooked his other arm over the rope. Even if he slipped the rope would be wedged under his armpit. Using one hand he pulled himself along the rope. The water reduced his weight but it was the undertow that tried to pull him down.

The woman saw how Grant was keeping the rope clamped to his side and did the same. She was tired but at least had two hands to pull herself along. Her eyes burned with fierce determination. Grant moved slowly so she could keep up. The last thing she needed was to feel separated from her sons. Seeing Grant holding her youngest gave her confidence. Looking into her eyes Grant could see that she finally believed this was going to work.

Cole was the stronger swimmer. With the facemask on top of his head and ignoring the mouthpiece he kept hold of the boy while tugging on the rope. The boy shifted his position on Cole's hip and tightened his grip. He looked up at Cole and even began to enjoy the journey. His eyes were big as saucers in the moonlight. He broke into a grin. This was fun. Cole nodded then focused on the rope. The woman was just in front of him. Grant was making good headway.

All was going smoothly.

A triple-header of waves surged towards the shore. It lifted Grant then dumped him three times. Crest of the wave then into the trough. Once. Twice. On the third swell a red spot of light danced in front of his eyes. He blinked to clear his vision and it disappeared. Then it was back again. Not in front of his eyes but across the surface of the water. The wave broke and spray from the white tops disguised a spout of water that shot in the air. Grant watched for the red dot again and suddenly realized what it was. He jerked his head towards the others following but before he could yell a warning there was another spout of water and the woman let go of the rope. The third swell became a trough and she slid quietly beneath the surface.

THIRTY-FOUR

*

Cole saw the woman go under and acted immediately. He closed the gap with Grant and swung the boy off his hip. Grant tucked him under the same arm as the youngest boy and held onto the rope with the other. Cole pulled the facemask down, clamped the mouthpiece in his mouth, and jackknifed underwater.

The world disappeared in a swirl of air bubbles and darkness. Searching for bodies in the waterways of Yorkshire had been all about methodical planning and fingertip searching. Trying to rescue a drowning woman in the Pacific Ocean was a much bigger task. It was a much wider search pattern and a more urgent timescale. He struck out for her last known position and then down where he thought she might have gone. Down into the murky depths. No, not murky. It was completely dark. It was like searching with your eyes closed. It would be blind luck if he found her. He was counting on being lucky.

*

On the surface Grant felt the swell lift him up. The boys felt weightless under his arm but he didn't have them in a good grip. The youngest was secure but the other was only half clasped in Grant's arm. Grant tried to shift him onto his left hip but the smaller boy was already sitting on the bony outcrop. He felt tiny hands grab at his clothing and a loose kick caught him between the legs. He ignored the pain and kept his right arm clamped on the rope. Using his free hand he pulled for shore, dragging two boys and himself along the rope.

The swell rushed past him and dumped him into a deeper trough. The older brother's head went underwater then broke the surface gasping for air. The younger boy began to cry. Another wave swept them forward and the trough was even deeper. More coughing water. More crying. The older boy slipped from under Grant's arm and Grant had to grab hold with his hand while keeping the arm clamped around the brother.

He risked a look towards the shore. They were halfway there. He glanced back to see if Cole had resurfaced with the woman. There was no sign of either of them. The stars twinkled in the pitch-black sky. The moon shone. Looking at the shore again Grant could make out the waves breaking on the shingle. He could see the beach cottages over to the left and the silhouettes of houses on the hilltop above them. Could anybody see him from there? Was it worth shouting for help?

The rope tightened when the swell lifted him up and slackened in the troughs but it was a lifeline to safety and he clung to it with all his strength. He pulled himself along one painful foot at a time.

Grip. Pull. Relax.

One foot.

Grip. Pull. Relax.

Two feet.

Grip. Pull. Relax.

Three feet.

It was slow and arduous work and every six feet felt like a mile.

Grip. Pull. Relax.

After ten feet he paused for breath. His arms felt heavy. The muscles in his shoulders and back screamed but he wouldn't let go. Another swell. Another trough. Another bout of coughing and spluttering. The boy struggled in panic. He waved his arms and kicked his legs. Grant held tight but could feel himself losing him. He tucked the rope under his armpit and used the hand to reach for the boy. It was no use. The boy was round the other side, pulling Grant's left hand away from the younger brother.

A fresh wave lifted them up and Grant almost lost the rope. He grabbed hold again and squeezed with his armpit. They weathered the swell and the trough that followed but Grant was struggling to keep hold of both boys. He glanced towards the shore. They were two thirds of the way there but there was still unfathomable depth beneath them, more than enough to drown them all. Deeper than the bath that Matt King had drowned in. Deep enough to drown twenty-three Mexicans and not even break a sweat.

Grant tugged on the rope. The solid feel of it was the only thing that gave him hope. The rope was everything. His left hand squeezed tight on the elder brother's arm and he got back into the rhythm.

Grip. Pull. Relax.

Then the rope went slack. No strength in it at all. Just a flapping length of cord that didn't hold anything and they all went under.

*

COLE WENT DEEP BUT still didn't touch bottom. He quested left and right and up and down. Even with the mask he couldn't see anything. Adjusting to the light was okay when there was some light to adjust to. Down here there was nothing, just a drowning woman and a futile attempt to find her. The moonlight only penetrated so far. If he'd glanced up he would have seen it glinting off the waves.

He could have seen the rope and the figures clinging to it. He didn't look up. What little night vision he had would have been ruined. So he went deeper and hoped his questing arms would find her before it was too late.

*

GRANT BROKE THE SURFACE but didn't gasp for breath. To do that would have sucked in a mouthful of water. He waited until he'd steadied himself and then took a deep breath. First rule of saving somebody is to save yourself. If you drown then you can't help anybody. His sergeant had taught him that back in driver training. Drive fast but drive safe because if you don't get there you can't catch the bad guys. Grant wasn't catching bad guys today, he was trying to keep hold of two boys who had just lost their mother.

Except he was only holding one of them.

He jerked his head around to find the older brother. There was nothing. No splashing or kicking or spluttering. He had gone. The rope had gone. All that was left was Grant and the younger boy trying to stay afloat.

It was the hardest decision Grant had ever had to make. Save who you can and mourn the rest. He shifted onto his side and held the boy's head above water, using his body as a floatation aid. He swam one-handed, kicking his feet for extra traction, and struck out for shore. The rolling waves helped propel them forward. Now that they weren't confined to the rope they could ride the waves in and it wasn't long before he felt the sloping beach beneath his feet. Two more strokes and they were far enough in that he could stand in the waist deep water.

He staggered upright and hefted the boy onto one hip. Without the ocean to buoy him his body felt heavy and weak. Carrying the boy was like hefting the weight of the world. He reached the high water mark and collapsed into the shallows. Water lapped around his legs. The boy stopped crying, not because he was safe but because he was exhausted.

Grant looked out to sea. There was nothing on the surface except rolling waves and white tops. The jagged teeth of San Pedro Rock stood out in the distance. The moon sparkled on the water. Surf whispered along the beach then receded. Whispered then receded. The rhythm was peaceful. He kept looking out to sea. Looking for his brother. It felt like he'd spent a lifetime looking down the beach and knowing he wouldn't find him.

He glanced towards the rocks where he'd tied the rope. It was too dark and too far away to tell if it had come undone or if somebody had cut it. That thought threw up another. He looked up the hill to the houses on Kent Road. There were lights on in the huge picture window. A silhouette stood in the window. Somebody looking out? Or just a shape that his mind had turned into a man?

The red dot. Grant snapped alert and scoured the beach. There was no telltale spot from the sniper scope. Had there ever been one? He looked up at the house and then along the hillside above the cove. Trees and bushes and rocky outcrops. Too many places for a sniper to hide. Nothing Grant could do about it if he was the target now. He rolled onto his back and held the boy in his arms, using the heat from his body to keep the boy warm.

The surf whispered on. The rhythm was soothing. It was the only sound until Grant heard footsteps on the shingle and a shadowy figure loomed over him. Grant pushed himself into a sitting position and kept one arm around the boy for protection. Cole came out of the surf dangling the facemask from one hand. He was alone. Their eyes met and Cole recognized the unasked question. He shook his head and threw the mask onto the beach.

THIRTY-FIVE

*

BEN GARDNER CAME AWAKE from a dream about retirement when the knock on the door reached fever pitch. His first thought was, it's still dark outside. I never get up when it's still dark. His second was, that's a dawn raid knock. He swung his legs out of bed and pulled his pants on. The only people who knocked like that were cops. He wondered what was so urgent they had to do a dawn raid on the bungalow round back of the Linda Mar police office.

The knocking grew louder. It almost took the door off its hinges. A voice shouted above the noise. The voice brought Gardner awake in a flash. The accent was unmistakable, so his next thought was, what was an English bookseller doing knocking him up in the middle of the night? He shrugged into his shirt on the way to the door. "Okay. Okay. I'm coming."

When he opened the door he blinked his surprise. It wasn't one Englishman it was two. Carrying a Mexican kid who looked half dead.

*

URGENCY HAD CHANGED THE PLAN. With only the youngest boy left it was better to climb back up to the car and drive into Linda Mar.

Grant kept the boy warm while Cole drove. With immediate medical care needed the choice of who to tell changed as well. Grant's suspicions about Gardner had to be put on the backburner. Even he wouldn't harm a child in front of witnesses.

Cole parked the car round the corner. He didn't want to get the owner into trouble. Grant carried the boy, shrouded in blankets, and Cole knocked on the door. Grant was impressed. His brother hadn't forgotten the copper's knock. Cole was about to knock again when the door opened. Ben Gardner looked surprised to see them. Wait until he heard about the two who hadn't survived.

*

"WHAT THE HELL WERE YOU THINKING?"

Gardner had stepped up to the plate and shown that experience trumped higher education. Speed was of the essence. Instead of calling an ambulance he drove the injured boy three blocks to the Linda Mar Pediatric Clinic. It was small but well staffed and had all the medical equipment they'd need to stabilize the casualty. Now that the immediate danger had passed he stood in the waiting room and turned to the English cop. "Soon as you knew they were out there you should have called me. Goddamn it. The coastguard could have got them out by boat." He looked at Cole. "And you. I don't know what shit you're mixed up in but this is local. You don't go running off like Diver Dan doing search and rescue. That's what Search and Rescue is for." He kicked the door. "God damn it."

Grant leaned against a poster of a teddy bear having tea with a grasshopper and waited for the storm to die down. Gardner let out a heavy sigh and glared at the two Englishmen but didn't kick anything. Grant waited a beat to make sure Gardner was finished then pushed off from the wall. "You feel better now?"

It was the wrong thing to say. Gardner almost stamped his foot in anger. “No I bloody well do not. You’re a cop. Should know better.”

Grant held up his hands in surrender. “I know. Bad decision. But it doesn’t change what happened.”

Gardner raised his eyebrows. “The red dot and the sniper scope? You kidding me? Who on earth’s going to shoot a mother and her two sons?”

Grant crossed his feet at the ankles and leaned against the wall again. “Just the mother.” He looked at his feet. “I lost the boy.”

Gardner took some of the edge off his tone. “Did you see her get hit?” Grant shrugged but didn’t answer. Gardner toned it down even more. “Did you hear the shot?”

Grant shook his head. These were questions he’d already asked himself so he understood where Gardner was coming from. The local police chief drew the obvious conclusion. “A red dot and a splash. Hell, bang on the head gives me spots in front of the eyes. And a splash on an incoming tide?”

Grant folded his arms across his chest. “And the rope.”

Gardner stood beside a row of plastic chairs and a coffee table. “You check the anchor point?”

Again, the obvious question. Grant gave the only answer he had. “It was still dark and we were getting the kid to safety.”

Gardner nodded. “Protect life. Priority. I agree.” He stepped to the window and pulled back a section of curtain. “It’s getting light out now. What say we take a look?” He let the curtain fall shut. “Coastguard’s going to search the cove in daylight.” He looked at Cole. “You stay with the boy in case they’ve got any questions.” Then opened the door for Grant. “Let’s go check your knot.”

*

THEY TOOK THE SHORTEST ROUTE to Shelter Cove. Gardner parked the cruiser on Kent Road and went down the steps to the cottages then followed the beach towards San Pedro Rock. The cold light of pre-dawn bled the colour out of the shoreline. A coastguard boat was already sweeping the southern end of bay. The tide was out, barely whispering as waves lapped against the sand. Grant kept his eyes focused on the rocky outcrop where they'd set off last night. Everything looked different in daylight.

The sandy beach gave way to shingle and broken rock as they followed the crescent to the point. It crunched underfoot in the silence, the only sound apart from the distant surf and his own breathing. Grant was deep in thought. What could he have done differently? How much could he rely on the red spot and the splash? It had been dark and he was exhausted, a combination that could test the most experienced rescue worker. Grant's experience was more in combat. Had that coloured his thoughts?

Gardner reached the rocks first. "Okay. Which rock?"

Grant scanned the jagged points to see which one he'd tied the rope to. It was hard to tell in daylight so he checked them all. There was no sign of the rope. There was no severed end. Gardner picked up on that. "Nobody cut the rope then." He mimicked firing a sniper's rifle. "No hot shot red spot sharpshooting."

Grant put forward an alternative theory. "Could have come down and untied it."

Gardner put his hands on his hips. "So why'd he need a laser sight? If he's come down here to undo your knot?"

Before Grant could answer there was a double whoop from the coastguard boat siren and there was a crackling message on Gardner's radio. Gardner asked a couple of questions but Grant couldn't make out the answers. The boat heaved to in the shallows opposite the beach cottages. Gardner clipped the handset onto his shoulder and turned to Grant. “They got a floater. Same place as the others. A woman.”

Grant rubbed his chin. “Flotsam always wash up over there?”

Gardner started walking back along the beach. “Seems that way don’t it?” Then he stopped and turned to Grant. He lowered his head and braced his shoulders. The look on his face brooked no argument. “I don’t care if Thornton’s deep cover or not. You should have called me.” He jutted his chin forward. “And if this shit’s got anything to do with why you’re here…”

He didn’t finish the threat. It wasn’t the sort of thing Grant expected from somebody in Arlo Rankoff’s pocket. Unless this was nothing to do with Arlo Rankoff. Gardner set off along the beach again. “Come on. Let’s see if she’s full of holes.”

THIRTY-SIX

*

Skin looks pale and washed out after a long time underwater. Injuries look vicious and bloodless. Lying in a body bag on the beach the Mexican woman looked as if she'd spent too long in the bath but hadn't yet bloated into the longtime submerged. Her injuries didn't look like a bathroom accident either, they looked like she'd been attacked with a meat cleaver. Most of her head was gone. Savage cuts from razor sharp reefs beneath the surface had torn large chunks out of her right side and leg. Gardner zipped the body bag shut and stepped back. "That's that then."

Grant looked at the woman he had tried to rescue as her face disappeared beneath the zip. What remained of her face. He had seen plenty of dead people but most had been corpses he was investigating. Not somebody he'd seen alive just a few hours ago. That made it personal. More real. He knew what Gardner was thinking because he came to the same conclusion. "Insufficient evidence."

Gardner nodded. "I doubt even an autopsy could find a bullet wound in that lot."

Grant looked at the local cop. "Doesn't mean she wasn't shot."

Gardner returned his stare. "Doesn't prove she was."

Grant turned away and watched the coastguard boat continue its search for the boy. There would be no bullet wounds on him. Grant felt a phantom hand trying to hold onto his as the boy slipped away. The boy was dead because Grant couldn't hold on. The only consolation was that Grant had managed to save the boy's brother. He looked out to sea and listened to the quiet swish of the waves, the gentle throb of the boat. He looked down at the sand. It was a good beach for making sandcastles. He turned and walked back towards the steps. Gardner jerked his head up and set off after Grant. "Where d'you think you're going?"

Grant spoke over his shoulder as he approached the bottom of the steps. "Back to the clinic." He stopped and turned to face Gardner. "Whoever killed the woman wanted them all dead. The boy's the only one knows how they ended up in the cave. You asked about Cole being in witness protection. Well here's one witness that needs protecting."

*

GARDNER DROPPED GRANT at the clinic. Begrudgingly. He didn't look convinced that the boy needed a guardian angel and he wasn't convinced that a lone sniper had attacked the rescue party in the cove. He gave a reluctant concession, promising that he'd get one of his deputies to guard the boy until he was fit to talk. Then he headed back to the police office. If there was one universal truth about police work it was that everything a cop did generated paperwork.

Grant met Cole in the waiting room. A nurse brought coffee then left to give them privacy. Grant didn't have the heart to tell her he preferred tea. Cole stirred sugar into the cups while Grant looked out of the window. The clinic was on the corner of De Solo Drive overlooking San Pedro Creek, another dry riverbed that would only be full during the rainy season. He glanced to his right at the extended parking lot of the Linda Mar Shopping Center then turned to Cole. "How is he?"

Cole finished stirring. "Sleeping."

"He say anything yet?"

Cole handed a cup to Grant. "Nurse says he might not speak for a while. He's in shock. He's exhausted. And he's just lost his mother and brother. She's not even sure he knows that yet. Or if he's blocking it out."

Grant nodded and took a drink of the sickly brew. He was toying with an idea but wasn't sure how to broach the subject so he drank in silence and tried not to gag. Cole drank too. The pair fell into an uneasy dance, neither wanting to be the one to break the silence. Both felt responsible. Neither blamed the other. There had been too much water under the bridge for either one of them to give solace to the other. They were brothers in name only. The separation had been too traumatic to heal quickly. Cole spoke first. "It wasn't your fault."

Grant held the cup in both hands. "It was my idea to cut out the coastguard."

"Not the coastguard. Gardner."

"Same result."

"I agreed with you."

Grant snorted a laugh. "That's a first."

And right there was the problem. Everything between them came back to the beach, the bullies and the sandcastle. More importantly, the rift between them ever since Cole sided with their father and banished Grant to boarding school. Cole didn't respond. He felt guilty about their childhood so he concentrated on the present. He wasn't sure why Grant didn't trust Gardner but assumed it was to do with keeping Cole's identity secret. If that was the case then, by extension, cutting out the local police was on him and so was losing the mother and son. All he could do was repeat himself. "It wasn't your fault."

His words hung in the air. They could have been a confession from years ago. That hadn't been Grant's fault either. The room settled into another uneasy silence. Cole drank his coffee. Grant ignored his, simply using the cup to warm his hands. He ran the idea through his head again then decided to grasp the nettle. He put the cup on the low table and looked at his brother. "How much do you trust Holly?"

The change of subject caught Cole by surprise. "What?"

Grant lowered his voice. "Do you trust her?"

Cole drained his cup and put it down. "Who do you think leant us the car?"

*

FOR A MAN WHO DIDN'T believe in coincidences it was no surprise who got out of the patrol car when it pulled up outside the clinic. Grant had already left on his next enquiry. Cole heard the car door shut and looked out of the reception window. Ben Gardner had a choice of two deputies. It was fifty-fifty which one turned up. Cole tapped on the window and smiled as Holly crossed the front lawn.

*

"YOU SHOULDN'T HAVE SUCH long legs then."

"No, I'm not complaining. It was great. Thanks."

They were doing that little dance that bordered on small talk but was really about something more important. The Mexican family not the size of the car. Cole had already thanked her for the loan while not touching on the reason. Holly had been detailed to watch the boy so she already knew the reason. "Maybe you should have borrowed a boat."

Cole felt the sting of criticism but kept his tone friendly. "You don't have a boat."

Holly jerked her head towards the window as if her car was outside. "I might not have a car either. When Ben finds out."

Cole held his hands up in apology. Everything Holly said was true. He'd been reckless and foolish and that recklessness had cost two lives. It might also cost Holly her job let alone her car. He was feeling Catholic levels of guilt but her mention of Ben Gardner was just the excuse he needed, he wasn't ready to ask the question yet. He continued the dance. "How come the kid's staying here instead of the hospital?"

Holly was relieved to change the subject. "They say he's doing okay. Don't want to add to the trauma by moving him."

Cole tested the water. "Who's decision was that? Ben's?"

Holly shook her head. "Powers that be. The clinic I guess."

Cole made a face as if considering that. "Makes sense." Then he slid into a change of direction. "Do you need authority from Ben to make info requests?"

Holly looked puzzled. "Like owner enquiries and stuff?"

Cole tried to sound casual. "Land registry. Ownership. Planning. That sort of thing."

"No. I don't need him for that."

Cole prepared for the big question, the favor that would be hard to ask without sounding secretive and paranoid. The waiting room felt warm and claustrophobic. He looked out the window at the trees bordering the creek then turned to Holly. "I've got another favor. And I want to keep it between us for now."

Holly narrowed her eyes. "Between us, as in don't tell Ben?"

Cole nodded. "Until I see how it pans out."

Holly watched his face. "Go on."

Cole took a deep breath before he spoke. "Can you find out about Rankoff's holdings? What he owns and where? Especially to do with the planning application. For the road to Shelter Cove."

Holly didn't answer for a moment. She looked at the man she hoped to share a future with and wondered where he was going with this. She held the pause a few seconds longer then nodded. "I can make a couple of calls."

Cole let out a sigh and almost gave her a hug. "Thanks. You're an angel." He went to the waiting room door then looked back at Holly. "I see you brought the book."

Holly took the book from under her arm and held it in front of her. History Of The Ocean Shore Railroad. She touched the cover with her other hand as if greeting a friend. "Was going to read it while I'm stuck in here." She put it on the coffee table. "But I'd better make those calls first."

Cole opened the door and stepped into the corridor. Holly came out and walked him to the front door. The day was bright and sunny and Cole's day felt a lot brighter having Holly in it. He decided to come clean with her after all this was over. It was time to put down roots that weren't tainted by lies. A dark cloud drifted into his head. If that were the case there was somebody else he'd have to come clean with. He wondered how Grant's second visit to Arlo Rankoff was going?

Holly opened the door and let Cole out. They almost touched hands. Cole wanted to tell her how much she meant to him but this wasn't the time. It never seemed to be the right time. They said goodbye and Holly went back inside. Neither of them noticed the plaque on the wall.

This Clinic Supported By Local Donations
Many Thanks To Arlo Rankoff
Chairman Of The Board

THIRTY-SEVEN

*

GRANT'S SECOND VISIT TO ARLO RANKOFF started pretty much the same as the first. Policeman's knock. Short hard man ushers Grant into the living room. Arlo Rankoff shows off his wealthy lifestyle. It went downhill rapidly from there.

"Follow up enquiries? I'm beginning to feel harassed."

They were out on the balcony again, the sun heading towards its midday high. Grant was resting his back against the railing. Rankoff was standing in the middle of the patio. The tough looking doorman kept his distance, standing in the doorway of the triple-glazed patio windows. Grant ignored the doorman and concentrated on Rankoff. "Not as harassed as the fat guy and the surfer."

Rankoff seemed relaxed. Not threatened at all by the rogue cop from out of town. His tone betrayed nothing. "Are you still banging on about that?"

Grant smiled. "I haven't started banging yet."

Rankoff sounded indifferent. "Then what are you doing?"

Grant repeated his introduction. "Follow up enquiries."

He looked out across the bay then at the hillside along the back of the beach cottages. Trees and foliage and rocky outcrops. The same as before but different this time. He was looking for vantage points where the sniper could have hidden. He didn't think the red dot had come from here. Something caught his eye. He softened his focus to take in the sweep of the bay. Uneven and overgrown. Except there was a smooth line running in an arc halfway up the hill. Not something that stood out because it was covered in scrub and brush, like an overgrown road but only in snatches. When he didn't stare directly at it he could see the gentle curve, broken in places by shoulders of rock. He glanced down at the bushes beneath the balcony then back at Rankoff. "Between bathtubs and Shelter Cove, people keep drowning around you."

The doorman took a step onto the patio. Rankoff held a hand out behind him and the man stopped. The businessman came over to Grant and surveyed the cove. "The three who drowned last night?"

Grant looked at Rankoff to see if this was a test. "Two."

Rankoff feigned enthusiasm. "Yes, that's right. You saved one of the boys. Congratulations. You're a hero. I can get you some local press coverage if you like."

Grant turned sideways so he could see Rankoff and the cove. "I don't like press coverage."

Rankoff didn't move. "Follows you around though doesn't it? Boston. LA." He shrugged instead. "Everywhere. You're always in the news."

Grant focused on the businessman. "Last night wasn't on the news."

Rankoff gave a soft humorless smile. "It will be."

Grant's focus narrowed to Rankoff's eyes. "And yet you know about it already."

Rankoff waved a hand to encompass everything around him. "This is a small community. I hear about everything."

Grant pushed off from the railing and faced Rankoff. "How much did you see though?"

Rankoff looked up at Grant. Being the shortest man on the balcony didn't seem to bother him. Power made him taller in his own mind. Power, and employing short people to answer the door. "Is that what your follow up enquiries are about?"

Grant raised his eyebrows. "Police investigations are always the same. Check for forensic evidence and CCTV. And eyewitnesses. That would make you the eyewitness."

Rankoff glanced over the railing. "Except I didn't see anything."

Grant took a step towards the businessman. "I saw you."

"Really? Where was that?"

Grant nodded towards the huge bank of windows. "Right here. Silhouetted in the window. Looking out."

Rankoff looked across at the jagged teeth of San Pedro Rock. "From down there? In the dark? You must have good eyes?"

"I do."

"But what makes you think it was me?"

It was Grant's turn to give a humorless smile. "Too short to be your heavies."

If that stung Rankoff he didn't show it. He indicated the doorman. "David isn't tall."

Grant shrugged. "It's between you two then. So what did you see?"

David the doorman stood beside Rankoff but Rankoff answered. "As a cop you must have done this before, but let's assume you're describing the viewing position of a witness. You must have to record the time of day, the weather conditions, and the light. Right?" Grant didn't answer. Rankoff nodded. "It was after dark. The lights were on. And David or I were looking out."

Grant waited. He'd taken witness statements before. He knew what the conditions would reveal. Rankoff looked smug and happy to rub it in. "Do you know what you see when you are in a lighted room looking out?" Grant waited. Rankoff lowered his voice. "You see yourself."

He clicked his fingers and the doorman moved forward. "And if you could see yourself now, you would see yourself being ejected from my property. This interview is over."

The doorman surged forward to grab Grant by the arm. Grant stepped sideways and let David come. He grabbed the outstretched wrist and yanked it up the doorman's back while pushing him towards the railing. Forward momentum and leverage lifted him across the rail and he disappeared over the edge. Rankoff jerked back in shock. There was no scream, just a rustle of bushes and a thump and tumble from below. Grant dusted his sleeves and rubbed his hands together. "Stick to three, like last time."

Rankoff looked over the side at the crumpled figure in the bushes then back at Grant. He recovered his composure quickly. "The other two are busy."

Grant went through the patio door into the lounge. On the way to the front door he wondered what Rankoff had his heavies doing that was so important it left the businessman unprotected. He closed the door behind him but couldn't shake a nagging doubt that was creeping into the back of his mind.

THIRTY-EIGHT

*

WHAT THE OTHER TWO HEAVIES were doing was watching Holly West at the Linda Mar Pediatric Clinic. From the trees that bordered San Pedro Creek. They had initially parked in the shopping center parking lot but decided that was too public so they'd followed Cabrillo Highway and taken the slip road exit on the other side of the creek. It was quiet and secluded and only a short walk through the trees to the clinic. The riverbed was dry and empty. No wading required.

The big men stood at the edge of the tree line round the back of the building and looked through large windows that gave a perfect view of life inside. A receptionist was updating medical records at her desk. A nurse was taking a tray of medications down the main corridor. The female cop was hanging up the telephone at the reception desk and drumming her fingers on the counter. She picked up the phone and dialed another number.

The men looked at her then at the private room at the end of the corridor. They came out of the trees while she was still talking and headed for the fire exit.

*

HOLLY PUT THE PHONE DOWN but didn't resume drumming her fingers. The second call had been a direct result of what had been said during the first and as she stared at the reception counter she wondered if she had done the right thing. She was a strong and decisive woman but this was bigger than anything she'd dealt with before. The conflict of emotions was tearing her apart, her feelings for Cole versus her loyalty to Ben. She felt like she was walking a tightrope without a safety net.

A door closed further down the corridor and a nurse came back towards the front office swinging an empty tray from one hand. The receptionist was busy updating records on the computer. Holly felt like a spare part with no good reason for being here. A babysitting job. Not an assignment she felt qualified to take. The medical staff was looking after the boy. There was no imminent danger that she could see. This was Linda Mar. Hit men didn't go after kids here. That only happened in the movies not in a quiet backwater.

That thought stopped her dead. A quiet backwater? Where nothing ever happened? That might have been true three days ago but look at what had happened since then. A car through the bookstore window. Hospitalized with her injuries. The surfer drowned in his bath. Twenty-three Mexicans drowned at Shelter Cove. Another two drowned last night during a botched rescue attempt. The only survivor being treated for shock in a room at the end of the corridor. A backwater it might be but it had been anything but quiet lately.

She looked along the corridor towards the boy's room. The clinic was quiet. Even the receptionist barely made any noise as her fingers tapped the keyboard. The place was bright and clean and safe. Holly put her fears aside. Her decision had been made and now she'd have to live with the consequences. She hoped she'd made the right choice. In the meantime her assignment was to sit here and mind the child. She picked up the book from next to the telephone and sat in a reception chair facing the front door.

History Of The Ocean Shore Railroad

It felt like a long time since she'd stood in the bookstore with Cole and joked about his accent. She smiled at the memory then opened the book.

*

THE FIRE EXIT DOOR WAS SIMPLE. They were built for ease of opening, albeit from inside. The lock wasn't designed for security. Getting in had been easy but then they almost got caught by a nurse coming out of the room with an empty tray. Almost. The first man waited until she set off down the corridor then darted into an alcove next to the fire extinguisher. The second man joined him, pulling the fire door shut behind him.

A quick look around the corner. The nurse reached the office. The receptionist was out of sight. The female cop picked a book up from the counter then sat with her back to the corridor. Good. The clinic smelled of antiseptic and air freshener. Sunlight slanted in through vertical blinds. They waited a few seconds until they were sure nobody else was coming then crossed the hallway and entered the room.

*

HOLLY WAS LEAFING THROUGH the book when a photo caught her eye. She paused while she looked at it then, keeping her place with one finger, flicked back to the front. The cover photo was a scenic shot of a sweeping railroad track coming round the headland. It was a cropped version of the one she'd just been looking at. She opened the page again. The section of coastline looked vaguely familiar but she hadn't thought the Ocean Shore Railroad came this far.

A van that had been parked outside moved away, letting sunlight flood through the windows. It glinted of a polished metal plaque on the wall and Holly changed position to avoid the glare. From her new vantage point she could read the sign.

This Clinic Supported By Local Donations
Many Thanks To Arlo Rankoff
Chairman Of The Board

She looked at the plaque and then at the stretch of coastline in the book. She was putting two and two together when she heard the noise from the private room along the corridor. She folded the page over and put the book down. This wasn't a quiet backwater anymore.

*

HOLDING A PILLOW OVER THE boy's face shouldn't have been a problem for two men as big as they were. It was the easiest way to kill a half drowned Mexican kid, just finish what the Pacific had failed to do. Suffocate the little bastard. But they hadn't thought it through. Drowning kids always struggle to reach the surface, flailing with their arms and kicking with their legs. The second man had the arms covered. He forgot about the legs.

The boy kicked the bedside table over. It went crashing sideways spilling medication and flowers and a tumbler of orange juice across the floor. The tumbler was glass. It shattered making even more noise. The man struggled to contain the legs and finally stopped the boy kicking. The pillow was held firmly enough to stop the air without being hard enough to cause bruising. It was a kid. How hard could it be?

The door burst open and the female cop charged in.

*

HOLLY ALMOST DREW HER SERVICE weapon then realized she was as likely to shoot the boy as the men trying to suffocate him. She stamped on the back of the nearest guy's leg just below the knee. The joint collapsed and he went down like a crippled quarterback, pulling the bed sheets and the boy with him. More noise. Holly reached for her Taser but never got it out.

The first man swung a roundhouse blow that caught her on the side of her head. He was bigger and stronger than her and very angry. The anger added weight to the blow. She was flung sideways and hit the wall.

Raised voices sounded along the corridor. Somebody was shouting for the receptionist to call the police. Footsteps raced towards the private room. The sunlight and cleanliness didn't feel so safe anymore. The smell of antiseptic and air freshener lost its appeal.

Holly flopped like a boned fish onto the floor. She kicked out with both feet. The man she'd kicked got up and stood over her. The other one reached across the bed and grabbed for the boy but missed. The boy scurried under the bed.

The footsteps grew closer. The voices were louder. Holly tried to reach her shoulder mic but a kick in the stomach took all the wind out of her. She struggled to back away and came up against the door as the footsteps outside approached the private room.

The boy slithered around under the bed. The man couldn't get hold of him. His partner stood over Holly and kicked her again. Frustration and anger and the nurse dashing along the corridor proved too much. "Aw fuck this." He pulled out a gun, cocked the hammer, and pointed it at Holly.

PART THREE

Riptide

"Our family has always been trouble. But you can't get away from being family."
- Cole Thornton

THIRTY-NINE

*

COLE WAS LOOKING AT THE nautical chart of Shelter Cove when he got the news. Back at the house. On the kitchen table. The chart covered a three-mile stretch of the coast either side of the crescent bay and detailed the shoals and the depth and the tidal flows. Sarah was leaning against the cooker with her arms folded. "Bit late for checking the weather isn't it?"

Cole's fingers traced invisible lines across the chart. "Doesn't tell the weather."

Sarah let out a sigh. "What I'm saying is, what's done is done."

Cole didn't look up, focusing on the deep water and the shoals. "I'm interested in why."

Sarah sounded exasperated. "Because they couldn't swim."

Cole kept his place with one finger and looked up at Sarah. The look on his face spoke volumes. Sarah shrugged then unfolded her arms. "I'll tell you one thing for free. It's no surprise this shit went down the day after James Grant came to town. That man could bring trouble to an empty room."

Cole shook his head. "This isn't his fault."

Sarah wasn't convinced. "Check the news archives. Everywhere he goes, shit happens. Resurrection Man they call him. Christ, they should call him the Destruction Man."

Cole came to the defence of his brother. Something he should have done years ago. That was always going to be a mountain to climb. He doubted that he'd ever conquer it. "He wasn't even here when it started."

Sarah widened her eyes. "He was here when that first lot drowned."

Cole shook his head again. "It didn't start with the drowning. It was the car."

Sarah lowered her eyes while she considered that and then looked up again. "The one that crashed through the window?"

Cole nodded. "Driven by a surfer who drowned in his bath."

"Another drowning?"

Cole turned his attention back to the map. His voice became a whisper, as if he were talking to himself. "Worked for the man who owns most of Shelter Cove."

Sarah joined the dots. "Where the others drowned."

Cole's finger followed swirling lines with tiny numbers and arrows. He referred to a dog-eared book with rows of dates and times and tidal surges. He superimposed the numbers over the area where the bodies were found then ran the calculation again in case he'd missed something. He hadn't.

Sarah wasn't going to be swayed from her mission. "You're getting too involved in all this. You should take the money and run."

Cole closed the book and stood up. "And take you with me of course."

Sarah raised her eyebrows and smiled. "It makes sense."

Cole let out a sigh. Sometimes his brother's ex-wife was the most caring person he had ever known but at other times she displayed a mercenary attitude that didn't relate to the woman he used to love.

He would normally put that down to a hard life and a bad marriage but his brother had been through worse and he'd turned out okay. As if reading Cole's thoughts Sarah contradicted him. "James Grant is trouble with a capital T."

Cole dropped the tidal almanac on the table. "Our family has always been trouble. But you can't get away from being family." There was more to be said but he didn't say it. It was too painful. He couldn't get away from being family. They were brothers. He should have stood by him instead of siding with their father when his baby brother was sent to boarding school. He hadn't. He'd been too young to understand the importance of kin. He finally understood, now that it was too late, but he was still lying to his brother. As if drawn by the negative thoughts the kitchen door opened and Jim Grant came in.

*

"ARLO RANKOFF HAD A PERFECT view of the cove last night."

It was coffees all round again. Well, two coffees and a tea. They were sitting around the table with the nautical chart forming a tablecloth. Grant warmed his hands on the cup. "That son of a bitch knows more than he's letting on."

Cole took a drink and put his cup on the chart. "When it comes to around here. He knows everything about everything." He slid the cup to one side so he could demonstrate on the chart. "But here's something I bet he didn't bargain on." His fingers made deft and sweeping moves across the map. "The tidal flow in Shelter Cove is universal. It's the same every day. So are the currents and eddies. They're dictated by the shoals and the reefs and the deep water swell."

Grant had no idea what Cole was talking about but watched his brother's fingers make a swirling motion in the cove. "The boy and his mother. Coming from the cave. She washed up where she did because the current only goes one way." He moved his fingers beyond the point. "Anybody lost at sea would have been swept along the coast. Probably make landfall at Mori Point past Rockaway Beach." He shook his head then stabbed his finger at Shelter Cove. "But they washed up in the same place as the mother."

Grant pointed to the beach off Shoreside Drive. "Not all of them."

Cole waved the hand away. "As many as makes no difference." He did the swirling motion again, ending in Shelter Cove. "Only way that happens…"

Grant looked at the map. "You saying they all came from the cave?"

Cole made a vague sweep of the shore. "Not necessarily the cave. But somewhere on shore for certain."

The brothers fell silent, both looking at the map with renewed interest. Sarah kept quiet and drank her coffee. Steam drifted up from two forgotten cups as the enormity of what Cole was saying sank in. The telephone began to ring. The sound should have made them jump but it drifted in like a whisper until the third ring. Cole answered before the fourth.

Grant heard the urgent voice down the line and saw Cole's face drain of colour. Cole didn't speak. He put the handset in the cradle with a shaking hand. He looked shell shocked. Grant spoke quietly. "What?"

Cole's eyes came up with an effort. "There's been an attempt on the kid at the clinic."

Sarah put her cup down. Grant knew better than to press. Cole cleared his throat and steadied his voice. "It's Holly. She's…" But he didn't finish.

FORTY

*

THE CLINIC WAS CORDONED OFF. The crime scene tape that was draped across the corner of De Solo Drive fluttered in the breeze. Holly's patrol car was still parked at the curb. Two Pacifica Police Department cruisers were angled at either end of the cordon, emergency lights flashing. Grant badged his way past the lone officer manning the tape before the young cop had a chance to see where the badge was from. Cole wasn't even challenged.

The nurse came straight over once they were inside. She knew Cole from the bookstore and remembered him being with Holly earlier. She clasped her hands together as if in prayer. Ignoring Grant she spoke to Cole. "I am so sorry."

Cole was still pale from the shock. "Thanks for calling."

The nurse nodded gravely. "She would want you to know."

Cole puffed out his cheeks to help control his breathing. "Thanks again."

Grant looked around the reception area. One of the chairs had been knocked over. There was an empty tray on the floor. The rest of the staff was corralled behind the reception desk with the second cop. The corridor towards the private room was empty. There was no crime scene tape forming an inner cordon. The first responders hadn't secured the scene. Anybody could be trampling evidence. He flashed his badge at the nurse then pointed a finger along the corridor. She nodded. It didn't matter. Grant was going down there anyway. Cole thanked the nurse again then followed his brother.

*

THERE WAS NO BLOOD in the room. That was good. The boy had been found hiding under the bed. That was good too. But he was still unable to speak. If he'd been in shock from losing his mother and brother then being attacked in his hospital bed had simply piled on the trauma.

Grant quartered the room with a practiced eye. The hospital bed was at an angle away from the wall. The bedding and mattress had spilled over one side forming a den beneath the legs. A bedside cabinet had been knocked over. There was broken glass and splashed liquid on the floor. Grant stayed away from the liquid. Not blood but equally receptive to footprints. The window at the back of the room had been smashed during the getaway. There was no blood on the glass either. Another good sign. He glanced at the ceiling and checked for cameras. None. He nodded to himself. Whatever CCTV the clinic had it wouldn't be in the rooms. That would be an invasion of privacy and America was a litigious society. They wouldn't want to lay themselves open to accusations of perving.

The cop from the front office came in and assumed Grant was the detective they were expecting. Grant didn't enlighten him. He nodded to the corridor. "CCTV?"

The cop showed he wasn't completely inexperienced. "Live feed. It doesn't record. For staff protection not burglary."

Grant nodded. That made sense too. Premises being protected from overnight break-ins recorded their CCTV when the building was empty. The Linda Mar Pediatric Clinic was staffed 24hours a day. There was no need to record it, even with time-lapse photography. Grant looked at Cole but there was no way to sugar-coat his next question. He turned to the cop and lowered his voice. "The protection officer?"

The cop felt the weight of the situation. He'd been in the force long enough to know the seriousness of an officer down scenario. Cole listened but already knew the answer. It was exactly what the head nurse had told him over the phone. The cop shook his head. "She's gone."

Grant wanted to clarify the circumstances. "In pursuit?"

The cop shrugged. "We don't know. Just, when the staff forced their way in the room was empty."

Grant looked at the fallen cabinet. "Forced their way in?"

The cop followed Grant's eyes and confirmed Grant was right. "Yes. It was wedged between the door and the bed."

Grant scanned the room again. "But not completely empty."

The cop waved an apology. "Sorry. No. The kid was under the bed."

Grant took a breath while he gathered his thoughts. "He say anything at all?"

The cop shook his head. "Nothing."

Grant scanned the walls for bullet holes. There were none. Two of the framed children's posters were hanging askew. He moved them aside with the back of one finger. No bullet holes there either. "No gunshots?"

"No."

Another good sign. Whatever violence had taken place wasn't firearms related. Nobody had been shot. He looked at the pillow resting against the headboard. Three indentations stood out like memory foam, one in the middle on one side and two smaller ones on either side of the back. Two fists and the boy's face. This had been a stealth mission. Suffocate the boy then get out quietly. Grant gestured towards the corridor and they all left the room. "Point of entry?"

The cop indicated the fire exit at the end of the corridor. It was closed but Grant could see a section of splintering near the lock. He pointed at the door and then the boy's room. "Fingerprints?"

The cop nodded. "Crime scene guys are on their way."

Grant made a circular motion to include the fire exit, the room and the corridor. "Tape it off. Nobody else enters until forensics. Make a note of the common approach. Where we all walked."

The cop looked shamefaced. He realized he should have done that as soon as the danger had been controlled. Priority was always to protect life then arrest the offenders. That was the emergency response part. After that his duty was to preserve the scene and gather evidence. Another part of the evidence was witness testimony. Grant nodded towards the staff behind the reception counter. "They see anything?"

The cop held a hand out then gave a wavering gesture. "One of them saw two big guys crossing the lawn before it happened."

Grant clenched his jaw but kept quiet. There was a man living up the hill he wanted to talk with again even if there was no evidence to support it. Probable cause wasn't something he took much notice of. He reckoned he knew why Arlo Rankoff's goons had been busy.

*

COLE FELT HIS HEART SKIP a beat when they returned to the reception area. The chair was still lying on its side and the sun was still shining through the front door. It glinted off the plaque on the wall and he read the words with a sinking feeling.

This Clinic Supported By Local Donations
Many Thanks To Arlo Rankoff
Chairman Of The Board

It wasn't the plaque that made his heart ache though. Or the fallen chair where Holly had been sitting. He looked at the telephone on the counter and the book that was lying next to it.

History Of The Ocean Shore Railroad

That was when he got a hitch in his voice and he decided to stay quiet. He thought about Holly making jokes in the bookstore and him suggesting she could use the book instead of her Taser. "I never need my Taser," she'd said. Well, she could have done with it today. He wondered if she'd tried. Two big fellas in a confined space was the ideal time to use the electric zapper. There had been no gunplay. That was the only positive he managed to take from today's attack. Not for the first time he vowed to tell her how he felt when they got her back.

Grant looked at Cole holding the book to his chest and then at Holly's patrol car parked outside. She hadn't gone in pursuit unless it was a foot chase. If it had been a foot chase there'd have been some radio traffic. An assistance call. A location. At the very least a code zero, or whatever they called the panic button in America. He saw the look on his brother's face and patted Cole on the back. "Got to figure they took her because she saw their faces."

Cole let out a sigh. He was being realistic. "They could have just shot her. No witnesses then."

Grant dropped his arm. "Shots would have drawn attention.

Cole turned to face him. "They'd already drawn attention. Half the staff was running down the hall."

Grant kept his voice level. "If she recognized them it means they're local."

Cole hardened his eyes. "We both know who this is. And when I find him I'm gonna rip his head off and shit down his neck."

Grant nodded. That was pretty much how he felt. A squeal of tyres outside drew his attention. Another patrol car jerked to a stop and Ben Gardner got out. No flashing lights. No sirens. The nearest cop to the scene but the last to arrive. Grant set his jaw as he watched the local chief talking to the cop at the crime scene tape. Gardner looked towards the clinic, puffed his chest and straightened his shoulders. He crossed the sidewalk and waved for them to come out.

Grant opened the door and braced himself for an argument.

FORTY-ONE

*

"WHAT THE HELL YOU GOT HER INTO?"

Gardner had taken them round the side of the clinic. A low wooden fence separated the garden from the shopping center parking lot and a gap in the bushes at the back led to the banks of San Pedro Creek. Trees soaked up the traffic noise from Cabrillo Highway. All they could hear was the gentle swish of leaves in the wind and Ben Gardner being more aggressive than Grant had ever seen him. Gardner put his hands on his hips but looked like he wanted to pull his gun. "I swear to god. If anything's happened to her I will shoot you dead."

The threat shocked Cole. He held his hands up in defence. "Whoah. Ben. This isn't about me."

Gardner breathed heavily through his nose. It made nearly as much noise as the trees. He hunched his shoulders like a bull preparing to charge. "Damn right it's not about you." He shoved his chin forward. "But it's because of you. You piece of shit."

Cole lowered his hands. "How d'you work that out?"

Gardner turned away for a moment to quell his anger. When he turned back to Cole he looked more in control. "Because it's you asked her to look into Rankoff's holdings."

Grant looked at his brother. Cole held his hands up again. Gardner leaned forward and lowered his voice. “And told her not to tell me.”

Cole felt the air go out of him like a pricked balloon. Busted. His shoulders sagged and he lowered his arms. Grant stepped forward. He had questions of his own. “But she trusted you.”

Gardner looked at Grant. “Of course she did. She’s like a daughter to me.” He lowered his head to cover his eyes. He didn’t want these men seeing how upset he was. He had no family. Holly was more than an apprentice to him, she was the reason he stayed in the job. To guide her through life until she was strong enough to stand alone. When he looked back at the two Englishmen he wasn’t the local police chief any more. He was a concerned father. “She should have called me first.”

Grant kept his voice level and understanding. “But she didn’t.”

Gardner shook his head. “She made a couple of calls on her own. The word had already got out by the time she told me. I gave her a secure number to call.” Gardner let out a sigh that trembled on his breath. “That was the last call she made.”

Grant listened to Gardner then shook his head. “You saying this wasn’t about the boy?”

Gardner looked Grant in the eye. “He wanted to shut her up. On account of what she found out.”

*

GRANT RAN A FEW CALCULATIONS in his head. Timing calculations based on what he knew and what he could guess. Holly reported for duty at the clinic just after Grant had left but before he reached the house on Kent Road. That was when Cole had asked her to check on Arlo Rankoff, at Grant’s request. She had made the first call shortly after, while Grant was climbing the hill. Whoever she’d spoken to hadn't wasted any time because the two heavies had been dispatched before Grant knocked on the front door.

That was how Grant saw it panning out, with a healthy dose of speculation. He didn't know who she had called but it was likely to be somebody in local government or at police headquarters. They were the only departments she could use to learn about property ownership and planning permission. Since she was a cop it was more likely to be police headquarters. That meant that somebody over there was in the businessman's pocket, either the person she called or somebody who heard the request. That same somebody could also have passed on information about Grant, meaning the leak wasn't necessarily Gardner. He might have to re-evaluate the local cop's status. "And you know what she found out, how?"

Gardner looked at Grant as if he were stupid. "Because I called the source back to see if he'd helped her."

Grant didn't need to ask if he had. What he really wanted to know was... "So, what did she find out?"

Gardner split his attention between Cole and Grant while he decided whether to tell them or not. His heart said not but instinct told him this overseas cop was the best chance of getting Holly back. Somebody who broke the rules. Somebody lying about Cole being an undercover cop and who would have no compunction about lying to get Arlo Rankoff. Gardner focused on Grant and nodded. Decision made. "Rankoff submitted planning to rebuild the road to Shelter Cove."

He moved in front of Grant and turned his back towards the cop at the crime scene tape. It was a subconscious move that bolstered Grant's trust of him. Ben Gardner wasn't sure who he could trust. The beat cops were unlikely to be in the loop but the fact that Gardner was unsure enhanced his credibility. Gardner glanced at Cole. "A local business objected to the application."

Cole looked at Grant then back to Gardner and held his hands up. "Wasn't the bookstore."

Grant looked at his brother. "It was the bookstore the car crashed into."

Gardner waved the comments aside. "It was the Café De San Pedro across the road."

Cole raised his eyebrows and gave Grant an, I told you so, stare. Gardner waited until the brotherly bickering subsided before continuing. "Arlo Rankoff owns the Café De San Pedro."

Grant remembered Cole telling him that Rankoff had bought all the businesses along the route to Shelter Cove and assumed it had been to remove any objections to the planning application. Now it looked like something else. He frowned at the burly cop. "He's blocking his own application?"

Gardner nodded. "There's more. The road gangs lined up for the work?"

Grant couldn't help but ask. "He owns them as well?"

Gardner nodded again. "And he stood them down three weeks ago." Grant was out of questions so Gardner gave the answer. "He never wanted to build a road to the beach cottages."

*

THAT PROMPTED ANOTHER RE-EVALUATION by Grant. Up until now he'd been working under the premise that Rankoff was buying all the businesses that might stand in his way. Building the road would give access to the beachfront properties and inflate the value of the cottages he'd bought at a knockdown price. Now the run-down cottages didn't appear to be the prime motive. He remembered standing on the balcony and looking along the hillside while Rankoff gloated about the prospects of further development beyond the cove. "He owns all the land between the cove and the highway."

Gardner shrugged. "He'd still need the road for access."

Grant considered that for a moment. "Unless he wants to make sure nobody else has access."

Cole drummed his fingers on the book clasped to his chest. "But there's nothing there. We saw that climbing down last night."

Grant looked at Cole. "We weren't looking for anything."

Gardner kept his back to the barrier as he spoke. "Doesn't matter. Hasn't been anything there for as long as I've been here. And that's a long time. Not even any hiking trails."

Cole stopped drumming. "Good place to hide something then."

Gardner let out a sigh. "Like what?"

Cole thought it was time to mention the tidal charts. "Like twenty-three Mexicans."

Gardner blurted a disbelieving laugh. "They drowned. Didn't fall down the cliff."

Cole briefly explained what he'd learned from the coastal chart. The tidal surges and the underwater currents on the day the bodies washed ashore. Gardner fell silent, not sure if he believed the tale or not, but when you added that into the mix it made all the coincidences feel more than a little strained. He was struggling to believe it though and shook his head. "That's just too… I don't know."

They both looked at Grant but the Yorkshire cop had dropped out of the conversation. His eyes looked glazed but what he was really doing was staring at the book in Cole's arms. At the cover photo of the railroad track sweeping around the headland. He'd seen a similar sweep when he'd been standing on Rankoff's balcony. The overgrown roadway or path overlooking Shelter Cove.

Cole saw what Grant was looking at and took the book from beneath his arms. The cover was bent to the shape of his chest but the pages weren't completely shut. A page had been folded over. He opened the book at the page, a chapter about the northern section of the historic Ocean Shore Railroad. About a stretch of the line and the tunnels that ran right through Arlo Rankoff's land.

FORTY-TWO

*

A BRIEF HISTORY IN THREE PARTS. Cole didn't give the history lesson, they muddled through it themselves, leafing through the book sitting around Gardner's desk at the Shelter Cove police office. It was the obvious place to regroup. They were three blocks away from the Pacifica PD units at the clinic. There was coffee to aid their concentration. And there was a map of Linda Mar on the wall. When Grant saw the scope of the railroad he let out a low whistle. "Holy shit on a stick."

Gardner looked up from the book. "I hope that's not a religious reference."

Grant took a sip of milky coffee. "It's a Yorkshire saying."

"Meaning what?"

Grant shrugged. "I have absolutely no idea."

*

PART ONE – Construction.

THE OCEAN SHORE RAILROAD WAS intended to be built from San Francisco to Santa Cruz via a route along the Pacific coastline. Construction started in 1905 at both ends but the line was never completed. The 1906 earthquake in San Francisco caused major damage and delayed construction but numerous trestles and bridges were built and track was laid. Tunnels were blasted through the mountains to straighten the route but the line never connected to the southern stretch out of Santa Cruz.

Economics dealt the railroad a further blow. The northern stretch ran a freight service and passenger trains but when the Pedro Mountain Road opened in 1913 many of the farmers used their own trucks to transport produce to San Francisco. The mainline service was abandoned in 1921. San Francisco incorporated the final stretch into the city but the rest fell into disrepair. Much of the track was lifted and the stations sold off.

*

"YOU RECOGNIZE THAT?" Cole pointed to an archive photo of the Tobin Station at San Pedro Point. The building had changed dramatically but the location was the same. Shoreside Drive at the junction with Danmann Avenue. Across the field from Cole's bookstore and just down the coast from the blocked access road where emergency workers had spent two days trying to rescue twenty-three Mexicans.

Grant looked at the grainy black and white photograph. "The Boathouse Diner?"

Cole nodded. "Formerly The Station Café."

Grant skimmed forward half a page. "Should have called it Smuggler's Inn."

*

PART TWO – Prohibition.

WITH THE LINE SOUTH OF SAN FRANCISCO abandoned most of the track was removed and the trestles dismantled. The more substantial spans were converted into road bridges to carry the Old Pacific Coast Highway Trail but the tunnels were simply shut down and the entrances blocked. Removing the track from inside the tunnels was deemed too expensive so the Western Pacific Railroad, who ran the San Francisco line, cut their losses and left them in place.

But if one thing is true it's that nature abhors a vacuum. Prohibition filled it. Smugglers bringing booze ashore in Shelter Cove used the tunnels for storage and transport from one end of the bay to the highway. They didn't need rolling stock and engines. Crates of liquor were ferried up and down the tunnels using handcarts and maintenance trolleys. It only took two men working the hand levers on the carts instead of ten men carrying wooden crates. It was efficient and economical and meant the trucks could be loaded miles away from the boats. Storage chambers were cut into the tunnels for extra space. The cool damp conditions were ideal for preserving the stock.

*

COLE DRUMMED HIS FINGERS on the map where a curve in the scenic highway bulged out over the sea. The dusty layby looked smaller on the map than when he'd parked Holly's car there last night. He'd assumed the overlook had been cut into the hillside to provide sightseers with a view of the coast. It was longer and wider than a car would need but ideal for tourist coaches. And bootleggers' trucks. "Small world."

He looked at Grant who was thinking exactly the same. It had been right under their noses the whole time. The railroad tunnels on

Arlo Rankoff's land. They'd eaten breakfast in the diner at one end and parked in the scenic overlook at the other.

*

PART THREE – Invasion.

OR MORE ACCURATELY, defence against invasion. During the Second World War America became paranoid about Japanese invasion. After Pearl Harbor work began on shore defences and gun emplacements. Some were out in the open and obvious, intended to deter as well as defend. Others took advantage of natural outcrops and clifftops but the most impressive were the conversion of railroad tunnels dotted along the Pacific coast.

The bootleggers' storage chambers were enlarged and strengthened to form armories and munitions stores. The tracks were upgraded and reinforced. Fortified gun emplacements were cut into the hillside and connected to the railroad tunnels. If the Japanese tried to invade California they were in for one hell of a shock.

The Japanese didn't invade and the tunnels were once again decommissioned. The heavy artillery was removed and the entrances dynamited. The gun emplacements were collapsed and allowed to grow wild. The hillside returned to nature and the vacuum lay dormant. But, as we've already proved, nature abhors a vacuum. The question was, what had filled it?

*

GRANT HAD ONLY BEEN THINKING one thing for the last twenty minutes. "The train never came." Together with Cole and Holly they'd been scratching their heads about what that could mean. They'd run the gamut of Michael Caine in Zulu and the rhythmic crashing of the Pacific surf. None of it sounded like a train. All of it was wild speculation. Because there hadn't been a train line near Shelter Cove for over fifty years.

Grant ran a finger along an imaginary line from the highway overlook to the Boathouse Diner. The line cut through the mountains along the coast and the hillside above the beach cottages. "Looks like it's not keeping Japs out any more." He stabbed the finger at the heart of Shelter Cove. "It's bringing Mexicans in."

FORTY-THREE

*

"THAT'S QUITE A LEAP."

Gardner pushed his chair back from the desk so he could look past Grant at the map. It had been hanging from the wall of his office for as long as Linda Mar had a police station instead of being run from Pacifica but he'd never looked at it quite like this before. Grant stood firm. It was Cole who played devil's advocate. "But Rankoff hates Mexicans."

Grant threw another theory into the pot. "Twenty-three of 'em just drowned. That won't have upset him."

This time Gardner stood up. "That's an even bigger leap."

Grant moved between Cole and Gardner and sat on the edge of the desk. All three were looking at the map, Linda Mar, stretching from Rockaway Beach to Pedro Point. Holly West was somewhere on that map. That was the first order of business. Everything else was just speculation leading to a conclusion. If Rankoff's men had snatched Holly, where had they taken her?

Cole proved that brothers really are twinned. "Shouldn't we be out looking for Holly?"

Gardner leaned against the desk next to Grant. "PPD put her description out half an hour ago."

Grant looked across at the local police chief. "Is that the same Pacifica PD that got her snatched in the first place?"

Gardner shook his head. "There's a leak up there for sure. But the police department isn't in on this. It's a missing cop we're talking about here. You know how that works."

Grant did know how that worked. Officer down. Cop killer. Line of duty. Officer needs assistance. They were phrases that sparked the nerves of every serving police officer. Cops would bleed to resolve a situation like this. "Where do you think? Scrapyard? Thc house? Café De San Pedro?"

Gardner folded his arms and looked at the map. "He's got businesses all over town. Off the map too. But you don't kidnap a cop and take her to your house. Or business."

Grant nodded. "You don't shit on your own doorstep."

Gardner threw a sideways glance at Grant. "Is that another Yorkshire saying?"

Grant kept his eyes on the map. "It's universal."

Three pairs of eyes focused on the map. The room became quiet. Coffee smells and dried leather made the office feel homely. The situation was anything but. Grant folded his arms. Cole did the same. The three men leaned against the desk in the same pose looking at the same place with the same intense silence. Three pairs of eyes. One map. Grant kept his tone level. "Here's another universal truth." His eyes drifted west beyond the rundown beach cottages. "Do bears shit in the woods?"

Cole and Gardner followed Grant's stare. At the wooded hills between Shelter Cove and the scenic highway. The place Arlo Rankoff didn't want people hiking. The first place Grant wanted to look.

*

THE PLAN OF ACTION FORMED pretty quickly after that. Gardner surprised Grant again by showing local knowledge and community awareness. "There's a Wells Fargo ATM round back of the shopping center. They'll have cameras. Metro PCS as well. They're nearest to the clinic. I'll check what they've got on CCTV."

Grant nodded and scanned the office. "Good. You got a war chest?"

Cole looked uncomfortable. Gardner pointed towards the kitchenette. "Firearms locker's in the back. You licensed for California?"

Grant raised his eyebrows. "Does it matter?"

Gardner lowered his eyes. This was Holly they were talking about. Of course it didn't matter. He fished a bunch of keys out of his pocket and walked into the back room. He talked as he unlocked the metal cabinet fastened to the wall. "We can't risk having PPD check Rankoff's holdings but I know a few people."

Grant didn't look convinced. "You got a posse?"

Gardner looked at him. "Community spirit. They don't just turn out for search and rescue."

Grant remembered the volunteers who had helped scour the hillside above the beach. If you had that many people checking the streets you could find a needle in a haystack. They could certainly track a kidnapped cop and a getaway car. If CCTV provided the car.

Gardner swung the cabinet door open. There were two shotguns and four semi-automatics clipped into the firearms rack. Gardner tossed a shotgun to Grant then handed him a semi-automatic and a box of shells. He looked at Cole but Cole shook his head. "I'm a diver. Can't shoot for shit."

Gardner took one of the handguns out and handed it to Cole. "Learn."

Grant began to load the shotgun. Cole put the gun in his pocket. It felt alien against his hip. Gardner loaded the other shotgun and locked the cabinet. "Where you gonna start?"

Cole went to the map and found the spot he wanted. "The highway overlook."

The coffee and leather smells faded. Adrenaline charged the air. It smelled like static electricity and freshly struck matches. Cole tapped the layby then drew his finger back towards the woods. "Bear shitting time."

Grant nodded his approval. It was good having his brother on board. "We got any flashlights?"

Gardner shrugged. "It's daylight."

Grant turned from the map. "Tunnels."

Gardner nodded and went to another cabinet, this one in the main office. He took out two solid metal Maglites, used by police forces around the world. He handed them out and looked at the highway overlook. "Have you still got Holly's car?" Grant and Cole looked at each other. Gardner raised his eyebrows. "I know more than you think."

Everyone nodded. Nobody smiled. It was time to go to work.

FORTY-FOUR

*

THE SUN HAD MOVED ACROSS the sky by the time Cole parked Holly's car in the dusty layby. They hadn't talked much on the drive out from Linda Mar and they didn't talk at all as they got out of the car. Grant didn't want Cole to know that he thought finding Holly alive was a long shot. Cole didn't want to believe what he already knew, that the odds were stacked against them and that Holly was most likely dead already.

The brothers stood shoulder to shoulder at the edge of the road. They looked at the wooded hills rising above the highway. Down to the left the path they'd taken to the beach looked dry and empty. Surf broke along the shore with the easy regularity of nature. Up ahead, amid the trees and outcrops, there was a vacuum waiting to be filled. Grant intended to fill it with fury and vengeance.

The brothers looked up at the hills one last time and nodded in unison. Neither spoke. Then they set off into the woods towards a darker place.

*

THE TREES SWALLOWED THEM immediately. Down into a ravine and then up the hill on the other side. During his army days Grant had served in jungles and deserts. This felt like coming home. The difference was that his military service had been about overcoming the sandcastle bullies and distancing himself from his brother but today involved bonding and working together. This time Grant didn't need his brother to protect him. He was more than capable of defending himself.

The slope was gentle but heavily wooded. After the deep ravine it climbed above the scenic highway to a ridge half a mile into Rankoff's land. Dense undergrowth between the trees snagged at their clothes and threatened to trip them. Grant kept his eyes on the ground, creating a trail for Cole to follow. Single file. Cole watched Grant's back as they forged ahead. Watching his brother made him consider his options, either keep quiet about the lies he'd told or come clean. In the end he went somewhere in between. The hard part was broaching the subject. He decided to slide in sideways. "You don't think she's alive do you?"

Grant kept walking. The foliage soaked up any noise from the outside world. All he could hear was the rustle of bushes and leaves. There was no birdsong. His breathing was loud in his ears. Cole's voice sounded distant and muted. Grant didn't raise his voice to answer, not wanting to disturb the peace and quiet. "I think it's a possibility."

Cole followed Grant's trail. "That she's alive or that they killed her?"

Grant kept going. "Either one."

He clambered over a rocky outcrop halfway up the ravine. It was large and overgrown and barely a rock at all. The slope was less steep but he had to climb over another outcrop further up the hill. The trees thinned out around the outcrops then thickened again up the hill. Grant threaded his way between them and listened to Cole's footsteps behind him. Cole was breathing heavily when he caught up with his brother. "This is going to end badly. Isn't it?"

Grant stopped and leaned against a tree. He glanced over his shoulder. "I don't remember you being this pessimistic."

Cole used the pause to catch his breath. The brothers stared at each other. With the lack of movement the woods fell into a deep silence. No birds. Not even the rustle of leaves. Dead blank stillness. Cole kept his voice calm despite what he was building up to saying. "You always looked on the bright side."

Grant was already calm. "Like when I was building sandcastles?" He lowered his voice. "Look what optimism got me." He didn't wait for a response, turning instead and starting up the hill again. Cole's footsteps crashed through the brush behind him, struggling to keep up. He barked his shin on a tree root and almost turned his ankle on a slippery growth. "Hold up. Jesus Christ. I'm sorry about that. How many times I got to say it?"

Grant didn't slow down. "Saying it doesn't change what happened."

Cole got his breathing into a rhythm so he could talk and walk without his voice breaking up. Any cracking in his speech was down to the subject matter and a lifetime of guilt. "You're right. And I'll go to my grave regretting what I did. But Jim…"

He reached out and grabbed Grant's arm. Grant spun round and almost squared off against his brother. The stare he leveled at Cole was hard and cold and angry. Exactly the opposite of a lifetime of guilt. He didn't trust himself to speak. Cole got his breath back. "I didn't like the way dad treated you. But I understood it. I missed mum. One minute she was there and then she was gone. You were there instead. I couldn't come to grips with it. Dad couldn't either."

Grant still didn't speak. Cole was almost pleading. "I've said things I regret." He let out a sigh. "I've done things I'm ashamed of." He looked at Grant. "Told you things I shouldn't have."

A branch snapped as he changed position. It sounded loud in the muffled silence. It should have signaled a flurry of wings but the woods were empty and lifeless. As quiet as the grave. Cole sagged against a tree. "The money didn't come from dad."

Grant looked up from where he'd been staring at his feet. He looked at Cole's pained expression and waited for him to confirm what Grant had always known. "I stole it from the drugs seizure."

*

THE CRACK OF A SNAPPED BRANCH echoed through the ravine. From when Cole changed position to make his confession. Grant was half thinking about that while Cole admitted to stealing the money. Part of him thought the echo in the muffled silence was strange but his mind was distracted by his brother's admission. "From the evidence locker?"

Cole nodded. "I figured it wasn't anybody's. Not like Joe Citizen." He shrugged. "And I needed to get away. It was killing me. The way dad cut you off. Back when we were kids. I needed a fresh start."

Grant kept his voice low and even. "You could have just emigrated."

Cole shook his head. "An anonymous start. You can only do that with money."

Grant was only half listening. His mind kept coming back to the echo. The lack of birds in the woods. The muffled silence that had only been broken by their footfalls and breathing and occasional snapped twigs. At no point during their climb had any of that echoed across the ravine. The trees and undergrowth had soaked it all up. There was only the quiet and the smells. Forest smells. And now that he thought about it, something else. Cole opened his mouth to speak but Grant held up a hand to silence him.

The quiet was complete. It was oppressive. Smothering.

Grant picked up a fallen branch and snapped it across his knee. The crack sounded like a gunshot. It echoed and bounced and came back reduced and distant. Not from across the ravine but from behind him. Grant turned around and looked at the slope. The trees had opened into a narrow clearing but bushes and creepers filled the void. Only they didn't fill it all. There was a gaping black hole in the middle. The remains of a collapsed tunnel. A toothless mouth that bounced the gunshot back from the depths of its blackness.

The echo tipped Grant off but it was the smell that grabbed his attention. He'd smelled it many times before and it had never signaled good news. It was bad and fetid and reeked of death. He looked down the slope. The rocky outcrops they'd climbed over were square and evenly spaced. Concrete foundations for the trestle bridge that once spanned the ravine. Without waiting for Cole to help, Grant scrambled up the landslip and began to tear at the rubble.

FORTY-FIVE

*

BEN GARDNER'S INVESTIGATION moved ahead in fits and starts. Moments of tedious procedure were interspersed with bursts of inspiration. The procedure part began at the Wells Fargo ATM. The final burst of inspiration came with the help of dozens of people working together.

*

"AND IT'S ALWAYS ANGLED DOWN LIKE THIS?"

"That's where the customers are."

Gardner was looking at a grainy computer screen inside the portable cabin that housed the ATM and a temporary Wells Fargo office. It had been dumped at an angle round the back of the shopping center and took up three bays in the parking lot. The manager seemed offended by Gardner's questions. Or maybe he was offended at being the manager of himself, since he was also the entire staff of the Wells Fargo, Linda Mar branch. Gardner waved at the space behind the ATM customers. "That's where robbers come from."

The manager shook his head. "The camera isn't about robbery. It's about fraudulent card usage."

Gardner let out a resigned sigh. "So, not the people coming up behind them?"

The manager pointed at a black and white customer on screen. "The person using the card."

Gardner had no better luck at the Metro PCS store across the parking lot. The countrywide cell phone company had internal and external CCTV to protect against burglary but the outside cameras pointed across the parking lot to cover the immediate area in front of the store. The Wells Fargo ATM was in the top right of the screen meaning that Metro PCS would be better for catching muggers than Wells Fargo but neither of them was any use for seeing what happened at Linda Mar Pediatric Clinic. An enthusiastic salesman pointed out the business next door and Gardner thanked him for his help.

Gardner could hardly pronounce Kuk Sool Won of Pacifica let alone understand what the martial arts training facility did but at least their camera faced the right way. The Third Degree Black Belt who showed Gardner the footage was more adept at throwing her own bodyweight than working the controls so Gardner scanned the recording himself. He found the time of the attack and pressed play.

Nothing.

The clinic itself was barely visible in the distance but the edge of the parking lot was sharp and clear. There was no movement. No vehicles crossed the screen or parked or maneuvered. Nobody walked towards the clinic or ran away from it. Gardner had drawn another blank. More in hope than expectation he asked about the internal clock. The Black Belt pointed at the time at the bottom of the screen. "That's your time right there."

Gardner waved a hand. "Is it accurate?"

The Black Belt stopped the playback and the screen returned to live feed. The clock showed the present time. Gardner checked his watch. The clock was accurate. He pressed play again then hit reverse. The world ran backwards, not that you'd have known from the recording. There wasn't enough activity at the far end of the parking lot to show any movement at all, just an occasional customer in the foreground walking backwards.

Gardner hit pause. He'd just seen a big black car cross the screen, stop for a moment, then drive off in reverse. He pressed play. The car returned in real time. The clock showed thirty minutes before the attack. The car stopped and a big guy got out of the passenger side, stood in the open door as he looked towards the clinic, then got back in. The car drove off. He hit rewind then play then pause. He found the zoom control and enlarged the image. The picture became grainy and indistinct. In small increments he changed the zoom until it was clear enough to make out the license plate then wrote it down.

The Black Belt tapped Gardner on the shoulder. "If that's where you're interested in." She waved a finger at the screen. "One of my customers lives over there on De Solo. Been having trouble with animals scavenging from her bins. Got a camera covering the back yard."

Gardner took the address and thanked her. Patience and persistence were about to pay off.

*

THE HOME SURVEILLANCE CAMERA wasn't as high tech or sophisticated as the bank or Kuk Sool Won but it was facing the right direction and up close and personal. It covered the waste bins round the back of her house and angled across her neighbor's property towards the trees. Her bungalow was on the back straight of De Solo Drive bordering San Pedro Creek. Her next-door neighbor was the Linda Mar Pediatric Clinic.

The woman let Gardner replay the hard drive recording. He could see through the trees towards the creek and a vague line of roadway but no traffic. The slip road off Cabrillo Highway didn't carry much traffic. The clock wasn't set right so Gardner had to rewind and play in short bursts until he was in the ball park then hit fast reverse while in play mode.

Two big guys dashed across the field of view. One was sticking a gun in his belt. The other was half dragging and half carrying a struggling figure. The uniform was obvious. Gardner felt a cold shiver run down his spine. The men crashed through the trees towards the roadway. The car was a distant blur but it was the same shape and size as the one from the parking lot. Gardner clenched his jaw and nodded his thanks.

Part one complete. The rest was police work. Back at the office he called a friend at headquarters to run the plate without it showing on the system. Doing that over the radio would have let anyone listening know who the owner was. Gardner wasn't surprised when the result came back. It was registered to L&L Hawaiian Barbecue, another local business owned by Arlo Rankoff.

*

COMMUNITY SPIRIT DID THE REST. Gardner met with the volunteers and gave them the licence plate. They put the word out. The jungle drums sounded. The grapevine did its work. Ninety minutes later Gardner had a sighting, a time, and a last known direction.

The car had driven up the peninsular towards Shelter Cove but cut left on Olympian Way. One street over from Kent Road. Unsurprisingly the car didn't go towards Rankoff's house, it turned up a dirt track into the hills. Into the wilderness overlooking the Pacific coast and the land where hikers were discouraged from exploring the Pedro Point headlands.

FORTY-SIX

*

GRANT PAUSED JUST INSIDE the mouth of the tunnel. Cole clambered over the rubble and joined him. Light from the hole they had made picked out carved stone walls and rusty tracks. Water dripped somewhere deep inside the mountain. The echo was almost musical after the quiet of the woods. Grant looked back at the dirty grey rocks of the landslip. Although there had been an opening when they arrived it wasn't big enough to climb through until they'd removed some of the rubble. Animals might have found their way in here but there hadn't been human traffic since the railroad was decommissioned.

Cole pulled the Maglite out of his belt but Grant held out a hand. "Save it. We don't know how deep this goes."

Keeping to the sleepers along the middle of the tracks he headed deeper into the tunnel. The light faded but his eyes adjusted as he walked. Stone chippings and railroad ballast supported the heavy wooden sleepers. In the gloom it was hard to tell but the oily discharge from the rolling stock had long since dried. The rails were dark with rust. No trains along here for a long time.

Thick black cables ran the length of the tunnel, festooned along the right hand wall like Christmas decorations. A hundred feet in there was a splintered wooden shed for tools and equipment. The door was hanging from its hinges. The tools had gone, salvaged when the railroad closed down. The dripping grew louder but the bad smell diminished. Either that or Grant was getting used to it. That happened. He'd witnessed many a post-mortem where he thought the smell would make him gag but eventually it became background noise. It helped having a pack of mints that everyone nicknamed Post-mortem Polos.

The tunnel was darker the deeper they went but then Grant noticed a lessening of the gloom up ahead, then another patch of light further than that. Air vents cut into the ceiling that came out in the wooded hills above the tunnel. It meant they didn't need the flashlights yet. Grant watched his footing, stepping from one sleeper to the next with a fluid movement that let him pick up the pace. Cole followed two steps behind him.

Time lost its meaning. Distance became hard to gauge. Halfway along the tunnel a gap appeared in the left hand wall. Grant paused. Dull green light filtered through the doorway. Grant sniffed the air. No bad smell in there. In fact the air smelled fresher than at any time since they'd entered the tunnel. He crossed the track, peered through the opening, and stepped back into a childhood coloured by *The Guns Of Navarone* and *Where Eagles Dare*.

The concrete gun emplacement also took him back to the east coast of Yorkshire and the long sandy beaches of Filey and Scarborough. Before the sandcastle and the bullies. Fortress England during the Second World War had been much like the Pacific coast in America. Fortified to keep the Germans from invading the same way America was defending against the Japanese. Yorkshire's coastal defences eventually crumbled into the sea with the rest of the cliff top erosion but not before the Grant brothers had time to explore the empty pillboxes.

Grant heard a gasp behind him. Cole was having the same thoughts. No matter where they went it always seemed to come back to Yorkshire and the beach and the defence of James Grant's castle. This castle was empty but the embrasures stood testament to a time when big guns defended the world from tyranny. Grant took a deep breath of woodland air through the foliage that covered the firing slits, hefted the shotgun in his hand, then went back into the main tunnel.

*

MORE DRIPPING WATER. Another broken tool shed. Two more air vents in the ceiling and one final gun emplacement. That was what they had to endure before they reached their destination. The tunnel had been collapsed more completely at the far end than the entrance but that wasn't the only difference. As they'd progressed along the track the rails had shown less rust and more signs of recent usage. The rails had a dull shine to them. Not regular railroad silver rails but definitely used occasionally and more recently than World War Two.

The other thing that signaled the end was the smell. It was ripe and bad and harder to ignore. Grant wished he had a pack of Post-mortem Polos to distract his taste buds. Despite standing under one last air vent the smell clung to his clothes like a bad autopsy.

The reason why the rails were shiny stood against the rubble and scree of the collapsed exit. A big solid railroad handcart. The seesaw handles were big enough for two men on either side. The flat metal circles of the spring-loaded bumpers hadn't clashed with buffers in a long time but the twin orbs said railroad as much as any child's train set. Three links of solid greasy chain hung from the chassis. An old wooden crate with faded letters stenciled on the side stood on the load bed. Maybe used to feed the big guns further down the tunnel. Or used to transport moonshine during prohibition.

There was a door cut in the wall to the left. Wide stone steps led down a dark passage. The bad smell drifted out of the entrance. Something else too. Grant listened to make sure he wasn't imagining things. Cole whispered the obvious. "Voices."

Grant reinforced the stupidity. "Mexicans."

FORTY-SEVEN

*

THE SECONDARY PASSAGE WAS WIDE enough for two people and just about high enough to stand without crouching. Until you started going down the uneven steps cut out of the stone. Grant went down the steps one at a time, slowly, head bowed to watch his footing. Forward movement banged his head against the sloping ceiling. He adjusted his knees to lower his center mass. The light faded behind him. There was no more light to aid his night vision. He was about to pull the Maglite from his belt when a gentle curve in the stairway revealed dull yellow light.

Grant stopped and listened. The voices didn't sound any closer but the smell was worse. Cole stood beside him and the brothers looked at each other. Cole raised his eyebrows. Grant shrugged. He had no answers. Instead he edged forward to look around the corner. Caged bulbs were fastened to the ceiling, joined by lengths of rusty metal conduit. The light fittings were cracked and dirty, barely throwing enough light to reach the walls. The passage widened and became an antechamber with three narrow passageways leading off.

It was the antechamber that caught Grant's attention.

The walls were stacked with wooden crates and jerry cans.

Several of the crates had split and spilled vintage shells and explosives across the floor. The jerry cans were painted dull green and smelled like a leaky gas station. They were old and rusty and not entirely watertight. It wasn't water that had leaked out. Faded stencils on the crates gave unit designations and calibers. The jerry cans were blank. Whoever had organized the evacuation of military equipment and personnel had left the small stuff behind. There was enough small stuff to blow a hole in California but not enough to trouble the war effort. At the time they had bigger things to worry about. Like invading Europe and fighting the Japanese.

The smell of petrol almost disguised the other smell but not quite. Grant sniffed the air. The smell was coming from the left hand passage. The voices were coming from the right. Intermittently. In little snatches of conversation. Quietly. Not the urgent panicky voices of people in immediate danger. Grant chose the left hand passage.

*

THERE WERE NO MORE STEPS. The passage was narrow, forcing Grant and Cole to walk single file. It sloped gently but was straight and true and not very long. The conduit was fastened to the side wall instead of the ceiling and only fed two light fittings. One of the bulbs was out. The other was even dirtier than the rest. Cobwebs festooned the cage. Grant couldn't imagine there'd be much for spiders to eat down here.

The passage opened into a bowl shaped chamber with a hole in the floor. A heavy wooden trapdoor had once covered the hole but age and decay meant it was little more than a few scraps of wood and a rusty hinge leaning against the back wall. The dripping noises from the railroad tunnel had receded. The voices had gone. Light from the one remaining bulb didn't reach the hole but the smell from the hole reached Grant.

He tilted his head to listen. When going into enemy territory the rule was look, listen and smell. There was no sign of movement. There was no sound of enemy personnel. There was only the smell. Grant knew what the smell meant even before he approached the hole. He edged forward. He didn't want to confirm what he already knew but there was no moving forward until you identified the past. He'd been trying to avoid that with Cole ever since he came to Shelter Cove. There was no avoiding the hole in the floor.

Grant stood two feet from the pit. Cole came up beside him. Neither spoke. Both drew their Maglites and leaned forward. The two flashlights came on together but it was Grant who bent his head and looked into the hole. He jerked his head back and turned away. Cole didn't need to look but he did. His reaction was just as instant. One look was all it took. The image would stay with them for the rest of their lives.

The pit was a charnel house. It had been carved deep and wide out of the rock coming to a neck at the top like a fat round bottle. The floor was invisible. It was piled high across the entire width of the pit with rotting corpses and bones. Not as naked as the atrocities of the WW2 death camps but no less terrible for the fact that they were still clothed. There was no colour. The clothes had faded into dirty greys and browns. Any blood had soaked into the ground in an ugly black stain. Blank dead eyes stared from the latest corpses. Eyeless sockets glared from the fleshless skulls of the long deceased. The stench was thick and heavy and physical.

Grant backed along the passage out of the bowl shaped chamber. When he reached the main antechamber he leaned against the wall and closed his eyes before turning the torch off. Cole did the same. Both knew about preserving night vision. When they opened their eyes again the dull yellow light was enough. Sometimes seeing less was better. Grant jerked his head towards the charnel pit. "Pipeline stops here."

Cole nodded. "Preserving America for Americans."

Grant tried not to breath deep. "You said he didn't like Mexicans but… This." He shook his head and slid down the wall until he was sitting on the floor. Cole stood over him like a protective brother. Years too late but at least it was a start. He rested a hand on Grant's shoulder. "He's bringing 'em in but not sending 'em on. What kind of business is that?"

Grant looked up at his brother. "A profitable one." He stood up. "How much you reckon he charges to smuggle someone into the States?"

Cole wracked his brain for a figure but couldn't come up with one. "A lot."

Grant looked along the passage towards the pit. "Counting the bodies. That's a lot times a lot. A fortune." Both became aware of the voices at the same time. Quiet mutterings coming from the other passage. Grant walked to the middle of the antechamber. "And that makes them the next batch."

He glanced at the ceiling and noticed the extra conduit for the first time. It was a thicker heavier pipe running from the main passage towards the whispering chamber. Where quiet Mexicans gave each other platitudes to keep their families calm. The bodies in the pit weren't just adult males. There were women and children too. Like the woman and her sons in the cave. A nightmare vision shot through Grant's brain. The bodies piled in the charnel pit. The death camps of WW2. He pointed at the thick grey pipe. "Gas chamber."

Before he could decide what to do next a light flickered from the railroad tunnel. A torch beam jerked and danced across the carved stairs and footsteps echoed down the passage.

FORTY-EIGHT

*

THE LONE FIGURE PAUSED at the top of the stairs and looked down into darkness. He knew the men he was looking for were down there. They certainly weren't in the railroad tunnel and they weren't still coming along the tracks. He'd stopped and listened several times. Footsteps would have echoed in the silence. They weren't behind him. That meant they'd already gone down the carved stone passage.

They were armed. So was he. The men coming from the other side would be armed too. This could go bad in a heartbeat. He turned the flashlight on and played it across the stairs. There was no avoiding going down there. He rested the shotgun across the forearm holding the flashlight and set off down the steps.

*

GRANT HAD TO THINK FAST. He glanced at the bottom of the staircase then at the three remaining passages, one behind him continuing down the hill and one on either side leading to the charnel pit and the whispering chamber. The passageways on either side were the darkest. Half the caged light bulbs were dead. They were the best places to hide. Grant leaned close to Cole and spoke quickly and quietly then they separated and melted into the shadows, one on the left and one on the right. Grant took the whispering passage. The voices fell silent. They could sense his presence. If fear had a smell he reckoned it would be strong here. He saw Cole edge along the opposite passage until he became a shadow among shadows.

The footsteps grew louder coming down the stairs. They bounced off the walls of the antechamber. The torch beam jerked and danced. There appeared to be no effort to keep quiet. Grant flexed his knees in readiness. Timing was everything. A man with a shotgun reached the bottom of the stairs. Cole dashed out of the opposite passage. The shotgun swung round, away from Grant. Grant took three swift steps and grabbed the man from behind, knocking the barrel upwards to neutralize the blast. The shotgun didn't fire. Ben Gardner recovered from the shock and found his voice. "Thought I'd find you boys here."

*

THE THREE MEN TALKED as they went up the passage towards the whispering chamber. It was a short passage. As with the charnel pit chamber the only bulb working was at the very end. Unlike the charnel pit chamber the end of the passage was blocked by a heavy wooden door that was bolted from the outside. Grant noted the locked door as he listened to Gardner.

"I lost them after the dirt track." Meaning the car they'd snatched Holly in. "They could have gone two or three ways. I took the wrong one."

Cole's voice was a hushed whisper. "But they've got Holly?"

Gardner nodded. "Neighborhood watch tracked them this far. Took me a while to find my way in. There's air vents all over the place. The one I found was near the collapsed tunnel."

Grant stopped and turned to face Gardner. “You sure they didn’t drop her at Rankoff’s?”

Gardner gave him a condescending look. “Would you?”

Grant didn’t back down. “He isn’t me.”

Gardner sounded impatient. “He isn’t stupid either. He didn’t take her to his house. There’s no connection from Olympian Way to Kent Road. The car came up Olympian Way.”

Grant was satisfied. He glanced at the thick gas pipe running along the ceiling. It went through the frame that supported the locked door. “They must be coming from the down the hill. Then she’ll be joining the rest.”

Gardner looked blank. Cole explained. “Gas chamber. Body pit’s down the other passage.”

Gardner screwed his face up in disgust. “Sick fuck.”

Grant looked at the local police chief. “Mexican hating sick fuck.” He did some internal calculations. “I’m betting the ones in the bay got out before the gas took full effect. Twenty-three don’t just drown. Somebody would have got ashore. Unless they were half dead already.”

Cole leaned against the wall. “Three of ‘em didn’t drown.”

Grant shrugged. “I can’t explain that. Maybe they avoided the gas. I don’t know.” He turned to the door and reached for the bolt. “Why don’t we ask them?”

*

THE CHAMBER WAS CRAMPED and degrading. It was tightly packed with smelly humanity that had no facilities and no place for modesty. The stone floor had a smattering of straw but that was the only concession to comfort. The toilet was a thicker patch of straw in the far corner. A single caged bulb shone on expectant faces that were beaming their gratitude, old men and young men and women and children. A babble of voices spoke over each other. Most spoke only Mexican. One managed some broken English. "Muchos gracias senor. I knew they would find help."

Grant looked into a dirty brown face with a broken nose and bloodshot eyes. "Who would find help?"

The Mexican waved a hand through the door. "The ones who escaped. When the train did not come."

Grant didn't ask which train. He'd seen the railroad tracks. They must have been promised onward transport on a train that was never going to arrive. He didn't have the heart to tell the man that the others hadn't escaped after all. That they had drowned in Shelter Cove, a place of safety that had proved to be anything but. He waved a hand at the door too. "Well, let's start getting..."

Before Grant could finish a gurgling noise shuddered through the overhead pipe. It rattled and coughed then uttered a quiet hiss. Gas. He jerked a hand at the door with more urgency. "Now."

Grant led the way, forming the refugees into an uneven line and directing them down the passage. Cole positioned himself halfway along to help guide the confused prisoners. Gardner stood by the door watching for stragglers.

The antechamber was a blessing of open space after the cramped cell. The smell of spilled petrol was like perfume after the stench of the great unwashed. Grant was guiding them left towards the stairs when he heard a noise from the main passage down the hill. A clatter of loose stones then a familiar sound. A gun being cocked. The gunshot that followed sounded like an explosion in the confined space. Sparks flew as the bullet ricocheted off the walls, then several guns fired at once.

FORTY-NINE

*

THE MEXICANS DROPPED TO THEIR knees and edged back along the passageway. A sensible precaution if you're being shot at. A collective decision if you've been terrorized and locked in a cell for days. Herd mentality. The gunshots were driving them back into their cell, the gas chamber that was waiting to claim them. Next stop, the charnel pit.

Grant pulled the gun from the back of his jeans and loosed off three shots down the main passage. He shouted to Cole over his shoulder. "Keep 'em moving. This way. I'll cover you."

He dropped to one knee next to an uneven shoulder of rock where the carved wall jutted out. He fired two more shots then waved for the lead Mexican to stay low and move fast. Towards the stairs and the railroad tunnel. "The train."

The old man grinned his excitement. Grant pointed at the stairs. "The train has come."

The old man nodded and darted across the chamber.

A fusillade of shots came out of the dark. From low to the ground in the main passage. The shots flew high, travelling upwards from a low position. Grant held the high ground, firing down at the attackers. A good defensive position if he were planning to defend his ground. Except he couldn't simply defend his position with the cell door belching gas into the whispering passage. The poisonous hiss was as deadly as a snake coming towards him. He couldn't smell it. He didn't know if it had a smell. The leaking petrol covered any telltale odor. He watched it trickle down the main passage. More shots ricocheted off the walls. Sparks exploded in the gloom. "Cole. Need some help here."

Cole ushered several women and children around the side of the chamber and up the stairs then came and knelt beside Grant. He took his gun out and looked at it like he'd never seen one before. Grant stuck his finger in the barrel. "The shooting end." Then he pointed down the slope. "That way."

Grant demonstrated. He fired three more shots down the passage and Cole followed suit. Gardner brought the last of the Mexicans into the chamber and crouched on the bottom step. He leveled the shotgun across the chamber and blasted two shots into the opposite entrance. There was an immediate shout of pain followed by another fusillade of gunshots. Sparks danced off the walls. An old man bringing up the rear went down.

Grant looked at Gardner and nodded. Gardner nodded back. He helped the fallen man up the stairs but before he disappeared he turned and tossed the shotgun across the chamber. Grant caught it one handed then looked at Cole. "Help get them on the handcart. Fast as you can."

Cole backed against the wall as a fresh round of gunshots ricocheted in the cavern. He looked at the jerry cans and the wooden crates of old munitions then turned to his brother. "What the fuck you you're gonna do?"

Grant kept his face calm. "What needs to be done."

Cole stared him in the eye. "No. I'm staying with you."

Grant shook his head. "Ben can't do it on his own."

Cole stared at Grant. "I'm not leaving you again."

Grant understood something then that he'd never realized before. Something he'd been hiding from himself ever since the sandcastle on Scarborough beach. Something that had been inside him the entire time. "You never did." He let out a sigh. "Honestly. Now go."

He felt light headed and thought it was only partly to do with the gas seeping into the chamber. He turned and fired three shots down the passage to cover Cole's getaway. A few seconds later he was alone in the killing jar. He settled on his haunches and slowed his breathing. Petrol trickled. Discarded ordnance spilled from splintered wood. Grant took one last look at Cole's retreating back then leveled the shotgun across one arm. He blasted the jerry cans at close range. The petrol cans exploded and flames engulfed the antechamber.

*

GARDNER HEARD THE MUFFLED explosion as he loaded a mother and her young daughter onto the handcart. He paused and lowered his head. Young Mexicans helped the older men onto the cart. It had a wide load bed for transporting bootleg liquor or ammunition. If they crammed tight they should all fit on. The mother held her daughter. The last of the young men clambered aboard and four of them stood either side of the seesaw cranking bars.

Cole came up the stairs at the run. His face was haggard and grey. Dark smears begrimed his cheeks. Gardner didn't think it was smoke. For the first time since he'd met the Englishman he felt sorry for the bookseller. He was beginning to realize what had seemed familiar about the two men from Yorkshire but this wasn't the time to mention it. "Give me a hand."

Cole stood beside Gardner at the back of the handcart and leaned his shoulder against the bumper. Gardner did the same. The cart didn't budge. It was solid and heavy and had been standing at the end of the tunnel for a long time. The two men at the raised end of the cranking handle pushed downwards. The other two pulled up. Cole and Gardner braced their feet against the sleepers and pushed.

The wheels squeaked. The crank groaned. Inch by agonizing inch the cart began to move, slowly at first but then with increasing momentum. Small arms ammunition began to pop and explode in the flames down the stairs. Soon the bigger shells and the explosives would catch fire. When that happened part of the California coast was going to change forever.

The pop and crackle from the staircase grew louder. Cole and Gardner strained as they pushed. The railroad cart built up speed. Then a third shoulder leaned into the push. Cole looked to his side and saw a singed and blackened Jim Grant pushing with him. The sight made him push even harder. The train was finally leaving the station.

*

"WE'RE NOT GOING WITH THEM?"

Cole stood with his hands on his hips as Grant gave one last shove and watched the handcart disappear into the shadows. Grant turned back towards the mouth of the stairs. Heat and smoke pulsed through the opening. The crackle of exploding small arms was beginning to include deeper pops and bangs. "Holly isn't at the end of the line. She's down there."

Cole jerked upright. "Shit. You heard her?"

Grant nodded. "When they were pulling back."

He pointed at the staircase. "Only way they can go is down."

A heavy thump shook the tunnel. Chunks of rock and dust fell from the ceiling. The debris blocking the exit vibrated and trickled small stones. The dark entrance to the stairs was feathered with an orange glow. Three small pops and a larger crump shook more dust from the ceiling.

"The only place they can go is Shelter Cove." Grant tossed the second shotgun back to Gardner. "So now would be a real good time to show us how you got in here."

Gardner didn't need asking twice. He went into a dark corner next to the wall of rubble. There was a narrow entrance, maybe three feet square. A passage sloped upwards towards the surface. A rusty grill had been kicked off the hole. An air vent or a maintenance tunnel, Grant wasn't sure which. He didn't care. He bundled the police chief into the hole and pushed Cole in behind him. The two men crawled into the dark.

The ground shook as a deeper explosion blasted fire and smoke into the railroad tunnel. The rest of the ammunition was about to go, the grenades and the bullets and the heavy artillery shells from the gun emplacements.

Grant scrambled into the shaft and began to climb. It was pitch black after the glow from the antechamber. He couldn't see the two pairs of feet above him. Then he became aware of a lightening of the gloom up ahead. A light at the end of the tunnel. A way out of the killing jar. He tried to crawl faster but the narrow space restricted him. He was starting to believe they were going make it when the loudest blast he'd ever heard shook the earth and the world turned upside down.

FIFTY

*

ARLO RANKOFF STOOD AT THE back window of the beach cottage and watched a chunk of his land being blasted into oblivion. Halfway up the hillside and across the top of the ridge. Fire and smoke and debris took the top off the hill like preparing a boiled egg for dipping. Nobody would be dipping toast into the inferno overlooking Shelter Cove. "What the fuck did they do?"

The knifeman with the bruised face was the only person listening. He didn't think his boss wanted an answer so he kept quiet. Having failed at the bookseller's house he'd been demoted to rear echelon support. Judging by the landslide coming down the hill he was glad he wasn't front line. He had no doubt what the fuck they'd just done and he had no doubt who'd done it. The big cop from England.

The houses on Kent Road and Olympian Way were safe but the trails and woodlands heading into the hills had taken a body blow. A crater stood at the heart of the destruction but a stretch of hillside had been cut open where the railroad tunnel began. A shoulder of rock further along was leaking smoke through the gun embrasures. The second gun emplacement had been spared along with the rest of the tunnel towards the scenic highway. Most of the damage was centered on the storage chamber that Rankoff had been meaning to clear for years but never found the time or the incentive. The stores had been there since WW2; he had no reason to believe it was going to be a problem until now. Removing that amount of munitions would have been difficult to hide anyway.

Rankoff went out onto the frail wooden porch and stepped aside. The knifeman followed suit. The empty beach cottage was built into the bottom of the hill, the end house furthest from the peninsula. The back wall was a façade hiding an access tunnel that lead all the way up the hill. The tunnel door was open.

Rankoff turned away and covered his mouth and nose. The smoke and dust took a few minutes to work its way down from the explosion but when it finally came out of the tunnel mouth it filled the cottage and drifted onto the porch. It took a few more minutes for the smoke to clear then he stepped back to the porch door.

Hesitant footsteps echoed down the passage. There was swearing and coughing and groans of pain then huddled figures staggered out of the dust. Two big men and a woman. The woman was being held by one arm until the big man holding it threw her to the ground. Holly West dropped to her knees and coughed her lungs up. She dry spat but there was no moisture in her mouth. Her throat was on fire. Her eyes were stinging but she resisted rubbing them.

Rankoff stared in disbelief. "What you bring her back for?"

*

SMOKE CLUNG TO THE BASE of the hill like fog on a winter's morning. It drifted along the row of abandoned beach properties but the calm afternoon air couldn't move it. Surf whispered on the sandy beach as the water reached low tide. The sand was hard packed and damp. Perfect for making sandcastles. One of the big men sat on the porch with his back against the wall. The second brought a water bottle from the kitchen and they drank to clear their throats.

Holly sat just inside the door. She held a hand up for a drink and the big man gave her the dregs at the bottom. She took a sip and swilled it around her mouth then spat it out. Once her mouth was clear she finished the bottle.

Rankoff looked at the part time cop then at the man standing over her. "She was supposed to be gassed with the others." He shook his head. "Now you're giving her water?"

The big man took the bottle back and stood with it dangling from one hand. "We didn't reach the chamber."

Rankoff waited for an explanation. When one didn't come he frowned. "And?"

The big man looked sheepish. He didn't want to say this. "The old cop and the English guys were letting the wetbacks out."

"Gardner?"

"Yeah."

"Shit. They get 'em all out?"

The big man waved a hand up the hill. "Nobody got out. There's nothing left."

Rankoff nodded at Holly. "So why the fuck you bring her back?"

The big man shrugged. He didn't have an answer but made a suggestion. "Throw her in the sea?"

Rankoff put his hands on his hips. It made the little fat man look comical but his tone of voice wasn't funny. "You brought her all the way down from the towering inferno so we could drown her in the bay?" He let out a huff that bordered on a laugh but there was no humour in it. "I'm gonna have to update your CV. From moron to head moron."

The man sitting outside got up. He stretched his legs, avoided the cuts and grazes down the side of his face, and decided to support his colleague. The bottle fetcher held one arm across his front as if in a sling. A gunshot wound. Nobody was unscathed. The big man had taken a gunshot to the arm but he wasn't complaining. It was only the short round businessman who was complaining. As powerful as their boss was, the men decided to stand together. Scar face shrugged. "It was a fluid situation. We didn't have time to think."

Rankoff turned on him. "Well think on this. Twenty-three Mexicans, who should have been locked up and gassed in the chamber, got out and drowned in the cove. You think a local cop washing up in the same place might not look a bit suspicious?"

Scar face looked crestfallen.

Rankoff threw him an olive branch. "Yeah. I know. Combat situation. Under fire. I understand all that. So let me do the thinking. Take her back up the hill and throw her in the fire." He jutted his chin out. "Purifying flames. Make sure she's completely purified."

The big man with his arm in a sling slumped against the wall. Scar face spoke for both of them. "Come on boss. We didn't sign up for killing no cops."

They were all on the porch now, round the side of the cottage near the steps down to the beach. The porch continued all the way to the back of the house where it met another set of stairs up to the access road across the back of the beach front properties. The road was still shrouded in dust. The quiet was thick and heavy and complete. Rankoff's voice was a harsh whisper. "Well, listen to this. You signed up for drowning surfers in their baths and Mexicans in the bay. Not to mention a ton of rotting flesh up there in the tunnel. So let me ask you. How many times you think they gonna hang you?"

Rankoff stepped back and leaned on the railing. The silence was heavy with meaning. They all knew Rankoff was right but nobody wanted to admit it. Nobody spoke. The dull thud of approaching rotor blades sounded to the north. Then another voice came from the road above the cottage. "You won't make it to be hanged."

FIFTY-ONE

*

THREE MEN EMERGED FROM the mist on the road. Grant maintained the high ground looking down at the warped planks of the side porch. Cole and Gardner spread out either side of him. Two shotguns were aimed loosely down the hill. Cole let his gun dangle at his side. Grant tightened his grip on the shotgun, ready for the next move.

Rankoff's gunmen moved fast, the one with blood down the side of his face and the other with one arm in a makeshift sling. Grant stopped them in their tracks with two blasts of the shotgun, six feet in front of the leading man. It blasted the shaky porch into a cloud of splinters and dust. The rest of the porch groaned and leaned to one side.

Grant leveled the shotgun at Rankoff. "If it's gallows you want."

*

HOLLY PUSHED AWAY FROM the wall when she heard Grant's voice. If the Yorkshire cop was here then Cole would be with him. She glanced through the side window and saw three men standing on the road above the cottage. Ben Gardner was with them. Her heart filled with pride.

The shotgun blasts shook her out of her reverie. The stilts holding the cottage groaned and swayed. She got to her feet and went out the door as Grant mentioned something about gallows. She came round the corner and ran straight into Rankoff's arms.

*

RANKOFF GRABBED HOLLY AROUND the neck and pulled a small silver pistol. He was short but he was still a few inches taller than Holly. He clamped her neck in an arm lock and shoved the gun into the soft flesh beneath her right ear. Sirens sounded in the distance. An air horn signaled that the fire department was speeding to the scene. Having a volcano erupt at Pedro Point was better than sending up a flare.

Grant kept the shotgun on Rankoff. The gunmen kept their guns on Grant. Gardner stepped aside to give himself a better angle, leveling his shotgun at the man with the sling. Cole stepped to the other side and brought his gun up, only vaguely towards the other gunman. It was enough. Everybody had everybody else covered. Grant took two steps down the hill. "Mexican standoff."

Rankoff took two steps backwards. "Mexicans don't know how to standoff."

The gunmen backed away with their boss. Cole and Gardner kept station with Grant. The entire group moved like synchronized dancers, towards the stairs to the beach then down. Grant moved around the holes he'd blasted in the porch. The stilts groaned again. The integrity of the crossbeams was compromised and the beach cottage leaned to one side. Rankoff started down the stairs.

One step. Two steps.

Rankoff kept his arm locked around Holly's throat.

Three steps. Four.

The gunmen backed down the top step.

Five steps. Six.

Grant reached the top of the stairs just as Rankoff reached the beach. The short man who looked like a Mexican backed away towards the distant surf. His men backed off with him. Grant stepped onto the damp sand. His shoes left footprints that oozed water. The sirens grew closer, almost drowning out the heavy thud of the helicopter coming along the coast. Twenty-four hour news never sleeps. Grant shouted above the noise. "You gonna swim for it?"

The thwup, thwup, thwup of the rotor blades became a deep rhythmic thud that shook the ground and pounded Grant's head. He'd been here before, standing off an armed confrontation in front of the news cameras. It never ended well. He didn't want this to go wrong too. He lowered the shotgun and dropped it in the sand. He held both arms out to show he was unarmed then waved a hand over his shoulder. "On live television?"

Rankoff looked at the hills behind Grant. The thudding grew louder. "It's a funny thing about TV news."

The downdraught became a physical presence. It cleared the smoke from the road and buffeted the already weakened beach cottage. Water that had puddled on the beach formed concentric circles as the downdraft forced it away from the middle. Spray stung Grant's eyes and he covered his face with one hand. The helicopter was directly overhead. Rankoff had to shout to be heard. "You never know who's sponsoring it these days."

The chopper drifted into view behind Rankoff and hovered six feet off the ground. It was decorated with a news logo Grant had never heard of. A sliding door on one side was open. There were no passengers. There was no film crew. Just the pilot waiting for instructions from his boss.

Rankoff kept Holly in front of him. A human shield. The gunmen formed a skirmish line either side of him. If Grant allowed Rankoff to get Holly on board she was as good as dead. He'd been here before as well. Having to choose between shooting the hostage or letting everyone die. The choice was never easy but it had always been his choice. This decision impacted on his brother. That made it more difficult but there was really only one choice.

He lowered his arms and reached behind his back. The gun came out fast and he swung it up in two hands. The helicopter jiggled as the pilot saw the gun. Rankoff's eyes widened then Cole stepped between the two men and everything changed again.

*

THE FIRST BULLY KICKED the parapet and the entire south wall collapsed. The second kept his knee on James Grant's chest to stop him getting up and the other two completed the destruction of the castle. And Grant's childhood. The sand was firm but damp. Standing in the trench that Grant had dug as a moat the bully's feet squelched and sank. When he moved he had to tug against the suction. He lost his shoe forcing Grant to smile. Bullies seemed less frightening when they were struggling to pull a shoe out of the mud.

It wasn't the sandcastle that hurt. It wasn't the beating either. It was watching his brother's back recede in the distance as he walked towards the surf. The pain became anger and the anger became rage. Grant was too young to know how to channel it, so he took the beating that day. From then onwards though he became an angry man. He'd learned how to control it nowadays but sometimes the beast slipped the leash.

*

"YOU CAN HANDLE THIS. Keep it in check." Cole pressed an open hand gently on Grant's chest. "Don't go ripping your shirt and turning green."

Grant kept the gun pointed at Rankoff. "I never turned green."

Cole kept his hand up. "No. You turned ballistic."

The thudding rotor blades made it hard to listen. Cole was shouting but keeping it close. This was about brothers. It was about him. "You said you're a better man now. Prove it."

Grant shook his head. "He gets her on the chopper. She's dead. Turning green's the only way."

Cole lowered his hand. "No. Getting sand kicked in your face provokes rage. Rage is blind. We need to think and see and work together."

Grant looked at his brother. "Tag team?"

Cole nodded towards Gardner. "Three Amigos."

Grant looked into Cole's eyes and blinked his agreement. He stepped aside and Cole raised his gun. He covered the man in the sling. Gardner aimed at the man weeping blood down the side of his face. Grant focused on Rankoff who was waving frantically for the pilot to land. The pilot shook his head. Rankoff jerked the gun towards the ground. Land. In the end the power of Rankoff's wealth triumphed over good sense. Grant knew where that would lead and turned his attention to the gunmen. "You really think he'll take you with him?" Cole and Gardner stepped forward. Grant raised his voice. "You really think we're gonna let him?"

The helicopter swayed as it settled towards the ground, far enough away that the group was outside the rotors' arc. Grant still felt like bowing his head. Everybody else did too. The blades were ten feet above the ground but instinct is a powerful force. Grant's instinct was to duck. The gunmen's instinct was to survive. Staying with Rankoff was a no win situation. They lowered their guns. Cole and Gardner quickly disarmed them. That only left Arlo Rankoff, a desperate man with a gun to Holly's head.

The helicopter landed. Its weight settled on the runners and oozed water from the hard packed sand. Rankoff pushed Holly up through the sliding door and climbed aboard. He kept her in front of him, not foolish enough to think he was safe until they were airborne. He jerked the gun skywards and the pilot took his cue. The motor changed tone. It strained to take off but the suction pulled the bully's shoe into the mud.

The bully looked worried. The pilot tried harder. The engine noise became a screaming whine. Grant shoved the gun in his belt and picked up the shotgun. Rankoff watched nervously. The getaway wasn't going according to plan. Between each thrust to lift off there was a reciprocal settling of the runners into the sand. The suction was too strong. The helicopter was too heavy. Grant moved to within six feet of the rotors arc and had to shout to be heard. "Funny thing about bullies on the beach." He looked at Rankoff but he was speaking to Holly. "Kicking sand in the face stings everyone."

Holly understood and closed her eyes. Grant pointed the shotgun at the beach and fired. The shot impacted the damp surface and blasted sand towards the helicopter. The hard wet particles slammed through the open door like a house being sandblasted. Holly ducked left leaving Rankoff to take it full in the face. His eyes were peppered with improvised buckshot. His gun went off, hitting the pilot in the shoulder. The getaway driver was out of action. The getaway car was stuck.

Holly dodged and rolled through the door. Rankoff did the worst thing he could have done. Even for a short man. He jerked the opposite door open and jumped out blindly towards the surf. Going out that side wasn't a problem. Pushing up with his legs was. He cleared the lip and sailed into the air. The only part that landed was his legs and torso and one arm. The rest of him was mashed into a bloody spray of meat and bone. The rotor blades didn't miss a beat. The beach was painted red.

Rankoff landed on his back and soaked into the sand. For a short man who hated Mexicans he was the wetback now. Grant walked back up the beach towards Shelter Cove, a safe haven that had become a killing jar. As if to emphasize the point the beach hut on stilts groaned one last time and collapsed onto the beach.

FIFTY-TWO

*

"THERE'S ONE OTHER THING." Cole was finding it difficult to say goodbye to his brother after finally reconnecting. They'd just had a farewell breakfast at Denny's and were standing at the Greyhound pickup point on Linda Mar Boulevard. Two blocks from McDonalds and the police office. The police office had been busy the last couple of days. Gardner had more to deal with now than school crossings and missing dogs. Grant had been busy too. Working out how not to arrest his brother.

*

BREAKFAST HAD BEEN THE AMERICAN equivalent of a Full English. Grant thought the traditional English breakfast of cereals followed by bacon, egg, beans, sausage, mushrooms, tomatoes, hash browns and fried bread was bad enough. What Americans tucked away for breakfast could feed a small country. Grant vowed not to eat anything else until supper in San Francisco.

The broad windows looked out across Cabrillo Highway to the beach. It seemed that everything the brothers did ended up at the beach. Grant waded into some kind of pancakes with syrup. Cole looked out of the window. "Why San Francisco?"

Grant paused between mouthfuls. "I want to see the hills where Steve McQueen jumped his car in Bullitt."

"That's all?"

"And the town hall steps where Dirty Harry goes up to see the mayor."

"City hall."

"Yes, that." Grant leaned back in his seat before the main course. He puffed out his cheeks. It was time to set the record straight. He looked across the table at Cole. "Okay. Here's how it is."

Basically Grant lied on his report back to England. He stated that Andrew Grant had been eliminated from enquiries and that he had nothing to do with the theft of the drugs money. He was living under an assumed name for a fresh start due to family friction. Case closed. Cole let out a sigh. "And the start up money for the bookstore?"

Grant shrugged. "Inheritance."

Cole was building up to something but he wasn't there yet. "That won't get you in trouble?"

Grant shook his head. "I don't work for them anymore. It was a special request. I did what they asked. Now they can close the file."

Cole toyed with his coffee. "What about Sarah?"

"What about her?"

"You two going to get back together?"

Grant pushed his plate aside. "She came here for you, remember? And you're engaged to the new Linda Mar police chief."

Cole turned his hands palms upwards. "Gardner hasn't gone yet."

Grant softened his eyes. "He's earned his retirement. And Holly's earned the job."

Cole laid his hands flat on the table. "And us?"

Grant looked across the table at the brother he'd blanked from his mind for most of his adult life. The smile he gave held a hint of sadness but at least it was a smile. "We've earned something too."

"What?"

Grant tilted his head to one side and shrugged again. "Something."

Before he could find the words a waitress came over with a tray as wide as the table. She rested it on a collapsible trestle and slid two plates across the fake wooden top. Cole welcomed the distraction. They weren't a hugging family. Kiss and make up was a difficult concept for both of them. Whether Grant would want to kiss and make up once Cole dropped his final bombshell remained to be seen. Eating a hearty breakfast delayed the inevitable. A condemned man's final meal.

Breakfast lasted almost to the time when the bus was due. Cole was running out of time. He plucked up courage as they went outside to the Greyhound pick up point in the parking lot off Linda Mar Boulevard. He reached one hand into his back pocket. "There's one other thing."

*

THE SILVER BUS SWUNG off Cabrillo Highway and pulled into the parking lot. It did an exaggerated circle to come back facing the road. Grant hefted the battered leather holdall in one hand and waited for his brother's parting shot. Cole brought his hand out of the pocket but Grant couldn't see what he was holding. Whatever it was, was hidden in the palm of his hand. Cole struggled to keep his breathing regular. "I wasn't entirely honest about the inheritance."

Grant waved the confession aside. "I know. The evidence locker. It's sorted."

Cole shook his head. "No about him dying. Dad."

Airbrakes hissed and the door swung open. Grant didn't move. Cole let out a sigh and finished his confession. "He isn't dead."

Grant stood still. Cole ran with it, eager now to get this off his chest. "He didn't completely disown you either."

He held his hand out and the dog-eared photograph unfurled. The one Cole had taken from the shoebox the day he tried to leave. Grant looked at the photo but made no effort to take it. The faded colour print must have been taken shortly after the one of his mother and Cole holding baby James. The one his father had taken. He must have found a nurse to take this one because the family was now complete. A tired looking mother, a sheepish brother and a grinning father holding them together with strong arms.

Grant still didn't move. His silence prompted Cole to fill in the blanks. "He's been following your career the whole time. Had the military pull your records. West Yorkshire Police too. I don't know about after you came to America but my guess is he's still watching over you."

Granted took the photo but kept his face straight. It wasn't easy. "Must have taken a lot of clout to pull that off."

This time Cole kept quiet. Grant looked him in the eye. "More clout than a naval commander's got."

Cole raised his eyebrows. "I think there's a lot we don't know about dad."

Grant nodded and put the photo in his pocket. "Thanks."

That was all Grant could manage. They weren't a hugging family. He took a deep breath, nodded once, then got on the bus. The door swung shut. The Greyhound swung out of the parking lot and Cole watched his brother leave Shelter Cove. A safe haven that had once been a killing jar but now held a future Cole never thought he'd have. He didn't wave. Grant didn't either.

AFTER WORD

This book was a long time coming but it took even longer to get it out there. It is the culmination of years of writing and seemingly endless patience. The years came with writing the first five books in the Resurrection Man series. The patience was mainly waiting to get book six published. And that's where my patience finally ran out.

Jim Grant has been a passion project ever since I introduced him in *Jamaica Plain*. I like his cop sensibilities and his Yorkshire grit. He has been well received by readers and reviewers and yet it was still hard to get each book published. The industry moves slowly and I write fast. The books were piling up while publication seemed to take longer. So, I decided to take matters into my own hands. *Shelter Cove* was published independently and I have to say it has been a very enjoyable experience. I am grateful for the professional help producing this book, including editing and cover design, but the decisions about style, choice of cover and timescale have all been mine. Going independent could prove to be the best decision I've ever made.

Whether that continues depends on how many people read it. So, the future is in your hands. If you like it, tell your friends. No author is any good without readers. You're the reason we write.

Colin Campbell
May 2018

ACKNOWLEDGEMENTS

This is the first time in a while that I haven't had an agent to thank but I would still like to acknowledge the help of my former agent Donna Bagdasarian in getting me this far. It's been a long hard slog and the book wouldn't be in your hands now without the hard work and professionalism of everyone at Lulu Press. I especially want to thank Ryan Herndon for getting in touch in the first place, and Sarah E Smith for shepherding Project 779148 through to completion. And to all those behind the scenes, I say thank you.

ABOUT THE AUTHOR

Colin Campbell is an army veteran and a retired police officer who served with the West Yorkshire police department for thirty years. He is the author of the UK crime novels, Blue Knight White Cross and Northern Ex, and US thrillers, Jamaica Plain and Montecito Heights featuring rogue Yorkshire cop, Jim Grant. Campbell resides in Otley, Leeds, Great Britain.